PETER
WATTS
is
an
Angry
Sentient
Tumor

PETER WATTS

IS AN ANGRY
SENTIENT TUMOR
{{ revenge fantasies and essays }}

T A C H Y O N

INTRODUCTION COPYRIGHT © 2019 BY PETER WATTS
COVER ART AND COVER DESIGN BY ELIZABETH STORY
INTERIOR DESIGN BY JOHN COULTHART

TACHYON PUBLICATIONS LLC
1459 18TH STREET #139
SAN FRANCISCO, CA 94107
415.285.5615
WWW.TACHYONPUBLICATIONS.COM
TACHYON@TACHYONPUBLICATIONS.COM

SERIES EDITOR: JACOB WEISMAN
PROJECT EDITOR: JILL ROBERTS

PRINT ISBN-13: 978-1-61696-319-4
DIGITAL ISBN: 978-1-61696-320-0

FIRST EDITION: 2019

9   8   7   6   5   4   3   2   1

"Known for his pitch-black views on human
nature, and a breathtaking ability to explore the
weird side of evolution and animal behavior, Watts
is one of those writers who gets into your brain and
remains lodged there like an angry, sentient tumor."
—Annalee Newitz, *io9*

C ... O ... N ... T ... E ... N ... T ... S

C...O...N...T...E...N...T...S

In Love with the Moment.
Scared Shitless of the Future.

By the bowels of Christ, man, *why?*

You can be forgiven for asking. It was certainly the first question on my lips when Tachyon's Jacob Weisman pitched the idea. Will I sound better the second time around, do my rants and musings—originally strung haphazardly across a couple of decades—somehow acquire more credibility when boiled down to a concentrate and released in a single high-octane package?

More to the point, who even reads blogs these days? Who slogs through long-winded essays when Twitter makes it so easy for everyone—regardless of background, spelling ability, or facility with CAPS LOCK—to reasonably discuss nuanced and complex issues in 280 characters or less? Even worse, who slogs through long-winded essays that have been staledating for years? The social currency of blogging has degraded over time, from cutting-edge to mainstream to webcomic punchline[1].

The 'Crawl—*No Moods, Ads, or Cutesy Fucking Icons*, if you're into formal nomenclature—has been there for it all.

I've forgotten exactly when it started. I've been able to track it back sixteen years at least: entries from 2004 still languish online if you know where to look, twin columns of type—one for personal news, one for science commentary—on a mauvey-bluish background. I didn't need no steenking third-party blogging service back then. I hand-coded the whole thing in html. It was a political statement of sorts: the 'crawl's very name an explicit raspberry blown at LiveJournal with its Mood fields and its ubiquitous ads and its, well, cutesy fucking icons. If spam and saccharine were the price of entry, I wanted no part of it.

Eventually, of course, I gave in. Moved from my own Web-1.0 protoblog to Blogger; from Blogger to Wordpress. The larger Rifters. com site—*No Moods*, yes, but also myriad alt-reality glimpses into the worlds of my novels—moved from Canada to California and offshore to Iceland, the better to avoid the intrusive, data-sharing jurisdiction of the Five Eyes nations. (Iceland's constitution enshrines the right to online privacy, did you know that? Some spook from Europe or North America shows up sniffing after your server logs, Iceland tells them to get stuffed. The more I learn about that place, the more I want to apply for refugee status there.)

Of course, while I was busy jumping from platform to platform and country to country, everyone else was jumping over to Twitter—a migration so widespread (one might even say *mandatory*) that literary agents have been known to turn down talented and brilliant authors for no other reason than that they don't have Twitter accounts[2]). I refuse to follow them. I've managed to steer clear of all social media except Facebook, and the only reason I surrendered that much was because I got sick of people saying *Dude, did you see what that person said about you on Facebook?* without being able to check it out[3]. If I am indeed fated to sink into this pit of surveillance capitalism with the rest of you, I'd just as soon limit my fantasies about eating the rich to a venue that doesn't shut you down the moment some community-standards algo thinks it sees an exposed nipple in a jpeg. The 'crawl abides. If you want my opinion, you know where to find me.

The question, of course, is how many people actually want my opinion.

It's a number that's changed over time. I know that much. I was pretty happy at the way my hit count spiked when I first got nominated for a Hugo, but that was a mere push-pin next to the spire provoked by my arrest (and subsequent trial) while fleeing the US back in 2009. And even that dwindled into insignificance once I'd posted graphic photos of a cavernous hole in my leg, flesh rotted away and debrided, calf muscle twitching like a striped bass along the floor of a gory chasm the size of Australia. For a while there I was as popular as any cute cat GIF, albeit for exactly opposite reasons.

Numerous foothills lie in the shadow of those peaks. I started giving my fiction away for free online. I got banned from the US. I raked in a pretty extensive list of award nominations and a significantly smaller number of actual wins. I grew inexplicably popular in Poland (foreshadowing a larger emergent pattern in which I sell disproportionately well in countries with a history of Soviet occupation—better than in countries occupied by the US, anyway). Necrotising fasciitis nearly killed me; when it didn't, I got married. I got involved in a Norwegian black-metal science opera about sending marbled lungfish to Mars. Started writing a monthly column for a Polish SF magazine (some installments of which await your attention in this very volume). I watched my whole family die off except for one creepy older brother whose interactions with children have not, traditionally, inspired confidence. (We don't talk much any more.)

You can read about some of that stuff here. Not all, by any means; out of the estimated 660,000 words I've poured into the 'crawl over the years, I sent a mere 180,000 on to Jacob. He whittled that down to an even merer 80,000. Almost ninety percent of the 'crawl was culled before you laid eyes on it here; take heart from the odds that anything making it through such a draconian filter should be at least readable, if not exactly ageless.

I might quibble with aspects of the final selection. I would like to have shared, one more time, the lovingly-detailed and intimate chronicle of my 2012 colonoscopy. It might have been nice to reiterate my disdain for *Interstellar*, my admiration for Soderburgh's unjustly-maligned *Solaris*, my ambivalence towards *Ex Machina* (although at least you get to discover my ambivalence toward *Blade Runner 2049* and my disdain for *Star Trek Beyond*). My take on Climategate contains a certain folksy charm, as does my perspective on that guy who uses pictures of cattle mutilation to predict political orientation. Archivists might have been interested in the review of *Person of Interest* that got me hired to write a tie-in novel for that series (before another blog post on the same subject got me fired). None made the cut. Pity.

On the other hand, you do get my thoughts on Zika as the potential savior of Humanity; on a courageous high-school teacher who nearly lost her job because she wanted to teach *Blindsight* to her English class; and on Daryl Bem's peer-reviewed findings on porn-mediated time-traveling ESP. You'll read about the Second Coming, which seems to have occurred in 2015—only this time the Messiah was hooked up to an EEG when it went down. You'll encounter more eulogies here than anyone really needs. A story about that one time I accidentally dissolved a toad.

Hey, don't look at me. I only wrote the damn things. You want someone to blame, Jacob decided what to print.

*

There's also a fair bit of anger in here: at the way we've fucked the planet, at our refusal to take responsibility for the messes we've made, at the idiotic self-adulation of Human behaviors that are, when you strip away the tech and the rationalization, scarcely different from what you see from the beasts of the field. If you squint you might notice a trend in my output over the past ten years or so. Back in the old days, my writing might have been suffused in a subtext of *Holy shit, people, we've got to turn this car around before it goes over the cliff.* These days I'm more likely to say:

> Reap the whirlwind, you miserable
> fuckers. May your children choke on it.

which is actually lifted from an essay that didn't make the cut.[4] I can see why Jacob left it out; insults aren't generally regarded as the best way to attract potential converts, especially when so many of those readers are in such a pathological state of denial to begin with. If, upon reading these words, you set down this collection and never pick it up again, that's okay.

You'll just be proving both points.

And yet the 'crawl comes with an epigram: *In love with the moment. Scared shitless of the future.* You'll notice I've co-opted it as the title for this Introduction.

Because The Moment *is* so very precious. Because the apocalypse shredding the planet hasn't touched me yet. Oh, I see it coming, so much faster than anyone expected. When it comes to climate change the optimists have always been wrong and the pessimists have always been too optimistic; even in my own back yard the changes are obvious. But the *costs*—displacement, starvation, loss of home and livelihood, death by disease or violence or straight-up hyperthermia—so far, those have always been borne by someone else. On a purely selfish level I'm happier than I've ever been in my life, happier than I deserve. Of course it won't last. I do not expect to die peacefully, and I do not expect to die in any jurisdiction with a stable infrastructure. At least I don't have to worry about the world I'm leaving behind for my children; I got sterilized in 1991.

The great tragedy, the monstrous ecocidal sin of our species is that we still make so many decisions with the gut—and to the gut, the Moment is always more real than the Future. I try so hard to look ahead, to just look *around*: at the firestorms and droughts and killer heat waves, the climate refugees in their millions, the rolling pandemics and societal collapse and a biosphere reduced to impoverished weedy tatters—but so often I fall short. My eyes see the writing on the wall, but my gut won't let me read it. We're programmed for delusional optimism. Even facing apocalypse, we fantasize about being Mad Max. Who fantasizes about being one of the skulls piled up in the background?

I'm destined to be one of those skulls, just like you are—but today there is still joy to be found, even here. The 'crawl may serve as a harbinger of doom but it also serves as a playground of ideas. You can see me giddily unwrap scientific discoveries, turn them this way and that, figure out how I might incorporate them into stories of my own construction. You can watch as I pick apart the latest *Aliens* movie, for all the world as if I were back in grad school and the lot of us were sitting around a barroom table full of half-empty pitchers. If you don't blink you might even catch moments of optimism on the environmental front, glimmers of hope arising from political and technological developments that might yet hold for us a measure of redemption.

Even my most bitter diatribes might not be totally fatalistic. I've never given in to the quiet resignation and the go-gently-into-that-good-nightedness counseled by the likes of Jem Bendell and

Catherine Ingram. I contain far more rage than acquiescence. Maybe that means I haven't given up yet.

I've cheated here and there to make myself look better in hindsight, cut away bits from one essay if it overlapped too much with another. The *Nowa Fantastyka* columns contained a number of remarks aimed at Polish readers that wouldn't make much sense to you North Americans; those have been purged. I may have tweaked an occasional rant to incorporate (or at least acknowledge) new insights. You probably won't notice the difference unless you comb through the archives looking for trouble. I wouldn't advise it. The revisions are an improvement.

None of which answers the question I led off with: Why do this at all? I'm still not entirely sure. Maybe Blogoirs are a thing now, like Space Opera or Dumb Adult. After all, that Scalzi guy's anthologized his blog posts twice now and nobody's complained.

Jesus. I hope they don't expect me to go up against Scalzi. No way am I gonna win a popularity contest with that guy. He's so, so—*cheerful*. How do I compete with that?

I suppose I could cut back on the fucking profanity . . .

1 Saturday Morning Breakfast Cereal, if you must know.
HTTPS://WWW.SMBC-COMICS.COM/COMIC/FIXING-SOCIAL-MEDIA
2 True story. Happened to a friend of mine.
3 I know, I know. In my defense I use it mainly to link to my own blog entries—and on those occasions when I do feel compelled to Like someone else's posts, I make sure to use the Orange Emoji of Apoplectic Rage rather than the usual Thumbs-up. (I also tend to Heart foamy diatribes by climate-change deniers, just to keep FB's algos from getting a target lock.) The only real drawback is my friends keep wondering why I'm so pissed off at them all the time.
4 "The Adorable Optimism of the IPCC." Oct 26 2018.

Everything I Needed to Know About Christmas I Learned From My Grandma

BLOG DEC 25 2011

Christmas in a household of professional Baptists has always been a time to think about the joys of giving. In my particular case this has proven to be a double-edged sword, the flip side being that it is *not* a time to think about "getting". Devoting any neurons to the contemplation of what one might *get* for Christmas, you see, is unChristian; we are supposed to be concerned entirely with the selflessness of giving unto others, not whether you're going to get that Captain Scarlet SPV Dinky toy you covet. (I was never entirely sure how to reconcile this *virtue of selflessness* riff with the fact that the whole point of being charitable was to get into heaven while the Rosenbergs down the street ended up in The Other Place, but there you go.)

It was considered bad form in the Watts household to show any interest at all in whatever swag *you* might accumulate on the 25th. On the off-chance that someone asked you what you wanted for Christmas, you were honor-bound to keep silent—

or at the very least to shrug off the question with a disclaimer along the lines of *I haven't thought about it, really.* By the time I hit adolescence I'd figured out how to game this system (just give everyone a hand-made card telling them that "In honor of Christ's birth I have made a donation to Unicef in your name"— nobody was ever crass enough to ask for a receipt). But even that conceptual breakthrough didn't stop Christmas mornings from being generally grim affairs in which people sat around with fixed and glassy smiles, thanking each other for gifts they obviously hated, but which they could hardly complain about because after all, they'd never told anyone what they wanted. The gifts bestowed upon *me* during my childhood included pyjamas, an economy-sized roll of pink serrated hair tape, and a set of TV tables (which, as you all know, is the absolute fucking *dream* of every 11-year-old boy).

But the best gift I *ever* got was at the hands of my paternal grandmother, Avis Watts, may Ceiling Cat devour her soul.

Avis was an absolute master at economy. For example, since my birthday falls within a month of Christmas, she would frequently send me a single gift intended to cover both occasions. On the occasion of which I speak—my thirteenth birthday, I think it was—she even economized on the card. I didn't notice that at first: I tore the wrapping off the box and extracted a flat leather billfold from within, and—thinking that perhaps there might be some money inside (what else would you put in a billfold, hmmm?)—I spread its flaps wide enough for a little card to fall out of the spot where a more generous soul might have stuck a twenty.

It was not a Christmas card. It was not a birthday card. It was an invitation to a cocktail party: at least, it was festooned with cartoon pink elephants and martini glasses beneath the cheery inscription

HOPE YOU CAN MAKE IT!

Immediately beneath this, Grandma had added in ball-point pen:

To Christmas and your birthday!

I opened the card and read the note within:

> *Dear Peter,*
> *Somebody gave me this billfold, but I already have a billfold so I thought you might like it for Christmas and your birthday. Happy birthday!*
> *Love, Grandma*
> *P.S. Please tell your father that Uncle Ernie has died.*

I had already learned a great deal about Christmas during the preceding twelve years. What Avis taught me was a valuable lesson about family, and it was this: they suck.

It was a lesson that has stood the test of time across all the decades between then and now. Many have been the relationships I've co-piloted from blast-off to burn-out; many the collateral families thrust upon me like disapproving and destabilizing ballast mid-flight, my coerced attendance at their interminable Christmas and Thanksgiving get-togethers only serving to reinforce my conviction to never have one of my own (and, doubtless, their own conviction that their daughter could do *so* much better). The lesson I learned at my grandmother's knee has always stood me in good stead.

Until now.

Now, oddly, I have encountered a family that actually, well, *doesn't* exactly suck. In fact, it doesn't suck at all. It took a while to figure that out. They had to patiently lure me close in small stages, as though bribing a feral and skittish cat with small helpings of tuna. Suddenly I was curled up at the hearth and there wasn't a fundamentalist Catholic or a Burlington banker or a weaponized 9-iron anywhere in sight. So, reluctantly, it is time to put my grandmother's lesson away, to set it free, to bequeath it to others who might still find it useful.

I bequeath it to you. Treat it well. Heed its wisdom; it is right so much more often than wrong. In fact, it may be truer now than ever, since I might just have snatched up the last available kick-ass family on the planet.

Most families suck. Especially this time of year. It is okay to admit that; it is okay to tell them to their faces. Have a couple of drinks first: that'll make it easier.

Merry Christmas.

Oh fuck, I think. *I'm gonna get arrested again.*

There's a growing cluster of uniforms in the ravine abutting our property: city employees, police, a couple of guys wearing unfamiliar insignia. Two cops poke at the tent just the other side of our fence. Their cars are pulled up in front of the house: those ones with the new, aggressive gray-and-black styling because the old blue-and-whites didn't look enough like the Batmobile.

It was only a matter of time. Kevin spent most of last night screaming death threats to the trees again. Someone must have complained.

I switch on my phone's voice recorder, slip it into my back pocket, trudge grimly into the underbrush. I pass the two whose insignia I didn't recognize from the window: Salvation Army, as it turns out ("Gateway: The Hand of God in the Heart of the City"). They look concerned and ready to help. I wonder if they know that Kevin's gay; the Sally Ann's a notoriously homophobic organization.

"So what's going on?" I ask in passing. One of them shrugs, jerks a thumb towards the center of action.

The cops have ripped away the fly and are talking to the huddled figure rocking in the exposed shell of the tent. They look up as I approach.

"Hi. That's my tent." Maybe not the optimal ice-breaking line, but better than *back away from the homeless guy and no one gets hurt.*

They look at me.

"I gave it to him to keep him from getting rained on." There was a torrential rainstorm a few months back, punched a hole in our roof and soaked through to the living room ceiling. I came home that afternoon to find Kevin taking shelter on our porch. He apologized for the intrusion. It was the first time we spoke, although he'd been living rough in the ravine for a couple of months at least. "He's harmless, really. He yells a lot, but when he's leveled out he's actually kind of charming."

One of the cops is about as tall as me, and broader. The other is short enough to be susceptible to Napoleon Complex. He's the one who first tells me to back up, who says I'm *interfering with their job.*

"Kevin?" I say. "You okay, dude?" The figure in the tent keeps rocking.

They tell me, once again, to back off. "The problem," I say, "is that you guys have a *really* bad reputation when it comes to dealing with black guys[1] with mental issues (see: Sammy Yatim). I'm worried about what you might do to him." At some point during this exchange I've pulled my phone from my pocket and switched to video record.

"Look, you want your tent back, we'll give you your tent back."

"It's not about the tent, he's welcome to the tent—"

"You want to record this, go ahead and record. But you are *interfering with our job.* So back away."

Which, despite my gut instincts, I have to admit is reasonable. I take a few steps back.

"Further," says the littler guy.

Another step.

"Further."

I figure I'm far enough; certainly well out of Interfering Range. "I don't think that's gonna happen," I say, "I'll stay right here."

He doesn't push it.

And I have to admit, they seem to be trying their best at a tough job. Nobody's tasered or shot Kevin (or me) yet. They're not escalating in the way that ends with unarmed people shot in the back, or choked to death for selling loosies. They're actually trying to *talk* to the dude.

One of the Gateway guys has dealt with Kevin before. They bring him over to try and talk Kevin out of the tent. I end up chatting with the City people; against the law to camp on public property, they point out. They gave Kevin a week's warning that they'd be coming. Came by just yesterday to remind him, left a note when he wasn't there. And there are shelters. Gateway's got a bed for him.

But Toronto shelters don't allow pets, and Kevin has a cat: a skittish, overweight black-and-white shorthair named "Blueberry Panda". They used to live together in an apartment run by the Toronto Community Housing Corporation. Kevin had arranged with the government to have his rent deducted automatically from his disability income. He went for months thinking that his rent was being paid; he believed that right up until the day TCHC evicted him last spring. Apparently they'd refused to authorize the direct-deposit arrangement after being unable to contact him by phone for "verbal confirmation."[2]

I explain this to the City people; they're sympathetic but whatyagonnado. "Just hypothetically," I wonder, "what if Kevin moves into our back yard?"

They look at me as though *I'm* the one rocking back and forth in the tent. "Well he wouldn't be on public land, but there'd still be the disturbing the peace issue." And they're right, of course. The current situation is unsustainable. A few nights back I found myself standing out in the rain at 2 a.m., peering through the fence to see if the fire Kevin had lit was in danger of burning down our shed or setting the ravine alight. It wasn't; but obviously the guy needs help. I just don't know if the current system can give him any. In terms of mental health this place has gone to shit ever since the government decided to cut costs by classifying everyone as an outpatient. It's a lesser-evil sort of thing.

Gateway guy has made no progress; Big Cop (Officer Baird, I learn later) approaches me and says, "I think we got off on the wrong foot. You don't know me, you're judging me by the uniform. I'm honestly trying to help this guy; you say you have a relationship with him? Maybe *you* could try talking to him?"

"Well, sure," I say, suddenly feeling like kind of a dick.

We go back to Kevin's tent—*my* tent, until I gave it to him on the condition that he stop screaming death threats in the middle of the night (or at least that he make it really clear that those death threats were not aimed at *us*). I remember he smiled when I said that, looked kind of rueful. Now that I think back, though, I realize he made no promises.

He's originally from Trinidad. Speaks with this wondrous liquid accent. Back in the nineties he earned a degree from the University of Toronto: dual major in chemistry and philosophy. How cool is that?

Now he huddles half-naked in the woods, and rages against monsters at three in the morning.

"Kevin? Dude? Remember me?"

The tent stinks. There's a tear down one side where the local raccoons tried to get at Blueberry's kibble. A small mountain of Bic lighters spills across a dirty scavenged mattress. A drift of empty plastic bottles. Half-eaten meals gone bad in foil wrappings. A couple of empty prescription vials (big surprise there). Kevin's knapsack: the thin edge of a grimy Macbook peeking out from a nest of balled-up socks and underwear.

He sits in the middle of it all, half-clothed: a dirty sleeping bag wrapped around his shoulders, a forgotten cigarette burning down between his fingers. He looks a little like a performance artist channeling that mud-and-garbage Devil's Tower Richard Dreyfuss sculpted in his living room, back in *Close Encounters*.

After our first sodden introduction, Kevin would wave a cheery "Hello neighbors!" at the BUG and me during his comings and goings. Occasionally he bummed a twenty to pay for a shower and a roof at the local bath-house; once he woke us late on a Saturday morning to ask if he could use our bathroom. Every now and then he'd push it a bit—asked if he could keep my hammer with him in the ravine, asked our house-sitters for the household WiFi password while we were out of town—but he also took No for an answer. We were a bit worried, at first, about getting sucked into a camel-nose scenario, but the dude always respected boundaries. Always cheerful and charming, in the light of day at least.

A centimeter of ash drops off the cig and smolders on the mattress. I try to tap it out. Kevin flinches away and doesn't look at me.

I ask how he's doing, try to invoke past shared experience to bring him out of it: "Remember when we set this tent up? Fucking insects nearly ate me alive."

"Insects don't exist in Alzheimer Space," he snaps.

It's a start. It's more than he's said to anyone else. I slide a bit of aluminum foil towards him across the fabric: "Just to keep the ash from, you know, setting the mattress on fire."

"Ash does not exist in Alzheimer Space. Mattress does not exist in Alzheimer Space."

"Dude? What are you—"

"You do not exist. You do not exist in Alzheimer—"

Finally it clicks: *All time and space.*

"You do not exist in all time and space. Nothing exists in all time and space."

In principle it's a decent coping mechanism. On some level he must know that the voices he hears at night, the things he rails against when the rest of us are trying to sleep, don't actually exist. So he's rejecting false input, only he's—overgeneralizing. He's rejecting *everything* as unreal.

I am false data. Why would he believe anything I say?

I try a bit longer, take some small satisfaction that at least I've got him talking, even if only to deny reality. Finally I crawl out of the tent, turn to Baird & Bud: "He's gone totally solipsistic."

"What's sol—solistic?"

"He's not recognizing anything beyond himself as real. I think he thinks we're all hallucinations or something, like he's some kind of Boltzmann brain."

By now the paramedics have arrived. Officer Baird and I stand back and watch one of them squat down, ask Kevin to come out. "Just want to test your blood pressure, buddy"—which, if not a bald-faced lie, is so very far from the whole truth that it might as well be. And yet, what else is there to do? Kevin couldn't even pass a Turing test in his current condition.

"You know, the press paints us in a really bad light," Officer Baird remarks. "There are a few assholes, but most of us are good people. *I'm* a good person."

I actually believe him. That last part, anyway.

"I get that," I say. "The trouble is, you good people *cover* for the assholes. You have to, because you need to count on them when you're in a tight spot. I understand the dynamic, but you gotta admit that suspicion is a reasonable mindset to take into these things."

"I've had training in this sort of thing. I go for de-escalation." (I immediately flash back to a couple of other incidents in my past where LEOs, fully free to escalate, stepped back and chose to engage instead. And others where they, well, didn't. Funny how the latter interactions tend to loom so much larger in memory.) "I always try to resolve things peacefully," Baird continues.

"And ninety-five percent of snakes are harmless"—invoking my most-favorite ever biology-cop analogy—"but you still carry an antivenom kit when you go into the desert."

He shrugs and, I think, concedes the point.

Kevin's been contained. The paramedics wheel him past on a stretcher. He's buckled down and strapped in. His hands are cuffed behind his back. He looks around, lost. "Could you take the cuffs off, please?" he asks. "I'm not a violent person."

Three minutes, tops, since nothing existed in all time or space. Just moments ago he was stuck in a loop that denied the very existence of external reality. Now he's perfectly coherent. He doesn't understand why he's being treated this way.

They don't take off the cuffs. I don't blame them. It breaks my heart anyway. I tell Kevin I'll take care of Blueberry while he's away (the little pudgeball fled into our backyard while all this was going down). Officer Baird and I wander after the gurney; he gives me his badge and phone number, and his email in case I want to follow up ("I probably won't be able to give you any details—that's Kevin's confidence—but I can at least tell you he's okay.") I wonder if he's the kind of guy who'd be willing to answer a few background questions if I ever put a cop in one of my stories.

The city employees move in with garbage bags and blue latex gloves. They say I can have my tent back if I want but it's a write-off; I salvage the hollow bones (gotta be able to find a use for those somewhere) and let them collect everything else for disposal.

The ambulance drives away.

There are two people in Kevin's brain. They don't play well together; only one is in control at any given time. Some kind of switch toggles between them. I hope Kevin can find a way to keep his hand on it.

In the meantime, a black shape lurks in the underbrush and glares at me with yellow eyes. She's lost her best and only friend; Kevin may have his issues but those two have been together for almost ten years, and he chose to sleep without a roof over his head rather than abandon her. So we won't abandon her either. She still doesn't trust us as far as she could throw an ibex, but she creeps out of cover to eat the food we serve, once we've gone back inside.

I guess it's a start.

---

1 HTTPS://WWW.THESTAR.COM/NEWS/GTA/2017/07/21/SIU-CHARGES-CIVILIAN-IN-BEATING-OF-TEEN.HTML

2 This is typical of the TCHC; they treat their tenants with contempt and every request as a shiftless attempt to game the system. I lived there for years, fighting rearguard against bedbugs and bad electrical wiring. When I asked them to deal with the black mold in my bathroom or the meter-wide hole in my ceiling, they literally laughed in my face.

And So It Begins.

BLOG JUN 23, JUL 3 2010

They could have held the whole damn G20 summit in Huntsville, like the G8 immediately before it; the infrastructure was already in place. But they didn't. They decided to stick it in the heart of downtown Toronto, and then build an indoor wading pool with fake plastic trees and wall-sized pictures of the Muskokas so visiting dignitaries and journalists could get a feel for Canada's Great Outdoors.

Or, if they *had* to do it in Toronto, they could have used the brand new facilities at Exhibition place. Right on the lake, state of the art, much easier for security. Designed explicitly for just this kind of thing. But no: too unobtrusive.

Instead, they've walled off a huge section of the downtown. Nobody gets in or out without ID and security screening. Train and streetcar routes have been chopped in half like worms. UK-level camera networks have been installed throughout the core, and the fuckers aren't even *pretending* that those will be coming down when the festivities are over; we've jumped into a whole new surveillance-state bracket over the course of a single extended photo-op. Half the city (including the Ministry of the Attorney General) has been told to just stay home for the rest of the week. Bay Street execs have been warned not to wear suits and ties to work: such attire constitutes "posing as a dignitary", you see, makes you suspicious by virtue of the fact that you're dressing to *blend in* with all those world-class entourages deep in the Forbidden Zone. (Of course, if you *don't* wear a suit and tie in the heart of TO's business section you look like a protester, and I don't have to tell you what's in store for *those* poor bastards.)

Local journos have been outfitted with gas masks and body armour by their employers. None of them expect to be shot or gassed by protestors; the Fourth Estate is protecting its own against the gentle protections of local law enforcement, who have been out in force for some time now. The core is infested, the police are literally moving in packs; we encountered two separate gangs of them just walking home the few blocks from dinner last night. Tourists caught taking snapshots of the Great Wall are forced to delete their files or be arrested. The sound of helicopters outside my building has been incessant and deafening; I barely noticed the earthquake this afternoon.

Way back on Monday night I was coming home from dinner with a fellow whose acquaintance I recently made via Squidgate; he's in town running satellite feeds for the network coverage. (Some of you may know him as uplinktruck; interesting guy, good dinnertime companion, and one of those folks you want to keep around to remind yourself that not everyone thinks the way you do. I hope we get to do it again.) I live blocks away from the Forbidden Zone, and at the time it was almost a week before the summit actually started; but this is what I encountered parked across the street from my apartment:

I took out my camera. At which point I was immediately accosted by these two gentlemen:

"What are you doing?"

"I'm taking a picture." I even smiled.

"You're taking a picture of these vehicles."

"Yes."

"Why are you taking pictures of these vehicles?"

"I live here. It's unusual to come home and find four paddy-wagons parked outside your bedroom window. I take it this is for the summit."

Nod.

"Say, can I take *your* picture?"

"No."

"How about *yours*, then?"

"No."

"Then I guess we're done here."

And we were, too. Except for the picture I took from the laundry-room balcony on the fourth floor, once I was safely home (I've arrowed the vantage point on the pic above). Night setting, no flash, digital zoom, taken by someone who doesn't know Aperture Science from an F-Stop, and it still turned out pretty well; you gotta love the Canon Powershot.

This nasty, belligerent thing my city is turning into? This place where wearing a suit has suddenly become a suspicious act, and unsmiling dead-eyed orcs emerge from the darkness to try and intimidate you for the act of taking a snapshot on a public street?

That, you don't gotta love so much.

Dress Rehearsal

A dispatch from a place we haven't quite got to yet:

A newsfeed running in one corner of his display served up a fresh riot from Hongcouver. State-of-the-art security systems gave their lives in defense of glassy spires and luxury enclaves—defeated not by clever hacks or superior technology, but by the sheer weight of flesh against their muzzles. The weapons died of exhaustion, disappeared beneath a tide of live bodies scrambling over dead ones. The crowd breached the gates as he watched, screaming in triumph. Thirty thousand voices in superposition: a keening sea, its collective voice somehow devoid of any humanity. It sounded almost mechanical. It sounded like the wind.

—*βehemoth*

A whole week later, and most of the world seems to have moved on. We're frogs, after all; take the stimulus out of our immediate perceptual sphere and we'll forget it ever existed. But suppose we were mammals? Suppose we were capable of adding two and two, of learning from experience. What take-home messages would we have distilled from the G20 festivities?

For one thing, we might conclude that the best way to avoid an altercation with the police would be to start smashing windows and trashing cars; Yonge Street was rampant with random acts of vandalism last Saturday, and myriad cops just stood around watching. On the other hand, if you were looking for a truncheon across the spine your best strategy might be to sit down in the street and start singing "Oh Canada"; our brave Boys in Blue didn't seem to have any trouble at all rushing *those* troublemakers from behind. Other strategies included penning in peaceful protesters with rows of shield-whacking riot cops, ordering them to disperse, and then refusing to let them leave (one of these incidents happened about two blocks from where I live); refusing to recognize the press credentials of the journalists you arrested on, well, no charge anyone admits to now; or just beating on random bystanders for no good reason.

They tried to put a couple of kinds of topspin on the aftermath. At first they took the line that "property can be replaced but lives can't", so their strategy was to simply let the protestors "wear themselves out" against the storefront windows (and presumably against those abandoned police cars set alight, curiously bereft—one might even say *stripped-down*—of the computer hardware that normally festoons the dashboards of such vehicles). When that didn't jibe with proliferating footage of unarmed civilians getting the ol' snatch-and-grab or a boot to the head, they told us that evildoing anarchists had doffed their black costumes and were blending in with the regular folks; what choice did the police have but to attack folks who looked regular, just to be on the safe side?

A cynic might suspect that the truth was a whole lot simpler: behind the truncheons and the tear gas and the riot helmets lurked cowardly chickenshits who didn't want to risk going up against someone armed with so much as a brick pried from the street. Someone who might actually fight *back* when attacked. Going after unarmed protestors sitting on the pavement is so much safer.

Police Chief Bill Blair didn't just admit to lying about sweeping and draconian laws that don't actually exist; he *bragged* about it, with a smirk on his face. Countless citizens—demonstrators, journalists, joggers, *grocery shoppers* for fuck's sake—were told that they would be arrested if they didn't submit to searches on the street, if they didn't hand over their papers on demand. Most submitted; many were arrested anyway, on whatever flimsy pretext the badges could sift from their illegal searches. If you happened to have a pen-knife keychain in your pocket you were guilty of possessing a "weapon of opportunity". If you happened to have a filtermask in your backpack—you know, those disposable things painters and pest control folks wear to protect their respiratory tracts from fumes and smog and solvents—you were attempting to "disguise" yourself. (One woman arrested on that pretext had a filtermask because she was an artist—who did freelance work for the Toronto PD.) I'm given to understand that one dude was hassled because he was coming back from a soccer game carrying a vuvuzela[1]; it could have been used, he was told, as a "call to violence". (Of course, this was before he identified himself as a crown attorney. For some reason he was not among the nine hundred ultimately arrested.[2])

The take-home message from these reports and images might be: if we didn't want to mow those armed and helmeted stormtroopers down before, we sure as shit do *now*. When the people charged with upholding the law lie to the citizenry about what that law even is; when they give "lawful commands" to disperse and then prevent anyone from dispersing; when they detain, search, arrest, and attack jes'-plain-folks for no better reason than that *the Cylons look like us now*—maybe we've passed the point at which we should be letting these thugs and bullies stomp all over us. Maybe we should start stomping *back*.

It's an easy reaction to have, given the evidence of our own eyes, the smug admissions of the authorities themselves. It's hard not to feel the blood boil. The problem with fighting back, of course, was articulated very eloquently by a dude posting under the name AngusM[3] following my rant about the BP spill: every act of violence on the part of us little people can be used to justify "increased repression in the name of 'security'. The attackers can be painted as 'extremists' and 'fanatics', while the state presents itself as the guardian of 'peace' and 'stability'. Terrorist attacks strengthen rather than weaken despots."

I don't think there's any denying the truth of AngusM's argument. It bears pointing out, though, that it really isn't an argument against the use of violence at all. It is an argument *for* violence—or rather, an argument that highlights the unparalleled effectiveness of violence as a means of getting your own way. When the state cracks down, after all, it doesn't do it with daisies and fluffy kittens; it cracks down with guns and gas and snipers. The problem is not that violence doesn't work; it's that it works too damn well, and the other side has cornered the market. No matter how many guns any individual might stockpile, next to the state we are as naked as newborns.

But if violence plays into the hands of the repressors, *non*violence does exactly the same thing. I don't think we have in this country any realistic possibility of bringing about real change by working within the political process, simply because it's impossible to mount a political campaign without corporate sponsorship. You can't get elected without getting your message out; you can't get your message out without backing from wealthy benefactors; potential benefactors got wealthy in the first place because the status quo works just fine for them, thank you very much, and they're not about to throw their support behind any candidate who's likely to force them to clean up the messes they make.[4] In fact, they will do everything within their power to ensure that such candidates never rise to power. Hell, look at Obama down in the US; potentially the most radically innovative president in generations, and in terms of his performance on matters of civil rights and governmental transparency you'd be hard-pressed to tell him from Dubya.

Bureaucratic and political organisms are like any other kind; they exist primarily to perpetuate themselves at the expense of other systems. You cannot convince such an organism to act against its own short-term interests. So we seem to have a situation in which working for change within the system is futile; rising up *against* the system (even non-violently) provokes greater repression from the state; and protest itself is only permitted if it is ineffectual and if (in the case of the recent summits) none of the targets of discontent are ever even line-of-sight to the discontented.

It's not really news, but we seem to be living in a soft dictatorship. The only choices we're allowed to make are those which make no real difference.

But there is one possibility that might give some cause for hope; the chance that deep down, as strange as it may seem, they are more afraid of us than we are of them. The chance that ironically, it might have been that very fear that made them rub the G20 in our faces, even when other sites would have been so much less disruptive. The chance that disruption of the little people was, to some extent, the whole point of the exercise.

They didn't just have to show *us* who was boss, you see. They had to convince *themselves*.

For once, this isn't an offering from my own fevered paranoid little brain. I'm cadging it from a dude called Geoff Dow (aka Edifice Rex)[5]. His intriguing conclusion about the choice of locale for the G20 summit is that, consciously or unconsciously—but nonetheless, *deliberately*—it was "designed not so much to cow the nation's citizens . . . but to *comfort* our so-called leaders".

His reasoning makes a scary kind of sense. Surely by now, the world's leaders have seen the portents: the collapsing infrastructure, the financial meltdowns, the countless environmental disasters which—absurdly and against all their cherished beliefs—are actually wreaking economic havoc *already*, long before they're safely dead and the next generation is left to foot the bill. If their conscious minds haven't yet acknowledged the smell of rising sewage, their brain stems at least must be serving up some diffuse sense of dread as they lie in the dark each night between their zillion-thread sheets. On some level, consciously or not, they know that something is seriously *wrong* here, and—consciously or not—they're scared shitless.

Dow again:

> . . . Stephen Harper deliberately "made a bloody mess" of downtown Toronto not only because he could, but because doing so made him feel strong; exercising the power to order 19,000 armed men and women is a form of magical thinking which he "and his buddies" feel will translate into the power to order about the economy and the weather.

Consciously or not, Toronto was turned into an armed camp, because our "leaders" foresee a time when brute force will be all they have to hold on to the reins of their illusory power.

I don't know if I'm convinced by this. It credits the G20 leaders (or at least their brain stems) with a degree of insight I'm not sure is especially common amongst that crowd. But it's a plausible model at least, given the data; maybe these people really did build the Bastille in downtown Toronto last week.

Maybe what we witnessed was—on some subconscious level, at least—a dress rehearsal for the Revolution.

1 An offence deserving of incarceration, granted.
2 Neither were any members of the so-called *Black Bloc*, as far as I've heard. But by now, who's counting?
3 HTTPS://WWW.RIFTERS.COM/CRAWL/?P=1372#COMMENT-25156
4 To be honest, the majority of the population is also unlikely to *vote* for a candidate who tells them to stop living beyond their means, grow the fuck up, and rein in their standard of living to something a bit more sustainable.
5 HTTP://ED-REX.LIVEJOURNAL.COM/201222.HTML

I've had a fondness for Daryl Bem ever since his coauthored paper appeared in *Psychological Bulletin* back in 1994: a meta-analysis purporting to show replicable evidence for psionic phenomena. I cited it in *Starfish*, when I was looking for some way to justify the rudimentary telepathy my rifters experienced in impoverished environments. Bem and Honorton gave me hope that nothing was so crazy-ass that you couldn't find a peer-reviewed paper to justify it if you looked hard enough.

Not incidentally, it also gave me hope that psi might actually *exist*. There's a whole shitload of things I'd love to believe in if only there was evidence to support them, but can't because I fancy myself an empiricist. But if there were evidence for telepathy? Precognition? Telekinesis? Wouldn't that be *awesome*? And Bem was no fruitcake: the man was (and is) a highly-regarded social scientist (setting aside the oxymoron for the moment) out of Cornell, and at the top of his field. The man had *cred*.

It didn't really pan out, though. There were grumbles and rebuttals about standardisation between studies and whether the use of stats was appropriate—the usual complaints that surface whenever analysis goes meta. What most stuck in my mind back then was the point (mentioned in the Discussion) that these results, whatever you thought of them, were at least as solid as those used to justify the release of new drugs to the consumer market. I liked that. It set things in perspective (although in hindsight, it probably said more about the abysmal state of Pharma regulation than it did about the likelihood of Carrie White massacring her fellow graduates at the high school prom).

Anyhow, Bem is back, and has made a much bigger splash this time around: nine experiments to be published in the *Journal of Personality and Social Psychology*, eight of which are purported to show statistically significant evidence of not just psi but of actual *precognition*. *The New York Times* picked it up[1]; everyone from *Time* to the *Huffington Post* sat up and took notice[2]. Most of the mainstream reaction has been predictable and pretty much useless: *Time* misreads Bem's description of how he controlled for certain artefacts as some kind of confession that those artefacts weren't controlled for[3]; the *Winnipeg Free Press* simply cites the study as one of several examples in an extended harrumph about the decline of peer-reviewed science[4]. Probably the most substantive critiques hail from Wagenmakers *et al* (in a piece slotted to appear in the same issue as Bem's) and an online piece from James Alcock over at the Skeptical Inquirer website[5] (which has erupted into a kind of three-way slap-fight[6] with Bem[7] and one of his supporters[8]). And while I by no means dismiss all of the counter-arguments, even some of the more erudite skeptics' claims seem a bit suspect—one might even use the word *dishonest*—if you've actually read the source material.

I'm not going into exquisite detail on any of this; check out the sources if you want nuts and bolts. But in general terms, I like what

Bem set out to do. He took classic, well-established psychological tests and simply ran them backwards. For example, our memory of specific objects tends to be stronger if we have to interact with them somehow. If someone shows you a bunch of pictures and then asks you to, say, classify some of them by color, you'll remember the ones you classified more readily than the others if presented with the whole set at some later point (the technical term is *priming*). So, Bem reasoned, suppose you're tested against those pictures *before* you're actually asked to interact with them? If you preferentially react to the ones you haven't yet interacted with *but will at some point in the future,* you've established a kind of backwards flow of information. Of course, once you know what your subjects have chosen there's always the temptation to do something that would self-fulfill the prophecy, so to speak; but you get around that by cutting humans out of the loop entirely, letting software and random number generators decide which pictures will be primed.

I leave the specific protocols of each experiment as an exercise for those who want to follow the links, but the overall approach was straightforward. Take a well-established cause-effect test; run it backwards; if your pre-priming hit rate is significantly greater than what you'd get from random chance, call it a win. Bem also posited that sex and death would be powerful motivators from an evolutionary point of view. There weren't that many casinos or stock markets on the Pleistocene savannah, but knowing (however subconsciously) that something was going to try and eat you ten minutes down the road—or knowing that a potential mate lay in your immediate future—well, that would pretty obviously confer an evolutionary advantage over the nonpsychics in the crowd. So Bem used pictures both scary and erotic, hoping to increase the odds of significant results.

Note also that his thousand-or-so participants didn't actually know up front what they were doing. There was no explicit ESP challenge here, no cards with stars or wavy lines. All that these people knew was that they were supposed to guess which side of a masked computer screen held a picture. They weren't told what that picture was.

When that picture was neutral, their choices were purely random. When it was pornographic or scary, though, they tended to guess right more often than not. It wasn't a big effect; we're talking a hit rate of maybe 53% instead of the expected 50%. But according to the stats, the effect was real in eight out of nine experiments.

Now, of course, everyone and their dog are piling on to kick holes in the study. That's cool; that's what we do, that's how it works. Perhaps the most telling critique is the only one that really matters; nobody has been able to replicate Bem's results yet. That speaks a lot louder than some of the criticisms that have been leveled in recent days, at least partly because some of those criticisms seem, well, pretty dumb. (Bem himself responds to some of Alcock's complaints[9]).

Let's do a quick drive-by on a few of the methodological accusations folks have been making: *Bem's methodology wasn't consistent. Bem log-transformed his data; oooh, maybe he did it because untransformed data didn't give him the results he wanted. Bem ran multiple tests without correcting for the fact that the more often you run tests on a data set, the greater the chance of getting significant results through random chance.* To name but a few.

Maybe my background in field biology makes me more forgiving of such stuff, but I don't consider tweaking one's methods especially egregious when it's done to adapt to new findings. For example, Bem discovered that men weren't as responsive as women to the level of eroticism in his initial porn selections (which, as a male, I totally buy; those Harlequin Romance covers don't do it for me *at all*). So he ramped the imagery for male participants up from R to XXX. I suppose he could have continued to use nonstimulating imagery even after realising that it didn't work, just as a fisheries biologist might continue to use the same net even after discovering that its mesh was too large to catch the species she was studying. In both cases the methodology would remain "consistent". It would also be a complete waste of resources.

Bem also got some grief for using tests of statistical significance (*i.e.*, what are the odds that these results are due to random chance?) rather than Bayesian methods (*i.e.*, given that our hypothesis is true, what are the odds of getting these specific results?). (Carey gives a nice comparative thumbnail of the two approaches at the *New York Times*.[10]) I suspect this complaint could be legit. The problem I have with Bayes is that it takes your own preconceptions as a starting point: you get to choose up front the odds that psi is real, and the odds that it is not. If the data run counter to those odds, the theorem adjusts them to be more consistent with those findings on the next iteration; but obviously, if your starting assumption is that there's a 99.9999999999% chance that precognition is bullshit, it's gonna take a lot more data to swing those numbers than if you start from a bullshit-probability of only 80%. Wagenmakers *et al* tie this in to Laplace's famous statement that "extraordinary claims require extraordinary proof" (to which we shall return at the end of this post), but another way of phrasing that is "the more extreme the prejudice, the tougher it is to shake". And Bayes, by definition, uses prejudice as its launch pad.

Wagenmakers *et al* ran Bem's numbers using Bayesian techniques, starting with standard "default" values for their initial probabilities (they didn't actually say what those values were, although they cited a source). They found "substantial" support for precognition (H_I) in only one of Bem's nine experiments, and "substantial" support for its absence (H_0) in another two (they actually claim three, but for some reason they seem to have run Bem's sixth experiment twice). They then reran the same data using a range of start-up values that differed from these "defaults", just to be sure, and concluded that their results were robust. They refer the reader to an online appendix for the details of that analysis. I can't show you the figure you'll find there (for reasons that remain unclear, Tachyon is strangely reluctant to break copyright law), but its caption reads, in part,

> "The results in favor of H_I are never compelling, except perhaps for the bottom right panel."

Let me state unequivocally that the "perhaps" is disingenuous to the point of outright falsehood. The bottom right panel shows unequivocally support for H_I. So even assuming that these guys were on the money with all of their criticisms, even assuming that they've successfully demolished eight of Bem's nine claims to significance—they're admitting to evidence for the existence of precognition *by their own reckoning*. And yet they can't bring themselves to admit it, even in a caption belied by its own figure.

To some extent, it was Bem's decision to make his work replication-friendly that put this particular bull's-eye on his chest. He chose methods that were well-known and firmly established in the research community; he explicitly rejected arcane statistics in favor of simple ones that other social scientists would be comfortable with. ("It might actually be more logical from a Bayesian perspective to believe that some unknown flaw or artifact is hiding in the weeds of a complex experimental procedure or an unfamiliar statistical analysis than to believe that genuine psi has been demonstrated," he writes. "As a consequence, simplicity and familiarity become essential tools of persuasion.") Foreseeing that some might question the distributional assumptions underlying t-tests, he log-transformed his data to normalise it prior to analysis; this inspired Wagenmakers *et al* to wonder darkly "what the results were for the untransformed RTs—results that were not reported". Bem also ran the data through nonparametric tests that made no distributional assumptions at all; Alcock then complained about unexplained, redundant tests that added nothing to the analysis (despite the fact that Bem had explicitly described his rationale), and about the use of multiple tests that didn't correct for the increased odds of false positives.

This latter point is true in the general but not in the particular. Every grad student knows that desperate sinking feeling that sets in when their data show no apparent patterns at all, the temptation to inflict endless tests and transforms in the hope that please God *something* might show up. But Bem already had significant results; he used alternative analyses in case those results were somehow artefactual, and he *kept* getting significance no matter which way he came at the problem. Where I come from, it's generally considered a good sign when different approaches converge on the same result.

Bem also considered the possibility that there might be some kind of bias in algorithms used by the computer to randomise its selection of pictures; he therefore replicated his experiments using different random-number generators. He showed all his notes, all the messy bits that generally don't get presented when you want to show off your work in a peer-reviewed journal. He not only met the standards of rigor in his field: he *surpassed* them, and four reviewers (while not necessarily able to believe his findings) couldn't find any methodological or analytical flaws sufficient to keep the work from publication.

Even Bem's opponents admit to this. Wagenmakers *et al* explicitly state:

> "Bem played by the implicit rules that guide academic publishing—in fact, Bem presented many more studies than would usually be required."

They can't logically attack Bem's work without attacking the entire field of psychology. So that's what they do:

> ". . . our assessment suggests that something is deeply wrong with the way experimental psychologists design their studies and report their statistical results. It is a disturbing thought that many experimental findings, proudly and confidently reported in the literature as real, might in fact be based on statistical tests that are explorative and biased (see also Ioannidis, 2005). We hope the Bem article will become a signpost for change, a writing on the wall: psychologists must change the way they analyze their data."

And you know, maybe they're right. We biologists have always looked at those soft-headed new-agers over in the Humanities building with almost as much contempt as the physicists and chemists looked at *us*, back before we owned the whole genetic-engineering thing. I'm perfectly copacetic with the premise that psychology is broken. But if the field is really in such disrepair, why is it that none of those myriad less-rigorous papers acted as a wake-up call? Why snooze through so many decades of hack analysis only to pick on a paper which, by your own admission, is better than most?

Well, do you suppose anyone would be eviscerating Bem's methodology with quite so much enthusiasm if he'd concluded that there was no evidence for precognition? Here's a hint: Alcock's critique painstakingly picks at every one of Bem's experiments except for #7. Perhaps that seventh experiment finally got it right, you think. Perhaps Alcock gave that one a pass because Bem's methodology was, for once, airtight? Let's let Alcock speak for himself:

"The hit rate was not reported to be significant in this experiment. The reader is therefore spared my deliberations."

Evidently bad methodology isn't worth criticising, just so long as you agree with the results.

This leads nicely into what is perhaps the most basic objection to Bem's work, a more widespread and gut-level response that both underlies and transcends the methodological attacks: sheer, eye-popping incredulity. *This is bullshit. This* has *to be bullshit. This doesn't make any goddamned sense.*

It mustn't be. Therefore it isn't.

Of course, nobody phrases it that baldly. They're more likely to claim that "there's no mechanism in physics which could explain these results." Wagenmakers *et al* went so far as to claim that Bem's effect can't be real because nobody is bankrupting the world's casinos with their psychic powers, which is logically equivalent to saying that protective carapaces can't be adaptive because lobsters aren't bulletproof. As for the whacked-out argument that there's no theoretical mechanism in place to describe the data, I can't think of a more effective way of grinding science to a halt than to reject any data that don't fit our current models of reality. If everyone thought that way, Earth would still be a flat disk at the center of a crystal universe.

Some people deal with their incredulity better than others. (One of the paper's reviewers opined that they found the results "ridiculous", but recommended publication anyway because they couldn't find fault with the methodology or the analysis.) Others take refuge in the mantra that "extraordinary claims require extraordinary evidence".

I've always thought that was a pretty good mantra. If someone told me that my friend had gotten drunk and run his car into a telephone pole I might evince skepticism out of loyalty to my friend, but a photo of the accident scene would probably convince me. People get drunk, after all (especially my friends); accidents happen. But if the same source told me that a flying saucer had used a tractor beam to force my friend's car off the road, a photo wouldn't come close to doing the job. I'd just reach for the Photoshop manual to figure out how the image had been faked. Extraordinary claims require extraordinary evidence.

The question, here in the second decade of the 21st century, is: what constitutes an "extraordinary claim"? A hundred years ago it would have been extraordinary to claim that a cat could be simultaneously dead and alive; fifty years ago it would have been extraordinary to claim that life existed above the boiling point of water, kilometers deep in the Earth's crust. Twenty years ago it was extraordinary to suggest that the universe was not only expanding but that the rate of expansion was *accelerating*. Today, physics concedes the theoretical possibility of time travel (in fact, I've been led to believe that the whole arrow-of-time thing has always been problematic to the physicists; most of their equations work both ways, with no need for a unidirectional time flow).

Yes, I know. I'm skating dangerously close to the same defensive hysteria every new-age nutjob invokes when confronted with skepticism over the Healing Power of Petunias; *yeah, well, a thousand years ago everybody thought the world was flat, too.* The difference is that those nutjobs make their arguments in lieu of any actual evidence whatsoever in support of their claims, and the rejoinder of skeptics everywhere has always been "Show us the data. There are agreed-upon standards of evidence. Show us numbers, P-values, something that can pass peer review in a primary journal by respectable researchers with established reputations. These are the standards you must meet."

How often have we heard this? How often have we pointed out that the UFO cranks and the Ghost Brigade never manage to get published in the peer-reviewed literature? How often have we pointed out that their so-called "evidence" isn't up to our standards?

Well, Bem cleared that bar. And the response of some has been to raise it. All along we've been demanding that the fringe adhere to the same standards the rest of us do, and finally the fringe has met that challenge. And now we're saying they should be held to a *different* standard, a higher standard, because they are making an *extraordinary claim.*

This whole thing makes me deeply uncomfortable. It's not that I believe the case for precognition has been made; it hasn't. Barring independent confirmation of Bem's results, I remain a skeptic. Nor am I especially outraged by the nature of the critiques, although I do think some of them edge up against outright dishonesty. I'm on public record as a guy who regards science as a knock-down-drag-out between competing biases, personal more often than not.[11] (On the other hand, if I'd tried my best to demolish evidence of precognition and still ended up with "substantial" support in one case out of nine, I wouldn't be sweeping it under the rug with phrases like "never compelling" and "except possibly"—I'd be saying "Holy shit, the dude may have overstated his case but there may be something to this anyway . . .")

I am, however, starting to have second thoughts about Laplace's principle. I'm starting to wonder if it's especially wise to demand higher evidentiary standards for any claim we happen to find especially counterintuitive this week. A consistently-applied 0.05 significance threshold may be arbitrary, but at least it's independent of the vagaries of community standards. The moment you start talking about extraordinary claims you have to define what qualifies as one, and the best definition I can come up with is:

any claim which is inconsistent with our present understanding of the way things work. The inevitable implication of that statement is that today's worldview is always the right one; we've already got a definitive lock on reality, and anything that suggests otherwise is especially suspect.

Which, you'll forgive me for saying so, seems like a pretty extraordinary claim in its own right.

Maybe we could call it the Galileo Corollary.

1 HTTPS://WWW.NYTIMES.COM/2011/01/06/SCIENCE/06ESP.HTML

2 HTTP://WWW.HUFFINGTONPOST.COM/JULIA-MOULDEN/DO-WE-HAVE-ONE-EXTRA-SENS _ B _ 808417.HTML

3 HTTP://HEALTHLAND.TIME.COM/2011/01/12/WAIT-ESP-IS-REAL/

4 HTTP://WWW.WINNIPEGFREEPRESS.COM/OPINION/WESTVIEW/SCIENCE-JOURNALS-IN-DECLINE-113189344.HTML

5 HTTP://WWW.CSICOP.ORG/SPECIALARTICLES/SHOW/BACK _ FROM _ THE _ FUTURE

6 HTTP://WWW.CSICOP.ORG/SPECIALARTICLES/SHOW/RESPONSE _ TO _ BEMS _ COMMENTS

7 HTTP://WWW.CSICOP.ORG/SPECIALARTICLES/SHOW/RESPONSE _ TO _ ALCOCKS _ BACK _ FROM _ THE _ FUTURE _ COMMENTS _ ON _ BEM

8 HTTP://DEANRADIN.BLOGSPOT.COM/2010/12/MY-COMMENTS-ON-ALCOCKS-COMMENTS-ON-BEMS.HTML

9 HTTP://WWW.CSICOP.ORG/SPECIALARTICLES/SHOW/RESPONSE _ TO _ ALCOCKS _ BACK _ FROM _ THE _ FUTURE _ COMMENTS _ ON _ BEM

10 HTTP://WWW.NYTIMES.COM/2011/01/11/SCIENCE/11ESP.HTML

11 HTTPS://WWW.RIFTERS.COM/CRAWL/?P=886

Why I Suck.

BLOG JUNE 6, 2013

I've just sat through an entire season—which is to say three measly episodes, in what might be the new SOP for the BBC (see *Sherlock*)—of this new zombie show called *In the Flesh*.

Yeah, I know. These days, the very phrase "new zombie show" borders on oxymoronic. And yet, this really is a fresh spin on the old paradigm: imagine that, years after the dead clawed their way out of the ground and started feasting on the living, we figured out how to *fix* them. Not *cure*, exactly: think diabetes or HIV, management instead of recovery. Imagine a drug that repairs the mind, even if it can't fix the rot or the pallor or the eyes.

Imagine the gradual reconnection of cognitive circuitry, and the flashbacks it provokes as animal memories reboot. Imagine what it must be like when the sudden fresh remembrance of people killed and eviscerated is regarded, clinically, as a sign of *recovery*.

In the Flesh imagines. It also imagines government-mandated reintegration of the recovering undead ("Partially-Deceased-

Syndrome" is the politically-correct term; it comes replete with cheery pamphlets to help next-of-kin manage the transition). Contact lenses and pancake makeup to make the partly-dead more palatable to the communities in which they once lived. Therapy sessions in which the overwhelming guilt of freshly-remembered murder and cannibalism alternates with defiant self-justification: "We had to do it to survive. They blew our heads off without a second thought—they were *protecting humanity!* They get medals, we get medicated . . ." Hypertrophic Neighborhood Watch patrols who never let you forget that no matter how Human these creatures may seem *now*, a couple of missed injections is all it takes to turn them back into ravening monsters *in the heart of our community* . . .

What's science fiction's mission statement, again? Oh, right: to explore the social impact of scientific and technological *change*. Too much SF takes the Grand Tour Amusement Park approach, offers up an awesome parade of wonders and prognostications like some kind of futuristic freak show. It takes a show like *In the Flesh* to remind us that technology is only half of the equation, that the molecular composition of the hammer or the rpms of the chainsaw, in isolation, are of limited interest. Our mission hasn't been accomplished until the hammer hits the flesh.

In the Flesh rubs your face in that impact. It rubs my face in my own inadequacy.

Echopraxia has its share of zombies, you see. They show up at the beginning of the book, in the Oregon desert; through the course of the story, various cast members wrestle with zombiesque aspects of their own behavior. *Echopraxia*'s zombies come in two flavors: the usual viral kind sowing panic and anarchy, and a more precise, surgically-induced breed used by the military for ops with high body counts, ops for which self-awareness might prove an impediment. Both breeds get screen time; both highlight philosophical issues which challenge the very definition of what it means to be Human.

Neither really tries to answer questions like: *How do you deal with the guilt?* Or *How do you handle the dissonance of becoming a local hero through the indiscriminate slaughter of rabid zombies, only to have your son come back from Afghanistan partially-deceased with a face full of staples?*

In the Flesh does a lot of the same things I've done in my own writing. It even serves up a pseudosciencey rationale to explain the zombie predilection for brains: victims of PDS lose the ability to grow "gial" cells in their brains, and so must consume those of others to make up the deficit. (I'm not sure whether this is an inadvertent misspelling of "glial" or if the writers were savvy enough to invent a new cell type with a similar name, the better to fend off the nitpickery of geeks like me.) It doesn't hold up to rigorous scrutiny any better than *Blindsight's* invocation of protocadherin deficits to justify obligate cannibalism in my own undead, but in a way that's the point: they've taken pretty much the same approach that I have.

The difference is, they've done so much more with it.

I used technobabble to justify a philosophical debate about free will. *In the Flesh* used it to show us grief-stricken parents dealing with a beloved son after he's taken his own life—and come back. Side by side, it's painfully obvious which of us used our resources to better effect.

I only wish I'd have been able to see that without the object lesson.

The Black Knight. In Memoriam.

Two months ago my brother Jon—my senior by eight years—suffered a stroke which bled into his cerebellum. The time since has been, as his wife Tracy described it, a roller coaster: neuro-surgeons reluctant to operate while Jon was on heart meds, car-diologists unwilling to take him off those meds for fear of fatal clots. Periods of delirium and intervals of clarity. Organ systems spinning the daily roulette wheel to decide whose turn it was to shut down today. Brain damage—then No, *motor* damage but cognitive functions probably okay. Squeezed hands and eye movements on even days; total unresponsiveness on odd ones. Two, three occasions when all was lost and plugs were pulled and the fucker just kept living. A gradual, incremental climb out of the well, enough to justify a move from ICU to a long-term rehab facility where he could learn how to do things like swal-low again. Relapse. Liver and kidney failure, and recovery. The whole deal.

I couldn't be there for any of it: thanks to a gang of ignorant fucktards with far more power than brains, I am banned from my brother's adopted country. It never really mattered until now. In fact, it was a badge of honor. But for the past two months there's been nothing to do but wait, and hope, and squeeze whatever data we could out of Tracy's daily updates to see whether the line, on balance, was going up or down.

The line ended around 2:15am on Thursday, May 10. I don't know quite how to process it.

There's a part of me that just doesn't believe he's dead. This was hardly the first time the reaper came calling, after all. It was thirty years ago that some pernicious bug got past Jon's pericardium and ate away two-thirds of his heart muscle; the doctors gave him two years then, three at the most. Every birthday he celebrated since 1985 was spit in their eyes.

Things—deteriorated, though. Over the decades. Bad heart function, reduced peripheral circulation: diabetes and neuropathies, a plastic umbilical leading back to a little tank of oxygen that lived in the bedroom and accompanied him on his travels. A workaholic suddenly reduced to three or four productive hours a day, although he kept pushing it. One day he passed out and collapsed onto a water heater, burning a swath of his skin to a crisp: but the result-ing adrenaline shock kick-started his heart and kept him alive long enough for the doctors to get to him.

Even then, he seemed unkillable. Like Monty Python's Black Knight—no matter how many pieces he lost, he just laughed and kept fighting.

There were pacemakers then, and an armored emergency vest equipped with defib paddles, explosive bolts, and a wireless in-ternet connection—the idea being that in the event of another heart failure, the bolts would detonate and spread conductant goop across his chest; the paddles would then shock his heart back into action while the vest called online for an ambulance. After a while he ditched those training wheels and became a bona-fide cyborg, with the implantation of a Ventricular Assist Device: the same type of battery-operated demiheart that so paradoxically humanized Dick Cheney when *his* shriveled old pumper gave up the ghost. Jon traded in his pulse for a second shot, for more strength and energy than he'd had in years.

That may have been the one leap forward the poor bastard got, though. Everything else was rearguard. And yet I never heard him whine or complain about his own predicament, no matter how dire. He *was* the Black Knight: he'd disappear into ICU and he'd come back three steps closer to death and we'd talk on the phone and he'd *laugh. Pshaw. Just a flesh wound.*

There's so much to say about my brother, and the internet is only so large. The time the Feds cut off his disability benefits— *Hey, who cares if what we're doing is illegal? Without benefits, none of these people can afford to take us to court!*—and he took them to court. And *won* (although his victory was diluted somewhat by the endless series of "random" tax audits that followed.) Or that time he ran the winning campaign for the mayor of Hamilton. (I learned about attack ads at my brother's knee; by today's standards, his were subtle to the point of meta. They never even explicitly named the person they were attacking.) His good-natured descent into the dark side, his repudiation of all things Canadian and whole-hearted embrace of what some would call the American Health-care System. (Let's just say that the Watts brothers could not claim unanimity on the question of whether the quality of your medical care should scale to the size of your bank account.)

Actually, that's a big one: his delight in argument, for the sheer joy of the exercise. I hardly ever agreed with the guy on anything. (Actually, scratch that; I think when you came right down to it, we agreed on more than he'd ever admit to, but he just really liked yanking my chain on general principles.) Half the time he was full of shit, and he *knew* he was full of shit, and he'd throw it against the wall anyway just to see if it would stick. Once he tried to lecture me on seal-fisheries interactions off Canada's east coast, a subject with which I had more than a passing familiarity (a script I'd done on that subject had just won the Environment Canada trophy for Best Film on the Environment). He pulled his argument out of his ass; I busted him; he laughed. He was far more interested in the fun of the joust than in anything so boring as *winning*.

We didn't see each other often: he and Tracy down in New York state, me up here in Toronto. I'd drop by for a day or two on my way back from Readercon, perhaps. They'd come up here a bit more frequently, although Jon's health constrained his travel options. Caitlin and I had a chance to hang out at their place back in 2009, just a few months before the border slammed shut. We won't forget the feral peacock that had taken up residence in their back yard, or the neighbors' orange cat who spent far more time hanging out in Jon and Tracy's company than he ever did at his official home across the street. We won't forget the horde of raccoons advancing over the crest of the hill every night just after sundown, their beady little eyes glinting in the backyard light as they closed on the food that Tracy left scattered about the lawn to lure them in. The endless quantities of lobster bisque. The wine and companionship and late-night conversations/arguments. (Oh, and the scotch: when I wanted to thank my agent for sticking it out with me, it was Jon's expertise that pointed me to just the right single-malt to express my gratitude.)

That was the one and only time that Caitlin had a chance to see Jon in his native habitat before the US and I went dead to each other. Since then it's been Christmas, maybe once or twice in the summer, always in Canada. Mostly my contact with Jon was by phone or e-mail. We talked every month or so, exchanged dueling links on everything from Obamacare to Climate Change. He was never a frequent presence in my life but he was a vital one, always there for the high points and the low. A 47″ flatscreen in our bedroom was part of that legacy, a gift he and Tracy bought to celebrate my first Hugo nomination. He was researching Michigan lawyers within hours of my arrest at Port Huron. A man with a malfunctioning heart and maybe four good hours a day in him, he was on the phone to Caitlin at 1:30a.m. while the doctors were scraping rotten meat from the inside of my leg. (In fact I'm pretty sure he was on the phone to me, too, between operations; I seem to remember Caitlin's cell against my ear in the ICU, and Jon's voice mocking my position on climate change. I remember finding it vaguely unfair that he would take advantage of my drug-addled impairment. But morphine was involved, so details remain elusive.)

The BUG and I kept our marriage secret but that didn't stop Jon and Tracy from dumping a case of champagne on our doorstep the next time they were in town. And I'll never forget the letter he wrote me—the last letter, as it turned out—following the death of Banana: short and to the point, a reminiscence of some eighties-era episode when I'd taken a cat off his hands when Jon had found himself unable to continue providing a home for him. I'd long since forgotten. Jon never had, and had been watching from a distance ever since: "I have subsequently come to understand that this is one of his roles in life," he wrote. "Stepping in to take responsibility for those less caring, or less able to care, for the Fur Patrol of whatever race or phylum." Enclosed was a cheque that went a long way toward mitigating the financial cost of Banana's ending.

Two weeks after writing that my brother was in Tufts Cardiac Intensive Care Unit. He never saw home again.

Married three times or four—depending on whether you count common-law—starting at age sixteen. (You only have to spend ten minutes with Tracy to know that he kept trying until he got it right.) World-class organist—came in third in an international competition in Bruges, before arthritis truncated that future in his mid-twenties. Top-forty tweaker for MCA. Distributor of weird-ass glassware from his basement. Dean of the Hamilton College of Music. Christ knows what else; I know next to nothing of the lost years he spent on the west coast.

The faintest echoes persist on my blog; Jon posted comments here occasionally, under the handle "Finster Mushwell" (don't ask). They are pallid things, though. You can read them all and come away with no sense at all of the man he was: Fighter. Stalwart. Infuriating life-saver. Pain in the ass. The Black Knight, indomitable.

Until Thursday.

I don't know what to say. I don't even know what to think. Except, maybe this: Any number born to the Watts name can lay claim to being part of my family.

Jon, alone among them, *felt* like one.

Viva Zika!

There's this guy I know, Dan Brooks. Retired now, an eminent parasitologist and evolutionary biologist back in the day. He did a lot of work on emerging infectious diseases (EIDs, for you acronym fetishists) down in Latin America. A few years back I wrote some introductory text for an online database he was compiling. Part of it went like this:

> You will find no public health advisories about Lyme Disease in Costa Rica. On the face of it, this is perfectly reasonable; Lyme Disease has never been reported there, and none of the local tick species is known to carry the bacterium that causes it.
>
> Some of those ticks, however, are closely related to those in other regions which do carry that bacterium, and many pathogens are able to infect a far greater range of species than they actually occupy;

simple isolation is the only thing that keeps them from reaching their true infectious potential. Thus, while Costa Rica is free of Lyme Disease at present, potential vectors already occur in abundance there. The infrastructure for an outbreak is already in place: a single asymptomatic tourist may be all it takes to loose this painful, debilitating disease on the local population.

Lyme Disease is by no means unique. Climate change alters movement and home range for myriad organisms. Our transport of people and goods carries countless pathogens around the globe. Isolated species come into sudden contact; parasites and diseases find themselves surrounded by naïve and vulnerable new hosts. And so maladies literally unknown only four or five decades ago—AIDS in humans, Ebola in humans and gorillas, West Nile virus and Avian Influenza in humans and birds, chytrid fungi in amphibians, distemper in sea lions—have today become almost commonplace. Pathogens encounter new hosts with no resistance and no time to evolve any. In such a world EIDs are inevitable. They are ongoing. A month scarcely passes without news of some freshly-discovered strain of influenza trading up to a human host.

This month, it's Zika. Spread by the tropical mosquito *Aedes aegypti*, so we northern folks (as they assured us only last week) don't have to worry. Hell, even 80% of the people who *do* get infected never show any symptoms. The other 20% have to suffer through joint pain, fever, a mild skin rash before Zika gets bored and wanders off to bother someone else. Ebola this ain't; it's never even killed anyone, as far as we know. I'm guessing that's why no one's bothered to develop a vaccine.

The things it does to fetuses, though. Now *that's* pretty horrific, even if WHO is back-pedaling and admitting that no one's yet proven beyond a doubt that Zika causes microcephaly. (If it doesn't, someone's going to have to explain the fact that Brazilian cases of microcephaly shot up by a factor of twenty-five since Zika debuted there last year—from a long-term annual average of 150 cases to well over four thousand, and climbing. That's a pretty stark coincidence.)

Even granting the argument that rampant Zikaphobia has resulted in the erroneous tagging of garden-variety small-headed babies—of a sample of 732 diagnoses, only 270 (37%) turned out to be truly microcephalic[1]—we're still talking a tenfold increase over historical levels. (And that may be conservative; it implicitly assumes that even though so many recent cases were misdiagnosed, none of the previous decades' baseline cases were.) Claims that Zika wasn't confirmed even in the majority of the verified cases aren't especially reassuring given that tests for Zika in the hot zone are "very inefficient"[2]—not to mention the fact that French Polynesia experienced a similar correlation between fetal CNS malformations and a Zika outbreak just the year before[3].

Back last week—when all us N'Ammers were being told *we* had nothing to fear because *A. aegypti* never got out of the subtropics—the first thing that came to my mind was Dan's work on EIDs, and the ease with which certain microbes can swap hosts. "Sure, *aegypti* won't make it this far," I told the BUG, "but what if Zika hitches a ride with *Anopheles* in the overlap zone?" It was, for a science fiction writer and worst-case scenarist, an embarrassing failure of imagination. Because Zika *has* in fact found some new Uber driver to hitch a ride with over the past few days, and it isn't a mosquito.

It's us[4]. Zika has learned to cut out the middleman. It is now a sexually transmitted human disease.

And call me Pollyanna, but I can't help nurture the outlandish-but-not-entirely-impossible dream that we might be looking at our own salvation. We might be looking at the salvation of the planet itself.

Because there's no denying that pretty much every problem in the biosphere hails from a common cause. Climate change, pollution, habitat loss, the emptying of biodiversity from land, sea, and air, an extinction rate unparalleled since the last asteroid and the transformation of our homeworld into a planet of weeds—all our fault, of course. There are simply too many of us. Over seven billion already, and we *still* can't keep it in our pants.

Of course, nothing lasts forever. My money was on some kind of self-induced die-off: a global pandemic that left corpses piled in the streets, or some societal collapse that reduced us to savagery on the third day and a relict population on the three hundredth. Maybe a holy nuclear war, if you're into golden oldies. The problem with these scenarios—other than the fact that they involve the violent suffering and extermination of billions of sapient beings—is that we'd wreck the environment even more on our way out, leave behind a devastated wasteland where only cockroaches and stromatolites could flourish. The cure would be worse than the disease.

Many well-meaning folks have pointed out that birth rates decline as living standards improve; since so much of the world still lives in relative poverty, the obvious solution is to simply raise everyone's quality of life to Norwegian levels. The obvious fly in *that* ointment is that your average first-worlder stamps a far bigger boot onto the face of the planet than some subsistence farmer in Burkina Faso no matter *how* many kids she might have. Mammals like me don't need a brood of children to wreck the environment; we do it just fine with our cars and our imported groceries and our giant 4K TVs. Elevating 7.6 billion people to levels of North American gluttony does not strike me as a solution to anything other than fast-tracking the planet back to Scenario One.

But look at Zika. It doesn't kill you, doesn't even present symptoms in most cases. The worst you have to fear is a few aches and pains, a rash, a couple of sick days.

All it *really* does is stop you from breeding.

In a way it's almost secondary, all this hemming and hawing about whether Zika *causes* birth defects or whether it's just mysteriously *correlated* with them somehow. Fear hangs in the air, and the benefits are already starting to roll in. Just two days ago, WHO declared Zika a "Public Health Emergency of International Concern."[5] Brazil, Colombia, Jamaica, El Salvador and Venezuela have all publicly advised their citizens against getting pregnant—all the more remarkable for the fact that all but Jamaica are bastions of Catholicism, which normally champions the whole Biblical *fill-the-earth-with-thy-numbers* imperative. And now that this baby-monsterizing bug can be transmitted directly, human to human, through the very act of intercourse? Why, none of us are safe!

I look forward to a day when Zika—or at least, the fear of Zika—is everywhere. I look forward to a day when this benign baby-twisting bug inspires us to save ourselves, frightens us into necessary measures that mere foresight and intelligence could never inspire. There need be no societal collapse, no devastating pandemic or wretched nuclear winter. There need be no great die-off to save the planet. There need only be this additional cost, this *danger*, that makes you think twice before indulging your reproductive urges. In the space of a single generation, the numbers of this pest species could just . . . gently taper off. We could become *sustainable* again.

That is my dream. Of course, upon waking, I have to admit that now Zika is in the spotlight, the medical community will simply fall over itself in the race to find a cure. They will succeed. And we'll be back where we started—albeit with some new proprietary and lucrative drug in hand, available only from Pfizer or Johnson & Johnson.

That's the thing about being an optimist. You have dreams, and reality crushes them.

I could write an upbeat short story about it, at least. Too bad that none of those Shine-on *Let's do an SF anthology about **positive futures!*** people have ever approached me, for some reason . . .

1 HTTP://RIFTERS.COM/REAL/ARTICLES/NS-724-2015 _ ECLAMC-ZIKA%20 VIRUS _ V-FINAL _ 012516.PDF

2 HTTP://WWW.NYTIMES.COM/2016/01/28/WORLD/AMERICAS/REPORTS-OF-ZIKA-LINKED-BIRTH-DEFECT-RISE-IN-BRAZIL.HTML? _ R=0

3 HTTP://ECDC.EUROPA.EU/EN/PRESS/NEWS/ _ LAYOUTS/FORMS/NEWS _ DISPFORM. ASPX?ID=1329&LIST=8DB7286C-FE2D-476C-9133-18FF4CB1B568&SOURCE=HTTP%3A%2F %2FECDC.EUROPA.EU%2FEN%2FPAGES%2FHOME.ASPX

4 HTTP://WWW.CBC.CA/NEWS/HEALTH/ZIKA-VIRUS-SEXUAL-TRANMISSION-WHO-1.3431458

5 HTTP://WWW.WHO.INT/MEDIACENTRE/NEWS/STATEMENTS/2016/EMERGENCY-COMMITTEE-ZIKA-MICROCEPHALY/EN/

Zounds, Gadzooks, and Fucking Sisyphus.

BLOG AUG 30 2016

"Those who know what's best for us
Must rise and save us from ourselves." —Neil Peart, 1981

Did you know that *Blindsight* contains seventy-three instances of the word "fuck" and its variants? I've recently been informed of this fact by a high school teacher down in a part of the US that— well, in the name of protecting the identities of the innocent, let's just call it JesusLand.

The ubiquity of "fuck"—not just in *Blindsight* but in other contexts as well—carries a number of ramifications. For one thing, it implies that the characters who use it have better vocabularies and language skills than those whose mouths are squeaky clean[1]. It means they are more honest. It also means that they probably have a greater tolerance to pain[2].

And in the case of this particular teacher—here in the *Twenty-First Century*, for chrissake—it means she could lose her job if she taught *Blindsight*, unexpurgated, to her advanced English class. Apparently high school students in her part of the world are blissfully unfamiliar with this word. Apparently all sorts of calamities might ensue should that precarious state of affairs ever change.

It's a hard scenario to wrap my head around, even though I myself had a relatively genteel history with profanity back in childhood. Raised by Baptists, I must've been eleven or twelve before I even used words like "damn" or "hell" in conversation; even then, I could only live with such unChristian lapses by telling myself that at least I limited myself to "clean" swearing. I never lowered myself to the truly dirty stuff like "fuck" or "cunt" or "asshole."

It cut no ice with my mother, who—as First Lady of the Baptist Leadership Training School—had appearances to maintain. When I pointed out that my use of such mild expletives didn't hurt anyone, her response was always the same: "I find it offensive. That's all you need to know." I suspect it was this idiotic response—that unthinking preference of gut over reason—that inspired my defiant and long-overdue upgrade to F-bombery shortly thereafter.

While I changed, though, my parents never did. When my first novel came out decades later, there was Fanshun, sadly shaking her head—not angry, just very, very *disappointed*—wondering why her son, who had such a way with words, had to ruin a perfectly good book with all that profanity. Especially since she had, in years past, gone so far as to suggest non-offensive alternatives for me to use.

One of them, believe it or not, was "zounds."

Neither of us knew back then that "zounds" was the "fuck" of its day—a contraction of "God's wounds," referring to the stigmata of Christ and purged from yesteryear's polite literature the same way "fuck" is purged from mainstream outlets today (by spelling it "Z—ds!" and leaving readers to figure out the fucking omissions for themselves). *Gadzooks*—a similar contraction of "God's hooks" (i.e., the nails of the crucifix)—was apparently considered equally vulgar, back before it ended up as a common expletive in Saturday comics and Bugs Bunny cartoons.

All of which is a roundabout way of saying that taking offense at the word "fuck" is, objectively, no less nonsensical than objecting to "gadzooks" or "zounds"—in fact, those latter words should by rights be *more* offensive, since they hew closer to "taking the Lord's name in vain." (As far as I know, no part of scripture forbids taking the name of sex in vain.) Should be case closed. Case shouldn't have even been opened in the first place, in any rational universe.

Cut to the present, and here we were: me, author of a book I'm pretty damn proud of in hindsight; she, a teacher who wanted to share that book with a gang of unusually bright students. Standing in our way—reluctantly, I've been told—was a department head who quailed at the prospect of teaching a novel that gave so very many fucks. Apparently there'd been trouble in the past. Jobs lost. Parents throwing shit-fits over course material they might have described as *progressive*, if such folks had ever been able work their way up to three syllables. So, this teacher asked, would it be okay if her students read a bowdlerised version of *Blindsight*? One from which all the f-bombs had been expunged?

It was a tougher question than you might think.

On one hand, it's not as though I hammered out the novel thinking *Oh boy, I'm gonna introduce* fuck *to a whole new generation! That's what this book will be remembered for!* I didn't even think about the use of profanity, beyond the obvious need to ensure that my characters had consistent speech patterns. *Blindsight*'s essential themes could have been conveyed in language pure as the driven snow—and it's those themes that matter, not idioms of dialog. Here was someone who wanted to introduce her students to riffs on evolution and neurology and human nature that a lot of post-grads never dip their toes into. Here was someone who not only wanted to educate, but *challenge*. Christ knows I would have benefited from more teachers like that during my own slog through the educational process. I'm not seriously gonna throw a monkey wrench into her aspirations over a few expurgated curses, am I? Am I?

And yet.

It's not so much the change itself that rankles. It's the *demand* for that change. Where it comes from. Where it leads.

Because my work—whether you regard it as art, literature, or florid pulpy hackwork—is *my work*. You may love a painting or revile it, but you don't walk into an art gallery and demand that the curator put duct tape over all the yellow bits in various paintings—no matter how easy it would be to do that, no matter if the basic theme of those paintings survives the mutilation. If the sight of yellow elements in paintings offends you, the solution's simple: *don't go to the fucking gallery.*

But these vocal JesusLand parents, who have the staff of this school so terrified: they are evidently not the kind who say *I find this book offensive so I will not read it*. They are not even the kind who say *I do not want my children exposed to this so they will not read it*. (If they were, students whose parents objected could simply be excused from that part of the class—problem solved—but this was never presented as a option.) These parents—these hysterical, brain-dead dipshits with the room-temperature IQs—would say instead *I find the profanity in this book offensive so I will have it* removed *from the curriculum. I will have it removed from the library. I will have it removed from whatever parts of the world I can intimidate into bowing to my demands.*

I find it offensive. That's all you need to know.

But isn't that always the way it is? The line is rarely *Abortion's not for me* but rather *Abortion should be outlawed*. Fundamentalists who demand that their creation myths be inserted into science classes tend to look at you funny when you suggest that likewise, we could insert passages from *On the Origin of Species* into the book of Genesis. The Ayatollah did not simply opine that *The Satanic Verses* wasn't his cup of tea: he literally put out a hit on Salman Rushdie.

Maybe I'm going off the deep end here. Maybe I'm being a self-important dipshit myself, grandiosely equating a bit of petty bleeping with homicidal fatwas and the bombing of abortion clinics. Certainly there's no denying that *Blindsight*'s troubles down in JesusLand don't amount to a hill of beans compared to these other things, conflicts where lives are all too often at stake. But that's kind of my point: I'd hoped that we'd won this small battle at least, that we could move on to bigger fights. It's been a while since *Catcher in the Rye* was in the news. A few years back I read something about the fundies raising a stink over *The Handmaid's Tale*—but that article left me with the sense that those protesters were some kind of relic population, kept alive only because of a captive-breeding program (sponsored by the Smithsonian, perhaps). PEN still has its work cut out for it but it focuses overseas, on third-world totalitarian regimes that imprison or murder writers of "offensive" or "subversive" material.

I'd hoped that over here, we'd won on the profanity front at the very least. It's hard to imagine a smaller victory. There's still the on-going war to be fought against the creationists and the racists and homophobes and the trans—hell, let's just save ourselves a few lines and call them *phobics*, generic—but by all that's holy, *swear words*? We haven't even come *this* far, here in 21st-century N'Am?

Evidently not. Educators in this place literally fear for their jobs, because they want to teach a book containing the word "fuck."

I'm not claiming that *Blindsight*, stripped of profanity, would lose something essential. In fact, it's the very triviality of this censorship that bothers me; it seems like such a ludicrous thing to get worked up about, such a high price to pay for something that really doesn't matter. Such a little thing to risk one's livelihood over. So let's give in, and save ourselves the tantrum. Let's pay this small, unimportant price. And *Nineteen Eighty-Four*'s Newspeak dictionary will have one fewer word in it, and *Fahrenheit 451*'s grassroots dystopia will burn one more book that someone considers offensive (*that's all you need to know*). Only next time it *will* be the ideas and not the slang, it'll be the political statement you have to cut if you want to keep your job, and it'll be even easier this time because we've already taken the first step down that slope.

But that's okay. After a few more iterations the problem will solve itself—because none of us will have the vocabulary to express dissent any more.

Back here in the present I suggested some workarounds. Maybe they could run the bowdlerised edition off on a Gestetner that blurred the words unto illegibility (I figured, given the outmoded attitudes at play in that part of the world, maybe their educational equipment might be equally antique)—at which point the teacher could simply point them to my website where the original text lay in wait. I seized upon the department head's reported objection to teaching a "non-classic" book containing profanity; did this imply that books regarded as "classics" got a pass? (I'm pretty sure *To Kill a Mockingbird* gets taught without having been purged of the word "nigger", for instance.) As it happened, Omni had recently stuck my name on a list of "Greatest Sci-Fi Writers of All Time", right up there with Orwell, Wolfe, and Le Guin. It was completely bogus, of course—my name doesn't belong anywhere near those folks, not yet at least—but somehow it had slipped in, and maybe that would be enough to classify *Blindsight* as a "classic"? No?

Okay, then. Maybe she could replace every instance of the word "fuck" with the name of some local personality, evil and/or corrupt in some way—someone whose name could be used as a common epithet in some dystopian future. I didn't know who that might be—"Cheney," "Harper," and "Trump" would all be candidates on the federal scale, but I didn't know anything about the local one. Since the teacher knew the locals, though, I figured I could trust her expertise.

That's the option she went for.

And that, as far as I know, is where things stand. She says she's cool with me blogging about this (I've filed off the serial numbers), and I'm told the students themselves are privy to our email conversation. (She's also bringing *Mr. Robot* and the *BSG* reboot into the discussion, to illustrate various strategies by which one might get profanity past Standards & Practices; for this and other reasons, I think she's pretty cool.) I expect I'll be Skyping with the class somewhere along the line. There's little chance that any of those students will go home thinking that the characters in *Blindsight* used words like "heck" or "fudgemuffin." No one will be fooled; in that sense, nothing will be censored.

And yet, I still don't know quite how to feel about this. Some part of me still thinks I should've climbed onto some higher horse and refused to budge, out of sheer ornery principle. There's not much chance the book will read smoother without the fucks than with them; in that sense, the reading experience has probably been compromised. On the other hand, *Blindsight* is hardly the smoothest reading experience anyway, even for people with a degree or two under their belt. (I've told you all about the smartass who asked me when it was going to get translated into English, yuk yuk yuk, right?) I don't care how "advanced" this class is; if the biggest problem they have with *Blindsight* is the rhythm of its curses, I'll consider myself insanely lucky.

I should consider myself insanely lucky anyway. There are whole libraries of books that any teacher could go to if they wanted to turn their kids on to the joy of reading or the challenge of SF;

pretty much every one of those books would be more famous than *Blindsight*, easier to read, and way less work. And yet, this person has chosen to climb uphill, doing all the heavy lifting herself. She has become Sisyphus, because she believes that something I wrote might matter to people she teaches.

How often does an author get to say that?

1 HTTP://WWW.SCIENCEDIRECT.COM/SCIENCE/ARTICLE/PII/S038800011400151X
2 HTTP://JOURNALS.LWW.COM/NEUROREPORT/ABSTRACT/2009/08050/SWEARING _ AS _ A _ RESPONSE _ TO _ PAIN.4.ASPX

Actually, You *Can* Keep a Good Man Down . . .

BLOG SEP 7 2016

Or, more to the point today, a good woman. Turns out it's quite easy, in fact: all you need is a phone or an email account, and a certain kind of craven cowardice.

Quoting Sisyphus, whom I introduced in my previous post:

> Hello again, Peter.
>
> I enjoyed your blog post, though thank goodness I didn't suggest reading it in any way with my class. As it turns out, I am no Sisyphus, and before I even began to teach the novel, one parent had written an email, and another called the principal (neither spoke to me) both outraged at the idea of teaching a novel which had at one point contained such language. I told my administrator, who is a completely reasonable man, by the way, to call off the dogs. If it was this big an issue before we'd read a single redacted page,

it was going to become a catastrophe. I will continue to teach "Ambassador" in the future. And as for the kids who began reading the novel on their own, they were quite disappointed and asked if they might still be able to discuss the novel with you over Skype at some point.

Thanks for even considering this. It's unfortunate how things turned out; in the words of Kurt Vonnegut: so it goes.

So it is not enough to be a good teacher. It is not enough to be a challenging teacher. It is not even enough to be an *accommodating* teacher, one so dedicated that she sought me out and enlisted my support for an act we both regard as downright odious—but were willing to commit if it meant that students could be exposed to new ideas and new ways of thinking. It is not enough to hold your nose and slash the prose and spread your cheeks in an attempt to appease these ranting, rabid Dunning-Kruger incarnations made flesh. They will not be appeased.

It is not enough to gut a book of its naughty bits. That the book ever had such bits in the first place is offence enough.

We do not know the names of those who complained; they struck out bravely under cover of anonymity. I do know the name of the school at which this travesty went down, but if I spoke it here the teacher would be fired. I find it curious that those so full of self-righteous fury, so utterly convinced of their own virtue, would be so averse to the spotlight. Are they not doing God's will? Should they not be proud of their handiwork?

Strangely, though, these people don't *like* to be seen.

In the end, it probably doesn't matter. It's not as though this is an isolated case, after all; it hails from the heart of a country where more adults believe in angels than accept evolution, a country where—in the race to rule a hemisphere—an orange demagogue with zero impulse control is once again even in the polls with a corporate shill who revels in the endorsements of war criminals. The problem is not one outraged parent, or one school, or one county. The problem is the whole fucking country. The problem is *people.*

Naming names in one specific case—even if that *did* do more good than harm—would be like scraping off a single scab and hoping you'd cured smallpox.

But there she is, doing her goddamned best in the center of that shitstorm: Sisyphus, and all those like her. Today she lost the battle, but I know her kind.

The war goes on.

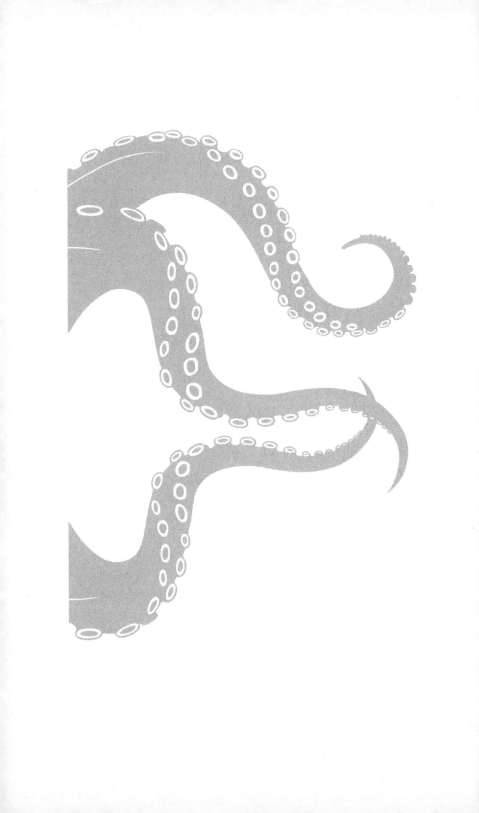

Shooting Back.

Blog July 11 2016

For at least three years now—probably longer—I've been worrying at a perpetually-unfinished blog post that tries to take an economic approach to murders committed by cops. I've never posted it, for reasons that should be obvious when I outline its essentials. The basic argument is that conventional attempts to reform police behavior are doomed to fail for two reasons:

1. the cost (to a cop) of gunning down the average black person in the street is low; and
2. the cost of not covering for your buddy when he guns down someone in the street is high.

I don't believe these are especially controversial claims. We all know how rare it is to see a cop indicted, even when there's video evidence of him choking the life out of someone or shooting them in the back. The astonishingly high rate of "equipment failure" experienced by body cams on the beat is old news. When you're used to that level of invulnerability, why *not* indulge in a little target practice if you're so inclined?

Likewise, the Blue Wall of Silence is news to no one. It is very difficult to get a cop to turn in their fellows because their very lives may depend on their partner having their back at a critical moment. You get a rep as a rat, your backup may just look the other way for that critical half-second when a *real* threat draws down on you. (I once compared civilian-police interactions to dealing with snakes in the desert: 95% may be harmless, but it's still a good idea to pack an antivenom kit when you head out. No, said the person I was talking with, the cops are worse: with snakes, at least the non-venomous 95% don't go out of their way to protect the other five.)

So: cost of murder low. Cost of turning in murderer high. These are the economics of Homicide: Cops on the Street. Seems to me, the only way to change the current pattern is to change those economic costs. For example, what if you increased the cost of *not* turning in a bad cop? What if, every time you didn't turn in a badged murderer, you yourself stood significantly higher odds of getting killed?

What if we started shooting *back*?

Not at the guilty cop, of course. He'd be too well protected, too on guard by the time the word got out. But what if, for every cop who gets away with murder, some other random cop within a certain radius—say, 200 miles—was shot in reprisal? It wouldn't matter that they were innocent. In fact, their innocence would be central to the whole point: to make the nonvenomous 95% stop covering for those "few bad apples" we're constantly being told are the heart of the problem. The point would be to raise the price of collusion enough make those 95-percenters think twice. Simple economics.

Of course it's not justice; you'd be killing an innocent person. But we're way past the point at which justice should have any say in the matter. There doesn't seem to be a whole lot of justice in the number of people who get gunned down by police on an ongoing basis (see: KILLEDBYPOLICE.NET). There's little justice in the statistical finding that on average in the US, unarmed blacks are 3.5 times more likely to be gunned down by cops than unarmed whites (over 20 times as likely in some corners of that benighted country)[1]. Anyone who tells you that you must remain polite, respectful, and most of all *nonviolent* while your fellows are being mowed down like mayflies has either chosen a side (hint: it ain't yours), or drunk about ten litres of Kool-Aid.

When it comes to game theory, tit-for-tat remains the most effective strategy.

I never published that blog post. Never even finished it. The solution seemed way too naïve and simplistic, for one thing. In a world of rainbows and unicorns cops might do the math, realize that murdering unarmed black people endangered themselves, and change their evil ways—but if we lived in a world of rainbows and unicorns, cops wouldn't be murdering with impunity in the first place. In *this* world, it seems a lot more likely that things would simply escalate, that police forces across the US—already militarized to the eyeballs—would go into siege mode, feel increasingly justified in shooting at every shadow (or at least the dark ones). They'd rather put the whole damn country under martial law than lose face by backing down.

It also didn't help that I've known some very decent people who happen to be cops—one a 9-11 first responder, another who actually reads my books and writes his own—and while that wouldn't change the logic of the argument one iota, random assassination is still a fate I wouldn't wish on good people. Because when it comes right down to it this *is* wish-fulfillment, for all the economic and game-theory rationales I might invoke. It was born in my gut, not my neocortex. Every time I read about another Philando Castile or Alton Sterling, I want to start throwing bombs myself. (My greatest disappointment in Bruce Cockburn welled up when he back-pedaled on "If I Had a Rocket Launcher".)

I want the fuckers to *pay*, and I know they won't.

Oh, maybe this month's killers have some rough times in store— the public documentation of *those* crimes was so incontrovertible that the politicians don't really have the option of sweeping them under the rug. But viral videos of murder in progress didn't send Eric Garner's killers to jail[2]. Nobody got indicted for the murder of Sandra Bland. The killer of Samuel DuBose is at least awaiting trial[3], but given the history of such proceedings dating back to Rodney King I'm not counting on any convictions. And those victims are the lucky ones, the ones "fortunate" enough to be gunned down on camera. What about the greater number whose deaths happen out of camera range, whose killers are free to make up any story that fits without fear of contradiction or scrutiny by a legal system which continues, unfathomably, to treat the word of a police officer as golden?

They keep getting killed. And we keep rending our garments and sending them our fucking *thoughts and prayers*, and the moment they block a road or stop a parade or express a fraction of the rage that is their due we back away and tell them that they won't get anywhere with that kind of attitude. We trot out the same insipid MLK Jr. quotes about the virtues of nonviolence, about peace being the only way to achieve "dialog" or "brotherhood"—as if the people who have them in the crosshairs give a flying fuck about any of that. We tell them to have patience, to let the system work because we've got the evidence now, everyone saw it on YouTube, no way those fucking cops will walk away from it *this* time—and yet they do. Time and time again. The cops walk away from it.

Why should the black community care about alienating us? Why should they give us another chance to express our shared anguish and deepest sympathies, only to have us wag our fingers at them the moment we're inconvenienced[4]? A quarter-century after Rodney King, why should they believe that the next time will be different, or the next, or the time after?

What's left to try, except fighting fire with fire?

That is where my game-theory imaginings came from: not some rational step-by-step multivariate analysis, but vicarious rage. And while I might be able to construct such an analysis to yield the same result; no matter how rationally I might put that argument; no matter how many of you I might even convince— all I'd have really done would be to craft a clever excuse to let my brain stem off the leash. I try to be better than that.

Which doesn't make keeping it to myself all this time feel any less like a betrayal of some principle I can't quite put my finger on.

Anyway, I never posted it. And now the scenario's been realized anyway: five cops dead, six others critical. All innocent, so far as we know (although if they were black civilians, I'm sure Fox News would already be pointing out that *they were no angels . . .*). All shot in direct retaliation for the murder of black people, for the sins of their brethren.

The only deviation from my own scenario is that the shooter didn't get away alive. They blew him up, used a robot carrying a bomb on its arm like it was delivering a pizza.

The usual aftermath. People "coming together." Pastors and politicians urging calm. The same old Kingisms and Ghandi-isms popping up like impetigo sores all over Facebook. Everyone expressing support for the members of the Dallas Police Force, chiefed by a black man who has, by all accounts, turned that department into a model of progressive policing[5] and perhaps the worst target

Micah Johnson could have chosen. (Although it bears mention that that same progressive chief, and those same progressive policies, are apparently quite unpopular with the DPF rank-and-file.) As usual, none of this seems to have had much impact on the tendency of certain cops to gun people down and lie about it afterward, e.g. the cases of Alva Braziel[6] and Delrawn Small[7] (I mean, Jesus—by now you'd think they'd dial back the shootings on account of the optics if nothing else). So far, nothing out of the ordinary.

Except now, here and there across the US, these *other* people have begun threatening reprisals against other cops. There've been some[8] actual shootings[9]. Copycat attacks, you might call them. Or perhaps "inspired reprisals" might be a better term.

Micah Johnson is becoming a role model.

So what now? Have we finally reached critical mass? Is this a smattering of isolated blips, or the start of a chain reaction? Have we finally reached a tipping point, will black lives matter enough to starting shooting back? Given the stats on the ground, who among you will blame them if they do?

For my part, I'm more glad than ever that I didn't make that blog post. At least nobody can blame me for the events of the past few days. (Don't laugh—following my post on Trump's burning of America, I had at least one long-time fan renounce me completely for "throwing [him] under the bus," as if my thoughts might have even an infinitesimal impact on the unfolding of US politics. Some people *seriously* overestimate my influence on the world stage.)

I have no idea what's in store. I'm not sure I want to find out.

All I know is this: if we are, finally at long last, starting to reap the whirlwind—no one can say it hasn't been a long time coming.

---

1 Ross, Cody T. (2015). "A Multi-Level Bayesian Analysis of Racial Bias in Police Shootings at the County-Level in the United States, 2011–2014." *PLoS ONE* 10(11): e0141854.

2 As of August 19, 2019, Daniel Pantaleo was finally fired by the NYPD. It's not prison, but it's better than nothing. Barely. HTTPS://WWW.NYTIMES.COM/2019/08/19/NYREGION/DANIEL-PANTALEO-FIRED.HTML

3 After two mistrials, prosectures declined to initiate a third trial; the officer later collected a $350,000 settlement. HTTPS://WWW.HUFFPOST.COM/ENTRY/FORMER-UNIVERSITY-OF-CINCINNATI-COP-WHO-KILLED-SAM-DUBOSE-AWARDED-350000-SETTLEMENT _ N _ 5AB521BDE4B054D118E26D7C

4 HTTP://WWW.THEGLOBEANDMAIL.COM/OPINION/THE-BULLIES-OF-BLACK-LIVES-MATTER/ARTICLE30746157/

5 HTTPS://WWW.THESTAR.COM/NEWS/WORLD/2016/07/09/DALLAS-KILLER-ATTACKED-POLICE-FORCE-KNOWN-FOR-PROGRESSIVE-REFORM.HTML

6 HTTP://THINKPROGRESS.ORG/JUSTICE/2016/07/10/3796941/ALVA-BRAZIEL/

7 HTTP://WWW.THEDAILYBEAST.COM/CHEATS/2016/07/08/VIDEO-SHOWS-OFF-DUTY-NYPD-COP-SHOOT-MAN.HTML

8 HTTPS://WWW.THESTAR.COM/NEWS/WORLD/2016/07/08/HIGHWAY-GUNMAN-TARGETED-TENNESSEE-POLICE-OFFICERS.HTML

9 HTTP://WWW.CBC.CA/NEWS/WORLD/POLICE-SHOOTINGS-PROTESTS-RETALIATION-1.3671806

> This is how you communicate with a fellow intelligence: you hurt it, and keep on hurting it, until you can distinguish the speech from the screams.
> —*Blindsight*

Believe it or not, the above quote was inspired by some real-world research on language and dolphins.

Admittedly the real-life inspiration was somewhat less grotesque: scientists taught a couple of dolphins how to respond to a certain stimulus (if you see a red circle, push the yellow button with your nose—that sort of thing), then put them in different tanks but still let them talk to each other. Show the stimulus to one, but put the response panel in the tank with the other. Let them talk. If the dolphin in the response tank goes and pushes the correct button, you can conclude that the two of them communicated that information vocally: you can infer the presence of language. What's more, you've recorded the vocalizations that carried that information, so you've made a start at *understanding* said language.

As I recall, the scientists rewarded correct responses with fish snacks. *Blindsight*'s scientists didn't know how to reward *their* captive aliens—they didn't even know what the damn things ate—so they used a stick instead of a carrot, zapped the scramblers with painful microwaves for *incorrect* responses. It was more dramatic, and more in keeping with the angsty nihilism of the overall story. But the principle was the same: ask one being the question, let the other being answer it, analyze the information they exchanged to let them do that.

I've forgotten whether those dolphins ever passed the talk test. I'm guessing they did—a failed experiment would hardly make the cut for a show about The Incredible Smartness of Dolphins—but then, wouldn't we have made more progress by now? Wouldn't we at least know the dolphin words for "red circle" and "yellow button" and (given that we *are* talking about dolphins) "casual indiscriminate sex"? Why is it that—while dolphins seem able to learn a fair number of our words—we've so far failed to learn a single one of theirs?

I was always a sucker for the dolphins-as-fellow-sapients shtick. It's what got me into marine mammalogy in the first place. One of my very first stories—written way back in high school— concerned a scientist living in an increasingly fundamentalist society, fighting funding cuts and social hostility over his attempts to crack the dolphin language because the very concept of a nonhuman intelligence was considered sacrilegious. (In the end he does get shut down, his quest to talk to the dolphins a complete failure—but the last scene shows his dolphins in a tank quietly conversing in their own language. They've decided to keep their smarts to themselves, you see. They know when they're ahead.)

Anyway. I watched all those *Nova* documentaries, devoured all the neurological arguments for dolphin intelligence (*Tursiops* brains are 20% larger than ours! Their neocortices are more intricately folded, have greater surface area!). I read John Lilly's books, embraced his claims that dolphins had a "digital language," followed his Navy-funded experiments in which people sloshed around immersed to the waist in special human-dolphin habitats.

By the time I started my M.Sc. (on harbor porpoises—one of the bottlenosed dolphin's stupider cousins), I'd grown significantly more skeptical. Decades of research had failed to yield any breakthroughs. Lilly had gone completely off the rails, seemed to be spending all his time dropping acid in isolation tanks and claiming that aliens from "Galactic Coincidence Control" were throwing car accidents at him. Even science fiction was cooling to the idea; those few books still featuring sapient dolphins (Foster's *Cachalot*, Brin's Uplift series) presented them as artificially enhanced, not the natural-born geniuses we'd once assumed.

We still knew cetaceans were damn smart, make no mistake. Certain killer whale foraging strategies are acts of tactical genius; dolphins successfully grasp the rudiments of language when taught. Then again, so do sea lions—and the fact that you can be taught to use a tool in captivity does not mean that your species has already invented that tool on its own. The expanded area of the dolphin neocortex didn't look quite so superhuman when you factored in the fact that neuron *density* was lower than in us talking apes.

So I passed through grad school disabused of the notion that dolphins were our intellectual siblings in the sea. They were smart, but not *that* smart. They could learn language, but they didn't *have* one. And while I continued to believe that we smug bastards routinely underestimate the cognitive capacities of other species, I grudgingly accepted that we were still probably the smartest game in town. It was a drag—especially considering how goddamned stupid we seem to be most of the time—but that was where the data pointed. (I even wrote another story[1] about cetacean language—better-informed, and a lot more cynical—in which we ultimately *did* figure out the language of killer whales, only to discover that they were complete assholes who based their society on child slavery, and were only too willing to sell their kids to the Vancouver Aquarium if the price was right.)

But now. Now, Vyacheslav Ryabov—in the *St. Petersburg Polytechnical University Journal: Physics and Mathematics*—claims that dolphins have a language after all[2]. He says they speak in sentences of up to five words, maybe more. The pop-sci press was all over it[3], and why not? I can't be the only one who's been waiting decades for this.

Now that it's happened, I don't quite believe it.

It wasn't a controlled experiment, for one thing. No trained dolphins responding to signals that mean "ball" or "big" or "green". Ryabov just eavesdropped on a couple of untrained dolphins—"Yana" and "Yasha"—as they chatted in a cement tank. We're told these dolphins have lived in this tank for twenty years, and have "normal hearing." We're not told what "normal" is or how it's measured, but concrete is an acoustic reflector; it's fair to wonder how "normal" conditions really are when you take creatures whose primary sensory modality is sound, and lock them in an echo chamber for two decades.

Leaving that aside, Ryabov recorded Yana and Yasha exchanging fifty unique "noncoherent pulses" in "packs" of up to five pulses each. Each dolphin listened to the other without interruption, waiting until the other had finished speaking before responding in turn. Based on this Ryabov concludes that "most likely, each pulse . . . is a word of the dolphin's spoken language, and a pulse pack is a sentence." He goes on to compare these dolphin "words" with their human equivalents. (Dolphins words are much shorter than human words, for one thing—only about 0.25msec—because their wider frequency range means that all the phonemes in a "word" can be stacked on top of each other and pronounced simultaneously. Every word, no matter how long, can be spoken in the time it takes to pronounce a single syllable. Cool.)

I find this plausible. I do not find it remotely compelling. For one thing, it doesn't pass the "tortured scrambler" test: while the pulses are structured, there's no way of knowing what actual information—if any—is being conveyed. If Yana consistently did something whenever Yasha emitted a specific pulse sequence— say, swam to the bottom of the tank and nosed the drain—you could reasonably infer that the sequence provoked the behavior, that it was a request of some kind: *Dude, do me a favor and go poke that grill*. Language. But all we have here is two creatures taking turns making noises at each other, and dolphins are hardly the only creatures to do that. If you don't believe me, head on over to YouTube and check out the talking cats.

Nobody denies that dolphins communicate. Lots of species do. Nature is full of animals who identify themselves with signature whistles, emit alarm calls that distinguish between different kinds of predators, use specific sounds to point out food sources or solicit sex. Killer whale pods have their own unique dialects. Honeybees communicate precise information about the distance, bearing, and quality of food sources by waggling their asses at each other. The world is rife with the exchange of information; but that's not grammar, or syntax. It's not *language*. The mere existence of structured pulses doesn't suggest what Ryabov says it does.

He does buttress his point by invoking various cool things that dolphins can do: they can *learn* grammar if they have to, they can recognize images on TV screens (responding to a televised image of a trainer's hand-signal the same way they would if the trainer was there in the flesh, for example). But all his examples are cadged from other studies; there's nothing in Ryabov's results to suggest a structured language as we understand the term, nothing to "indirectly confirm the hypothesis that each NP in the natural spoken language of the dolphin is a word with a specific meaning," as he puts it.

It's a tempting interpretation, I admit. This turn-by-turn exchange of sounds certainly *seems* like a conversation. You could even argue that a lack of correlated behaviors—the fact that Yana never *did* nose the drain, that neither pressed any buttons nor got any fish—suggests that if they were talking, they were talking about something that wasn't in their immediate environment. Maybe they were talking in *abstracts*. You can't prove they weren't.

Then again, you can say all that about YouTube's talking cats, too.

So for now at least, I have to turn my back on the claim that my life-long adolescent dream—the belief that actually shaped my career—has finally been vindicated. Maybe Ryabov's on to something; but maybe isn't good enough. It's a sad corollary to the very principle of empiricism: the more you want something to be true, the less you can afford to believe it is.

But all is not lost. Take long-finned pilot whales, for example. They were never on anyone's short list for Humanity's Intellectual Equals—the Navy loved them for mine-sweeping, but they never got anywhere near the love that bottlenosed dolphins and killer whales soaked up—and yet, just a couple of years ago, we learned that their neocortices contain nearly twice as many neurons as ours do.

Maybe we've just been looking at the wrong species.

1 HTTP://WWW.RIFTERS.COM/REAL/SHORTS/WATTSCHANNER _ BULK _ FOOD.PDF

2 HTTP://WWW.SCIENCEDIRECT.COM/SCIENCE/ARTICLE/PII/S2405722316301177

3 See: HTTP://WWW.CNN.COM/2016/09/13/EUROPE/DOLPHIN-LANGUAGE-
CONVERSATION-RESEARCH/, HTTP://WWW.CSMONITOR.COM/SCIENCE/2016/0912/
DO-DOLPHINS-USE-LANGUAGE, and HTTP://WWW.NATIONALGEOGRAPHIC.COM.AU/
ANIMALS/DOLPHINS-RECORDED-HAVING-A-CONVERSATION-NOT-SO-FAST.ASPX

HemiHive, in Hiding

Nowa Fantastyka FEB 2018

BLOG JULY 25 2018

If you've been following my writing for any length of time, you'll know how fascinated I am by Krista and Tatiana Hogan, of British Columbia. I've cited them in *Echopraxia*'s endnotes, described them in online essays; if you caught my talk at Pyrkon last year you might remember me wittering on about them in my rejoinder to Elon Musk's aspirations for "neural dust."

Can you blame me? A pair of conjoined twins, fused at the brain? A unique cable of neurons—a *thalamic bridge*—wiring those brains together, the same way the corpus callosum connects the cerebral hemispheres in your own head? Two people who can see through each other's eyes, feel and taste what the other does, share motor control of their limbs—most remarkably, communicate mind-to-mind without speaking? Is it any wonder that at least one neuroscientist has described the twins as "a new life form"?

If the Hogans don't capture your imagination, you're dead inside. I've been following those two from almost the day they were born in 2006 (the year *Blindsight* came out—and man, how that book could have changed if they'd been born just a few years earlier.) I've been trying to, anyway.

They don't make it easy.

Bits and pieces trickle out now and then. Profiles in the *New York Times*[1] and *Macleans*[2]. Puff-piece documentaries[3] from the Canadian Broadcasting Corporation, heavy on saccharine human-interest and cutesy music, light on science. Eleven years on, the public domain will tell you that Krista processes input from three legs and one arm, while Tatiana processes input from three arms and one leg. We know that they're only halfway to being a true hive mind, because there are still two of them in there; the thalamic bridge carries lower bandwidth than a corpus callosum, and is located down in the basement with the sensory cables. (We can only speculate what kind of singular conscious being we'd be dealing with if the pipe had been fatter, mounted higher in the brain.) We know they share thoughts without speaking, conspire nonverbally to commit practical jokes for example (although not in complete silence; apparently a fair amount of giggling is involved). The twins call it "talking in our heads." Back in 2013 one of their neurologists opined that "they haven't yet shown us" whether they share thoughts as well as sensory experience, but neurons fire the same way whether they're transmitting sensation or abstraction; given all the behavioral evidence I'd say the onus is on the naysayers to prove that thoughts *aren't* being transmitted.

We know they're diabetic and epileptic. We know they're cognitively delayed. We know that their emotions are always in sync; whatever chemicals provoke joy or grief or anger cruise through that conjoined system without regard for which brain produced them. We know Krista likes ketchup and Tatiana doesn't. We know—and if we don't, you can be sure the documentarians at CBC will hammer the point home at least twice more before the next commercial break—that they're God's Little Fucking Miracles.

If you look closely at the video footage, you can glean a bit more. The twins never say "we." I frequently heard one or the other refer to "my sister," but if they ever referred to each other by name, that never made it into the broadcast edit. They sometimes refer to each other as "I." They must have a really interesting sense of personal identity, at the very least.

But that's about it. After eleven years, this is all we get.

We're told about MRI scans, but we never get to see any actual results from one. (The most recent documentary[4], from just last year, shows the twins on their way to an MRI only to cut away before they get there; I mean, how do twins conjoined at a seventy-degree angle even *fit* into one of those machines?) There are plenty of Hogan references in the philosophical literature[5] (for obvious reasons), and even the legal literature[6] (for more obscure ones: one paper delves into how best to punish conjoined twins when only one of them has been convicted of committing a crime). They're all over popular science and news sites. Some idiot with the Intelligent Design movement has even used the Hogans to try and put lipstick on the long-discredited pig of dualism (i.e., souls).[7]

But actual neurological findings from these twins? Scientific papers? Google Scholar returns a single article, from a 2012 issue of the "University of British Columbia's Undergraduate Journal of Psychology"—a student publication.[8] Even that piece is mainly a review of craniopagus twins in the medical literature, with a couple of pages squeeing about How Much The Hogan Twins Can Teach Us tacked onto the end. A 2011 *New York Times* article describes research showing that each twin can process visual signals from the other's eyes, then admits that the results were not published.[9] And *that's it*.

Eleven years after the birth of the most neurologically remarkable, philosophically mind-blowing, transhumanistically-relevant beings on the planet, we have nothing but pop-sci puff pieces and squishy documentaries to show for it. Are we really supposed to believe that in over a decade no one has done the studies, collected the data, gained any insights about literal *brain-to-brain communication*, beyond these fuzzy generalities?

I for one don't buy that for a second. These neuroscientists smiling at us from the screen—Douglas Cochrane, Juliette Hukin—they know what they've got. Maybe they've discovered something so horrific about the nature of Humanity that they're afraid to reveal it, for fear of outrage and widespread panic. That would be cool.

More likely, though, they're just biding their time; sitting on an ever-growing trove of data that will redefine and quantify the very nature of what it is to be a sapient being. They're just not going to share it with the rest of us until they've finished polishing their Nobel acceptance speeches. Maybe I can't blame them. Maybe I'd even do the same in their place.

Still. The wait is driving me crazy.

And if any of you are on the inside, I'd kill for a glimpse of an MRI.

1 HTTPS://WWW.NYTIMES.COM/2011/05/29/MAGAZINE/COULD-CONJOINED-TWINS-SHARE-A-MIND.HTML

2 HTTPS://WWW.MACLEANS.CA/NEWS/CANADA/CONJOINED-TWINS-SHARE-EACH-OTHERS-SENSES/

3 HTTP://WWW.CBC.CA/CBCDOCSPOV/EPISODES/INSEPARABLE

4 HTTP://WWW.CBC.CA/CBCDOCSPOV/M _ FEATURES/THE-HOGAN-TWINS-SHARE-A-BRAIN-AND-SEE-OUT-OF-EACH-OTHERS-EYES

5 SEE: HTTPS://PHILPAPERS.ORG/REC/MRTPAT and HTTPS://LINK.SPRINGER.COM/ARTICLE/10.1007/S11098-014-0393-X

6 HTTPS://ACADEMIC.OUP.COM/MEDLAW/ARTICLE-ABSTRACT/19/3/430/988661

7 HTTPS://EVOLUTIONNEWS.ORG/2017/11/WHAT-THE-CRANIOPAGUS-TWINS-TEACH-US-ABOUT-THE-MIND-AND-THE-BRAIN/

8 HTTP://OJS.LIBRARY.UBC.CA/INDEX.PHP/UBCUJP/ARTICLE/VIEW/2521
9 HTTPS://WWW.NYTIMES.COM/2011/05/29/MAGAZINE/COULD-CONJOINED-TWINS-
SHARE-A-MIND.HTML

The Dudette With the Clitoris, and Other Thoughts on *Star Trek Beyond*

BLOG AUG 10 2016

I used to be a huge *Star Trek* fan.

I watched TOS reruns repeatedly and religiously in high school. Even watched the cartoons. Bought the James Blish episode adaptations, then the (better-written) Alan Dean Foster ones, then an endless series of mostly-forgettable tie-in novels (a few written by the likes of Joe Haldeman and Vonda McIntyre). I reread the Gerrold and Whitfield commentaries until the pages fell out of their bindings. I wrote *Star Trek* fanfic. The very first con I ever attended was a mid-seventies Trek con at the Royal York. I was pulling graveyard in the Eaton Center's IT department that summer; I'd work from 10 p.m. to 10 a.m., stumble down to the con for the day, stumble back to work again at night. (My most vivid memory of that weekend was Harlan Ellison introducing his then-wife as the love of his life on Friday evening, then publicly excoriating her as a faithless slut on Sunday afternoon. Not quite sure what happened in between. I may have dozed.)

I still have the original Franz Joseph blueprints of the Constitution-class starship hanging around somewhere, along with the Technical Manual and the Medical Reference Manual and the *Star Trek Concordance* and the *Star Trek Spaceflight Chronology* and—I kid you not—the official *Star Trek Cooking Manual* (authorship attributed to Christine Chapel). I always hated the third season but I blamed NBC for that, not the Great Bird of the Galaxy. I endured *The Motionless Picture*, breathed a sigh of relief at *The Wrath of Khan*, grimly held my nose and watched the first two seasons of *Next Gen* until they put Gene Roddenberry out to pasture so it could finally get good.

Of course, this was all seventies-eighties era. Eventually I got tired of lugging a steamer trunk's worth of paperbacks back and forth across the country and unloaded most of it onto Goodwill. I only made it halfway through *DS9*, got less than a season into *Voyager* before giving up on it (honestly, I wanted to throw in the towel after the pilot), and made it about as far as the easy-listening opening-credits song for *Enterprise* before deciding I'd had enough. I was clean and sober for years afterward, and proud of it.

Point is, I've earned a certain amount of *ST* cred. I didn't just know episodes, I knew *writers* (one of my happiest moments was when Norman Spinrad raved about my work in *Asimov's*). So I'd argue that my opinion, while watching these Abrams reboots coming down the pike, is not entirely uninformed. I mostly loved the first one even though it went off the rails in the third act, even though it arbitrarily relocated a whole damn planet (Delta Vega) from the very edge of the galaxy (where it lived in TOS's "Where No Man Has Gone Before") to mutual orbit around *Vulcan* for chrissakes, a planet which has no moon ("The Man Trap"). I mostly hated *Into Dumbness* for reasons I won't go into here.

A couple of weeks behind the curve, though, we finally checked out *Star Trek Beyond*, our hopes stoked by its stellar rating on

Rotten Tomatoes (no, I will never learn): 216 professional critics, 180 of whom applauded. And finally having seen it for myself, I gotta ask that Ratey-One Eighty: What the fuck were you *on*?

For starters, forget the bad science. Or at least, forgive it; *Star Trek* has never been the go-to franchise for rigorous verisimilitude, and that's okay. Forget the depiction of "nebulae" as impenetrable fogs of cloud and rocks jammed so cheek-to-jowl that they're forever colliding with each other. Just accept whatever weird biological mechanism grants you immortality by turning you into a horny toad (the lizard, not a sexually-aroused amphibian). Forget the fact that we shouldn't even be *using* starships any more, since *Into Darkness* showed us Federation transporters reaching from Earth to the Klingon homeworld without straining, and communicators that did the same without any noticeable time lag.

Let's put all that aside, and consider these questions instead:

Stripey-warrior-girl Jaylah is hiding from Krall's forces in the wreck of the *Franklin*, which she has cleverly cloaked to avoid detection. But the *Franklin* was originally *Krall's ship*; he was the one who crashed it on Altamid, back when he was Edison. So why doesn't he know it's there now, even though it's invisible? In fact, why doesn't the fact that his crashed starship has suddenly *vanished* raise all manner of red flags, draw attention to Jaylah's hideout rather than concealing it?

Krall—and presumably his whole merry band of lizard-faced minions—are actually human, physically modified as a side-effect of alien life-extension tech. (At least, if his minions *weren't Franklin* crew, someone please tell me where they came from; we're told that Altimid's original inhabitants abandoned the place centuries ago.) So what's this weird alien language they're speaking throughout most of the movie, the one that we require subtitles to comprehend? I'm pretty sure it's not French.

The last twenty minutes of the movie or so—basically, the climax—revolve around Kirk chasing a "bioweapon"—imagine that the Smoke Monster from *Lost* had its own Mini-Me— around the vast variable-gravity reaches of Starbase Yorktown. The weapon is on the verge of detonation. Kirk has to fly around and pull on a bunch of levers in a specific sequence to open a convenient airlock and suck it into space. One of the levers gets stuck. The clock ticks down. And not once does anyone say *Hey, we've got transporters—why don't we just lock onto the motherfucker from here and beam its squirmy black ass into space?*

I mean, seriously: transporter technology and warp drive are the two most iconic technologies of the whole 50-year-old franchise. *Not* using the transporter—not even *mentioning* it—is like putting an asteroid on a collision course with the *Enterprise*, then expecting us to believe that everyone on the bridge has just kinda forgotten they can simply move out of the way. Such scenarios do not inspire you to grip your armrests and wonder how our heroes will escape this time; they inspire you to cheer for the fucking asteroid.

Two of these three quibbles are mission-critical plot elements; the story falls apart without them, yet they make no sense. And there are other issues, smaller issues, that chipped away at my increasingly desperate attempts to squeeze a bit of enjoyment out of this rotten fruit. The lighting was incredibly dark, even in locations that should have been brightly lit; it was as if the theatre's main projector bulb had burned out and someone was filling in with a flashlight. The sound was almost as muddy as the lighting; at one point, Caitlin swore she heard someone make reference to "the dudette with the clitoris", and for the life of me I couldn't tell her what else it might have been.

Much has been made of *Beyond*'s "return to basics" in terms of characterization, which seems like a fancy way of saying that Spock and McCoy get to trade jabs again like they did in the old days. That's true; but these jabs are soft and flaccid things, never as funny or poignant as some of the sparks that flared between Kelley and Nimoy back in the sixties. "I do not blame him, Doctor. He is probably terrified of your beads and rattles"; "They do indeed have one redeeming feature. They do not talk too much"; "I know why you're not afraid to die: you're more afraid of living!"

Remember those?

Now take a moment to consider just what *Star Trek Beyond* has driven me to: it has driven me to praise (albeit in a relative way) the quality of the dialog in *sixties-era Star Trek*.

I could go on. I could complain about the absurdity of a soldier who felt abandoned by the Federation because "Starfleet is not a military organization"—despite the fact that Starfleet's ships are armed to the teeth, and carry out military engagements with the Federation's enemies, and are crewed by uniformed people assigned military ranks who follow a military chain-of-command. (Yup, no military organization here. Just the galaxy's best cosplayers . . .) I could remark upon the surrealism of two Starfleet captains locked in mortal combat while berating each other about their respective Captain's logs: *I read your diary! Yeah, well, **I** read **your** diary!*—

Evidently, in this timeline, Starfleet captains tweet their logs for all to see. You might be forgiven for wondering if this doesn't constitute some kind of security issue, were it not for the fact that Starfleet is not a military organization.

I could also go on at lesser length about the *good* things the movie served up. The FX were great, when you could see 'em. Nice to see a Universal Translator that needs to be programmed now and then, and which actually voices-over audible alien dialog instead of magically reshaping the speaker's sounds and mouth movements into English. I liked the almost-sorta invocation of nearest-neighbor algos to explain the schooling behavior of the alien swarm, even if they used a hokey made-up name and hand-waved the exploit. The acting was fine; the cast, for the most part, both honor and improve upon the legacy they've inherited. And—

Well, to be honest, that's pretty much it. Not great *Star Trek*. Not a great movie.

And you know what really doesn't make much sense? I'll still probably go see the next one when it comes out.

Maybe I shouldn't have tossed all those paperbacks after all.

A while back I was trying to explain "quality of life" to the pones—why sometimes it's okay to die young, why sometimes a long life can be the most terrible of fates. I invented a simple graphic to help make the point. Imagine time along the x-axis: quality-of-life along the y, but as a range not a scalar value (*i.e.*, the wider the range, the better the QoL). You can throw in a z-axis too, if you want two QoL metrics instead of one. I call it "The Life Sausage," and it's not height or width but *total area* that you want to maximize (or volume, if you're going the 3-axis route). You can live a hundred years if you never leave your home, never eat fatty foods, never risk love or sex for fear of failure and STDs—and your life sausage will be one long, emaciated pepperoni-stick of misery, hyperextended along one axis but barely registering on the others. You can fuck everything that moves, snort every synthetic that makes it past the blood-brain barrier, dive with sharks and wrestle 'gators and check out when your chute fails to open during the skydiving party on your sweet sixteenth. Your life sausage will be short but *thick,* like a hockey puck on-edge, and the sum total of the happiness contained therein will put to shame any number of miserable incontinent centenarians wasting away in the rest home. More typically the sausage will be a lumpy thing, a limbless balloon-animal lurching through time with fat parts and skinny parts and, more often than not, a sad tapering atrophy into loneliness and misery near the end. But in all these cases, the value of your life is summed up not by lifespan nor by happiness but by the *product* of these, the total space contained within the sausage skin.

Banana died in my arms yesterday: somewhere around 0630 counting from the time the pain stopped, maybe an hour later if you go by heartbeat. I do not know how long he lived in total; he came into my life as an adult with more miles on him that I'd care to imagine. But as far as I can tell, his Life Sausage looked something like this:

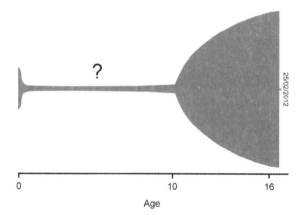

There must have been some joy there at the start, yes? He must have nursed at least, felt his tiny belly filling with milk, reveled on some dumb kitten level in the warmth and protection of a mom and litter-mates and an ambient bumble of purrs. Maybe he even had a Human home for a while; cats born feral are difficult at best to socialize to human company, and Banana's fearlessness in later years suggests at least some favorable interactions with us can openers during his formative months.

He must've gone through a whole shitload of Blue Mondays after that, though.

The vet couldn't tell me how old he was when he finally came into my care; all she knew for sure was that he was over ten years old, and most of those years had been mean ones. One of his ears was torn to shit, the cartilage permanently disfigured by his own furious scratching at what the vet described as the worst case of ear mites she'd ever seen. The other was folded back and literally *fused* to itself, flesh to flesh: that was frostbite. Most of his teeth were rotten and abscessed and had to be pulled; for the rest of his life, he would spray like a lawn sprinkler when he did that whole cat-head-shaky thing. Fur was missing in patches; the skin underneath was crusty with scabs.

I wasn't really looking to adopt another cat. Freshly single, about to relocate to a scummy little one-bedroom, and as financially-secure as any midlist author whose latest book had tanked like a Panzer, I didn't know if I'd be able to take on a long-term dependent. But *fostering* was different—a few weeks, a few months I could handle. So I renewed a lapsed acquaintance with Annex Cat Rescue—a local band of cat-lovers who capture ferals off the street, find homes for those who can be socialized, speuter and release those who can't. (They are good folks, and have an ingenious arrangement by which you can forward them your air miles using a special card; you avoid all that junk mail *and* provide kibble for homeless cats. Win win.)

Banana had worn out his welcome at his current foster home. Too used to a lifetime of hunger games, he was attacking anything he perceived as a threat to his kibble supply (which is to say, another cat who'd been living for years at the same address). So I took him back to my place, fell instantly in love, and wrote an adoption blurb which I maintain, even now, is the best piece of prose I ever wrote:

Are You Worthy?

Here's where we separate the superficial kitty-huggers from the serious lovers of real cats. Banana has had a really rough life. It shows. His ears are disfigured by frostbite, and by wounds sustained during the course of the world's worst ear-mite infection. Several of his teeth have broken against the hard life of the street. He drools sometimes. He hides a lot. Scars and scabs and shaved veterinary clear-cuts range across his body.

The fur will grow back, of course. The scabs are healing even now. And he's a solid cat. Everything that isn't scar tissue is muscle. His ears will be forever twisted, though. He is doomed to pad through the rest of his life being mistaken for a Scottish Fold.

But what a heart he has. Oh, what a heart.

Dragged from his refuge in the linen closet, he purrs instantly upon contact. Once you have begun scritching those twisted ears, he firmly and insistently head-butts you should your rhythm falter. Sometimes he will not eat unless he is being scritched; then he snarfs for a regiment (pausing now and then to glance around, as if fearful of the reappearance of old ghosts). When he comes to trust you he will lie on your bed with his belly to the sun and all four limbs stretched in ecstasy.

This cat is a goddamned hero. If you're looking for some cute and symmetrical plaything to go ga-ga over, something with the depth of Paris Hilton[1] and brains to match, move along. You don't deserve this one. But if you can provide a safe haven to a bruised and stoic predator, and treat him with the respect he deserves—if you ask not what Banana can offer you, but what you can offer Banana—then give us a call.

Maybe—just maybe—you have what it takes.

It wasn't even 24 hours before the calls started coming in. Twenty-four hours too long. In all truth, I was a goner before I ever wrote the blurb.

In the six years that followed we pumped Banana's life sausage almost unto bursting. We moved from one furnished bedroom in an aching empty house over to an accursed apartment where I had to fight back successive waves of invading bedbugs. Other cats started dropping by along the rooftop; one of them even officially joined the team as First Officer Chip, after an initial few weeks spent hiding under my bed and hissing at my ankles. Banana developed an uncanny knack for time-keeping; if his bowl hadn't been kibbled by 0800 he was standing on your chest by 0801, filling the room with the sound of his solicitation purr. If that didn't work, his claws would hook you through the internasal septum and he'd lead you down the hall to the place where his bowl gaped empty and innocent of food, a profound insult to the very idea of feline decency. (I started calling him "The Tum That Tells Time" about then.)

Sometimes I would go traveling, leave Banana in the care of a professional cat-sitter; upon my return he would huffily ignore me for perhaps five minutes, then break down and gallop like a small water-buffalo up the hall to hurl himself onto my chest as if to say *oh god I thought I'd never eat again that other can-opener only fed me twice a day oh please oh please never do that again.*

He never really lost that sense of insecurity—I think the legacy of so many starving years taught him that every meal might be his last, that you can never trust the future, that you have to eat not only for now but for all those hungry nights yet to come. Once he stole a whole BBQ chicken off the bed, got it halfway down the hall before I caught up with him; I had actually been defending his honor at the time, insisting to a mistrusting partner-of-the-moment that *He's not even **looking** at that chicken, how dare you accuse him of—**Banana!!*** When other cats started joining the team we had to feed Banana in a separate room, so he wouldn't shoulder-check them out of the way and eat their food as well.

Such precautions notwithstanding, it began to dawn on me that he no longer resembled anything so skinny as the banana for which he had originally been named. I contemplated changing his name to *Potato*, which would have been more descriptive of both color and shape (not to mention the nickname potential: *Spudnik!* Or in tandem with Chip the Fuzzbot, *Potato-Chip!*)—but although Banana had many fine qualities, a razor-sharp intellect was not among them. I did not want to tax his furry little brain with the demands of learning a whole new name.

We were two grumpy mammals against the world. He saw me through a half-dozen short-term relationships (with partners who understandably found him far more charming than me), and helped lure a longer-term one into range (ditto). We appeared together in *Nature*. We moved again: from Accursed Apartment to Magic Bungalow, replete with a front porch from which to survey Raccoon Alley; a wild English garden full of triffids to prowl in the back; a small ravine just off to the side, just in case he was feeling adventurous—although he rarely was, as he was in his mid-teens by now. Inside was adventurous enough: three other cats, two rabbits, a couple dozen tropical fish, and two adoring pones (the smaller of whom compulsively carried him around like a furry handbag; for reasons I will never fully understand, he did not seem to mind this in the least).

Banana and I developed a tandem fondness for half'n'half; mine in coffee, Banana's straight up in a little ceramic cup. His yowled demands for refills drew in the other cats every time I hit the kitchen to top up my mug; within a week every feline in the place was hooked on the white stuff. I was married now (Banana got a shout-out in Caitlin's vows), with real in-laws and everything; Banana got his own chair at family dinners. He would sit there looking back and forth, patiently following the dinnertime conversation between the bits of curried chicken or smoked salmon laid regularly before him by the can openers arrayed worshipfully to either side.

When I worked, he was curled up on my desk. He padded at my side when I went for the mail. He was an omnipresent obstacle that Caitlin and I had to maneuver around during sex, whether in the bedroom or the kitchen or bent over the treadmill; somehow he was always in the way, furry and unflappable.

I would have killed for that cat.

Sometime around 5:45a.m. this past Saturday, Caitlin returned to bed from an early-morning pee-break to find Banana curled up on the pillow beside me. She edged in under the covers, careful not to disturb him. I scritched his ears; he purred, half-awake.

At 5:50 he shot off the bed like a rocket and bolted from the bedroom, crashing into walls and furniture. I smiled at first. Just another cat kerfuffle, I thought, one of those psycho midnight boxing matches always breaking out amongst the Gang of Fur: with Minion, maybe, although I hadn't seen any of the others on the bed. "Stupid cat," I mumbled to Caitlin, and rolled over as something crashed into the kitchen garbage pail.

Caitlin sat up. "I think—I think he's having a *seizure*—"
Banana screamed, and didn't stop.

I've never heard a sound like that: like he was caught in a leg-hold trap, like something was tearing him apart from the inside. He would howl, and stop when he ran out of air, gulp a breath and cry out again. By the time we got to the kitchen he was convulsing on his side, back arched, legs thrashing, strings of foamy saliva smeared across the floor. His tail was puffed big as a raccoon's; his eyes were wide and sane and utterly terrified. And all I could think was *He's still in there. He* knows. *That puffy tail—that's not just some thrown clot, that's not a stroke, that's fight/flight, that's a threat display, that's what they do when something's coming at them and they're trying to scare it off.*

He tried to run, you see. Something happened, inside; something *broke*, and he felt it but he had no way to parse it except that somehow there was a mortal threat and he wasn't equipped to tell the difference between the things that kill you from the outside and those that kill you from within. All he knew was that his life was in danger, and he reacted the only way he knew how: he tried to run away.

Like a fucking idiot, I try holding him and making stupid comforting *shhh* noises. He screams and thrashes and pisses all over the floor. I leave him with Caitlin, boot up the laptop, Google desperately on *24-hour emergency veterinary Toronto*: get a hit down on Kingston Ave, click (fucking idiots, what kind of emergency clinic doesn't have phone number and address on the splash page *where's the fucking phone number?*), punch in the number. We've got a brown tabby late-teens mild heart murmur mild hyperthyroidism, otherwise healthy, good appetite normal behavior until about five minutes ago and he's convulsing, massive salivation, piloerection, can you hear the sounds he's making, here I'll hold the handset down—

No clue, they say. Could be anything. Bring him in. (Of course we're bringing him in, Caitlin's already on the other line and she's on fucking *hold* waiting for the cab dispatcher to pick up . . .)

The other cats hide or circle at a safe distance, unnerved, eyes wide. In the next room the rabbits thump out alarm signals like little bongos. I grab my Powershot to film the convulsions: probably stupid, probably just make-work but you never know, maybe there's something in those leg movements that could have diagnostic value. The Powershot isn't working: the digital display's been on and off for months, just never got around to taking it in. I run into the bedroom, get Caitlin's camera instead. By now Banana's running out of strength—still screaming, but the screams are weaker now, the convulsions edging down to frantic twitching kicks—but I take a few seconds of footage anyway, even though the light's shit, even though you can barely see anything on playback. I take an mp3 of the sounds too, just in case. We grab towels and clothes, bundle up, slam the door behind us as the cab pulls up outside. Banana's so much quieter, now; "He's dead," I say a block south of Danforth, but he squirms and lifts his head and gulps as if drowning.

We get him to the clinic. They put him on oxygen. He's not screaming any more, hasn't been screaming for minutes now but he's still kicking and for the first time I don't know if there's any light left in those eyes. Shit spills out of him. They wipe it up and hand me some paper to authorize an IV. They send us away to wait. I can still see them working around the corner.

When the vet comes out, he's all equivocation and soft-pedal. Could be thrombosis. Could be anything, really. No way to know. He's sedated now, see what happens. A few minutes into the spiel he tosses off something about no pupil response. *He's brain dead*, I say. The vet nods sadly. *Well you might have fucking said so up front; that has a certain central relevance, wouldn't you say?* He agrees.

Almost no chance of recovery, he admits when pressed. What do you mean *almost*? I ask, because there's hope in that word. What are the ballpark odds? He can't give me any. How long have you been in the business? I ask. Twelve years. And in all that time, have you ever seen a patient recover under these conditions?

He has not.

We go back in. Banana's lying on his side, IV dripping into one bandaged paw, breathing in short jerky gasps. His tongue lolls on the table like a little pink firehose; I never knew those things were so long. I tap at his nose right beside the eye; the lids blink a little, but the eyes themselves don't move. Something has already settled on the cornea, some thread or bit of dandruff. The vet grabs a hindpaw, squeezes out a claw, starts clipping. He cuts off pieces one after another, nail up to quick and beyond. He's cutting into tissue now; he must be cutting nerves. Banana doesn't twitch; maybe that's just because he's sedated, right? But, you know. Brain dead. Twelve years experience. Zero recovery.

Banana's already dead. We pay almost a thousand dollars, all told, to help his body catch up. Graveyard shift, remember: premium rates. The sun's up by the time we walk home, carrying what's left in a box sealed with white medical tape.

The pones are with their dad this morning. We ascertain, over the phone, that Mesopone wants to be present for the burial. Micropone blows it off. As has always been my custom, I wrap the carcass in an old Jethro Tull t-shirt (the *Living with the Past* tour; I've been saving it for years). I think I read somewhere that it's a good idea to let the deceased's peers encounter the body, so I leave the opened box in the dining room, Banana shrouded within. Nutmeg and Minion could care less but Chip, who has known Banana almost as long as I have, immediately takes up position beside his dead buddy and sits there for an hour or more. I have no idea if there's any significance to this.

I spend the time until Meso and Caitlin's sister arrive choosing what proves to be the most godawful root-infested part of the garden to dig the grave, and then hacking through roots as thick as my wrist with the edge of a shovel. I get the hole deep enough to foil any attempts by the local dogs or raccoons to disinter the body (or at least, if they *do* get down that far, they'll have earned their spoils). I go collect my glasses from across the yard where I hurled them in a fit of unexpected rage halfway through the excavation; we all line up in the cold. I lower Banana into the ground. Nobody has anything to say. We each drop a shovelful of soil into the hole. I retrieve the shovel and move the rest of the earth back into place. Mesopone pours a cup of half'n'half onto the dirt. We go inside.

I can't stop thinking about that puffed-out tail, about Banana's panicked terrified flight from the reaper. I can't stop thinking that he *knew* what was happening, and it scared the shit out of him, and I couldn't do fuck-all to make him feel even a little bit better. I spent six years making up for the ten that had gone before, making the life sausage of his retirement so fat that he'd forget all about the dried leathery string of jerky that preceded it. He went to sleep with us the night before, a furry pain in the ass somehow capable of monopolizing 70% of the bed with 10% of the mass; just minutes before everything turned to shit, he was purring under my hand. But in the end, he didn't die basking in the reflection of his golden years. He died in the present, in the thirty-minutes-to-an-endless-goddamned-hour when he felt something killing him from the inside, something that somehow effortlessly kept up no matter how fast he tried to run. I keep telling myself that those last minutes don't obliterate the previous six years. I will never be entirely convinced.

He's still here, of course, even though he isn't. I go into my office and he's asleep on the desk. I go into the kitchen and he's figure-eighting around my ankles. I reach down to scritch him here on the bed and it's only when the ears feel wrong that I look down and realize it's been Chip or Nutmeg or Minion all along.

The Gang of Fur goes on, leaderless for now. Minion continues to jump onto the bedside windowsill, pull the window open and jump down again without even going outside; she's always been less interested in going walkabout than in freezing me to death in my bathrobe. Chip continues to swat at me from atop the fridge, trying for a repeat of that long-past glory day when he scooped the contact lens right off my eyeball with a single claw. Nutmeg is still a furry slut. None of them are Banana, of course; just as Banana was never Zombie, or Cygnus, or Strange Cat. They're just who they are, and someday they'll all be dead. Chip's probably next to go. Positive for both Fe-leuk and FIV, he was supposed to be dead last summer, not running around robust and full of beans the way he is. And as I am typing these very words—I shit you not—the pones have just started yelling about *A Cat That Looks Just Like Banana!* trotting out of our back yard along the fence. And they're right: I just watched him cross the street. Same walk. Same well-fed tum. Same dirt-common brown tabby markings.

Different ears, of course. No one will ever again have Banana's ears.

The pones want to leave a bowl of kibble out on the porch tonight. I'm not sure what that means.

1 This was back when Paris Hilton was A Thing.

No Brainer

Nowa Fantastyka MAY 2015

BLOG JUL 28 2015

For decades now, I have been haunted by the grainy, black-and-white x-ray of a human skull.

It is alive but empty, with a cavernous fluid-filled space where the brain should be. A thin layer of brain tissue lines that cavity like an amniotic sac. The image hails from a 1980 review article in *Science*: Roger Lewin, the author, reports that the patient in question had "virtually no brain"[1]. But that's not what scared me; hydrocephalus is nothing new, and it takes more to creep out this ex-biologist than a picture of Ventricles Gone Wild.

What scared me was the fact that this virtually brain-free patient had an IQ of 126.

He had a first-class honors degree in mathematics. He presented normally along all social and cognitive axes. He didn't even realize there was anything wrong with him until he went to the doctor for some unrelated malady, only to be referred to a specialist because his head seemed a bit too large.

It happens occasionally. Someone grows up to become a construction worker or a schoolteacher, before learning that they should have been a rutabaga instead. Lewin's paper reports that one out of ten hydrocephalus cases are so extreme that cerebrospinal fluid fills 95% of the cranium. Anyone whose brain fits into the remaining 5% should be nothing short of vegetative; yet apparently, fully half have IQs over 100. (Why, here's another example from 2007[2]; and yet another.[3]) Let's call them VNBs, or "Virtual No-Brainers."

The paper is titled "Is Your Brain Really Necessary?", and it seems to contradict pretty much everything we think we know about neurobiology. This Forsdyke guy over in *Biological Theory* argues that such cases open the possibility that the brain might utilize some kind of *extracorporeal* storage[4], which sounds awfully woo both to me and to the anonymous neuroskeptic over at Discovery. com[5]; but even Neuroskeptic, while dismissing Forsdyke's wilder speculations, doesn't really argue with the neurological facts on the ground. (I myself haven't yet had a chance to more than glance at the Forsdyke paper, which might warrant its own post if it turns out to be sufficiently substantive. If not, I'll probably just pretend it is and incorporate it into *Omniscience*.)

On a somewhat less peer-reviewed note, VNBs also get routinely trotted out by religious nut jobs who cite them as evidence that a God-given soul must be doing all those things the uppity scientists keep attributing to the brain. Every now and then I see them linking to an off-hand reference I made way back in 2007 (apparently rifters.com is the only place to find Lewin's paper online without having to pay a wall) and I roll my eyes.

And yet, 126 IQ. Virtually no brain. In my darkest moments of doubt, I wondered if they might be right.

So on and off for the past twenty years, I've lain awake at night wondering how a brain the size of a poodle's could kick my ass at advanced mathematics. I've wondered if these miracle freaks might actually have the same brain *mass* as the rest of us, but squeezed into a smaller, high-density volume by the pressure of all that cerebrospinal fluid (apparently the answer is: no). While I was writing *Blindsight*—having learned that cortical modules in the brains of autistic savants are relatively underconnected, forcing each to become more efficient—I wondered if some kind of network-isolation effect might be in play.

Now, it turns out the answer to that is: *Maybe*.

Three decades after Lewin's paper, we have "Revisiting hydrocephalus as a model to study brain resilience" by de Oliveira *et al*[6] (actually published in 2012, although I didn't read it until last spring). It's a "Mini Review Article": only four pages, no new methodologies or original findings—just a bit of background, a hypothesis, a brief "Discussion" and a conclusion calling for further research. In fact, it's not so much a review as a challenge to the neuro community to get off its ass and study this fascinating phenomenon—so that soon, hopefully, there'll be enough new research out there warrant a *real* review.

The authors advocate research into "Computational models such as the *small-world* and *scale-free* network"—networks whose nodes are clustered into highly-interconnected "cliques", while the cliques themselves are more sparsely connected one to another. De Oliveira *et al* suggest that they hold the secret to the resilience of the hydrocephalic brain. Such networks result in "higher dynamical complexity, lower wiring costs, and resilience to tissue insults." This also seems reminiscent of those isolated hyper-efficient modules of autistic savants, which is unlikely to be a coincidence: networks from social to genetic to neural have all been described as "small-world." (You might wonder—as I did—why de Oliveira *et al* would credit such networks for the normal intelligence of some hydrocephalics when the same configuration is presumably ubiquitous in vegetative and normal brains as well. I can only assume they meant to suggest that small-world networking is especially well-developed among high-functioning hydrocephalics.) (In all honesty, it's not the best-written paper I've ever read.)

The point, though, is that under the right conditions, brain *damage* may paradoxically result in brain *enhancement*. Small-world, scale-free networking—focused, intensified, overclocked—might turbocharge a fragment of a brain into acting like the whole thing.

Can you imagine what would happen if we applied that trick to a normal brain?

If you've read *Echopraxia*, you'll remember the Bicameral Order: the way they used tailored cancer genes to build extra connections in their brains, the way they linked whole brains together into a hive mind that could rewrite the laws of physics in an afternoon. It was mostly bullshit, of course: neurological speculation, stretched eight unpredictable decades into the future for the sake of a story.

But maybe the reality is simpler than the fiction. Maybe you don't have to tweak genes or interface brains with computers to make the next great leap in cognitive evolution. Right now, right here in the real world, the cognitive function of brain tissue can be boosted—without engineering, without augmentation—by literal orders of magnitude. All it takes, apparently, is the right kind of stress. And if the neuroscience community heeds de Oliveira *et al*'s clarion call, we may soon know how to apply that stress to order. The singularity might be a lot closer than we think.

Also a lot squishier.

Wouldn't it be awesome if things turned out to be that easy?

1 HTTP://RIFTERS.COM/REAL/ARTICLES/SCIENCE _ NO-BRAIN.PDF
2 HTTPS://DOI.ORG/10.1016/S0140-6736(07)61127-1

No Brainer

3 HTTP://MYMULTIPLESCLEROSIS.CO.UK/EP/SHARON-PARKER-THE-WOMAN-WITH-
THE-MYSTERIOUS-BRAIN/

4 HTTP://RIFTERS.COM/REAL/ARTICLES/FORSDYKE-2015-BRAINSCANSOFHYDROCEPH
ALICSCHALLENGECHERISHEDASSUMPTIONS.PDF

5 HTTP://BLOGS.DISCOVERMAGAZINE.COM/NEUROSKEPTIC/2015/07/26/IS-YOUR-
BRAIN-REALLY-NECESSARY-REVISITED/

6 HTTP://RIFTERS.COM/REAL/ARTICLES/OLIVEIRA-ET-AL-2012-
REVISITINGHYDROCEPHALUS.PDF

The Yogurt Revolution.

Nowa Fantastyka SEP 2015

BLOG OCT 29 2015

Pick something you hate.

A government, maybe, or a church. Some multinational that treats its customers like shit. Any institution powerful enough to keep people under its thumb, to crush its competition (or at least fix prices with them) so you have nowhere else to go. Something you'd really like to see burned to the ground, although you know that's never going to happen.

A good example, here in Toronto, would be a telecommunications giant called Bell Canada. (Rogers would also be a good candidate—they suck almost as hard—but I think Bell owns more media.) If you've ever dealt with these guys—and you probably have, if you've ever watched Canadian TV—the following scenario might warm you up at night:

Gustav runs a cellphone kiosk for Bell. Walking home from work one night, a passing stranger notices the perky corporate logo on his employee polo shirt—and punches Gustav in the face.

Gustav goes down. "Fucking *Bell*," his assailant growls, kicking him in the ribs.

Gustav's no dummy. He knows everyone hates Bell. He knows all about the bandwidth throttling, the extortionate overpriced contracts, the abusive telemarketing and contemptuous customer service, the routine surveillance of customers for the benefit of any government snoop with her hand out. But—"*That's not me!*" he cries around a mouthful of broken teeth. "I don't make those decisions—*I just sell phones!*"

"It . . . doesn't . . . *matter*!" the attacker spits out, emphasizing each word with another vicious kick. "You . . . *knew*. You . . . *chose* . . . to . . . work . . . for . . . them . . . ." Eventually he tires himself out and wanders away, leaving Gustav to bleed out on the pavement.

Just a psycho with anger-management issues, you might think if you're a Bell CEO reading about it the next day. Nothing for *you* to worry about, even if you did just cut Tech Support's budget by another 10% because you want a fatter year-end bonus. The peasants will never get to you; you're safe up here on the 50th floor. Shame about poor ol' Gustav, though.

But then it happens to Shirley. And then Piotr. And Mahmoud, and George. All those underpaid drones hawking your wares at the local malls are suddenly getting the shit kicked out of them by random strangers. It's the weirdest thing. None of the attackers even have criminal records.

Now no one wants to work for you. Drones quit in droves for fear of being kicked to death like dogs in the street, and not even the unprecedented promise of a decent wage can lure in replacements. Management's safe—they don't deal with the public—but how can the top of a pyramid stay standing when the base just up and leaves? Bell has but two choices: go broke, or stop pissing off their customers. For the rest of us, it's win-win.

Isn't that a wonderful little scenario? I call it "The Justice Plague," and I fully intend to write it as soon as I can come up with an actual storyline. So far it's all premise and no plot.

It's a terrific premise, though. It hinges on yogurt—more precisely, on the ways gut microbes affect your behavior.

Of course, we've always known that your gut affects your mood. But the extent and complexity of those effects is only now coming to light—and it goes way beyond the cramps you get from salmonella, or the tryptophan drowsiness that lays you low after a turkey dinner. It's not much of an overstatement to say that your gut bacteria are a large part of what makes you *you*, psychologically. Transfer gut biota from one animal to another, and you transfer personality traits as well.

Think about that. You can literally transplant personality traits via feces. To that extent, we all have shitty personalities.

How does it work? For starters, your gut has a mind of its own: a standalone neural net with the computational complexity of a cat brain (no surprise there—cats are basically stomachs sheathed in fur anyway). Your gut microbes pull its strings by feeding it a complex cocktail of hormones and neurotransmitters; gutnet, in turn, tugs at the brain along the Vagus nerve. (Gut bacteria also have a more direct pipe into the brain via the endocrine system. Most of your brain's neurotransmitters—half the dopamine, most of the seroto- nin—are actually produced in the gut.) Via such avenues, your gut bacteria influence the formation of memories, especially those with strong emotional components. They affect aggression and anxiety responses by influencing neuroinhibitors in the prefrontal cortex and amygdala (which is responsible for fear, aggression, and the in- tensity of one's response to personal-space violations). You can make rats more or less aggressive by tweaking their gut biota.

You see where I'm going with this. Engineered gut bacteria— spread through shipments of spiked yogurt, perhaps—tweaked to promote violent, uncontrollable rage in their hosts. It's barely even speculation; rabies does that much, and it's not even engineered.

The big problem is targeting, of course—how to trigger reflexive aggression at the sight of a specific corporate logo. Corporations actually give us a lot of help here; they spend millions designing logos that are simple, striking, and immediately recognizable. So you could tweak responses in the V1 and V2 areas of the visual cortex—those pattern-matching parts of the brain that identify specific shapes and edges. If you could bend such circuits to your will, you could provoke a response in anyone who saw a given shape.

But it would be a lot simpler to let the brain do all that heavy lifting on its own, targeting instead those circuits that connect a general sense of "recognition" to the emotional response one feels at the sight of a given brand. You'd have to be familiar with that brand for this trigger to work—it keys on feelings of recognition, not the specific geometry of the stimulus—but who *doesn't* recognize the logos of major corporations these days? The best part is that all those recognition/response macros are located in the dorsolateral prefrontal cortex and in the—wait for it—

The amygdala. Back down in the limbic system, where gut bugs *already* affect aggression.

Why, we might be able to pull this whole thing off without ever leaving the basement. We don't even have to *create* the response; just magnify pre-existing resentment and let it off the leash. A thousand, a million disgruntled customers: turned into weapons of mass corporate destruction with a little help from the yogurt industry.

Hey, all you basement biologists. All you DIY Lifehackers. Looking for a project?

[**Postscript 2019:** And it took a while, but I finally wrote the damn story. "Gut Feelings" appeared in the *Toronto 2033* anthology edited by Jim Munroe, for Spacing Media. Good luck finding it, though.

A Ray of Sunshine

Nowa Fantastyka JULY 2015

I'm going to try some optimism on for size. I think it might be a bit tight around the middle.

Of course, if you've read any of the interviews I've given over the years you might remember that I've always claimed to be an optimist. I build dark futures full of no-win scenarios, critics clutch their bosoms and wonder how anyone with such a nihilistic outlook can even get out of bed in the morning, and I say *But my characters try to do the right thing! It's not their fault they're stuck in such a hellish future, that they have to kill a thousand people to save a million; that's the future we're building for them* right now. *If I ignored that fact I'd be writing wish-fulfillment fantasy instead of SF!*

Real people are scum, I continue. *They launch jihads; they rob the poor to further fatten the rich; they trick countries into going to war just to line the pockets of their oil-industry buddies! And if they're not scum, they're* idiots! *Nobody in* my *novels would deny the reality of evolution or climate change. Why, when it comes to human nature, my writing is almost* childishly *optimistic!*

All of which is true—about my fiction. My outlook on the real world, though, is somewhat dimmer—because the real world *is* infested with religious nutbars, and corporate sociopaths, and well-dressed puppets who prance upon the World Stage pretending to move by themselves while multinationals pull their strings. Species die off orders of magnitude faster than they have since Chicxulub took out the dinosaurs; droughts and firestorms sweep across the faces of continents, having somehow turned from transient events to permanent fixtures while we weren't looking. Glaciers melt—always so much faster than even the most pessimistic predictions—and slide into the rising sea.

Here in the real world, we're pretty much fucked. There's a reason my blog is subtitled "In love with the moment; scared shitless of the future."

And yet here I am, trying on some optimism. Because here in the real world, I can't help noticing a few hopeful developments amongst all the impending doom:

- A half-dozen Pacific Island nations, especially vulnerable to the impacts of climate change, have launched a campaign to take developed nations to court over their disproportionate production of greenhouse gases.
- The Netherlands has just lost a class-action lawsuit at the District Court in the Hague, which ruled illegal its plans for a measly 14–17% reduction in greenhouse gas emissions by 2020; the court has ordered more rigorous reductions of 25%.
- The Pope—of the very same Church of Rome that's come down on the wrong side of everything from birth control to the heliocentric solar system—has released an encyclical summoning the faithful to combat climate

change, and decrying the turning of our planet into a "pile of filth." I have, in years past, stood awestruck by the magnificence of European cathedrals that took centuries to build; I've wondered what might be accomplished if such multigenerational devotion were turned to the pursuit of good instead of evil. Perhaps we're about to find out.

- The production of solar energy has grown exponentially for at least two decades, far faster than any conventional energy source; it's expected to achieve grid parity across 80% of the global market within two years, and has already passed that point in somewhere around 30 countries including much of Europe. (And that's not even counting the impact of other renewable sources like wind and geothermal; Costa Rica recently powered itself entirely on renewables for 75 days running).

That last item probably carries the greatest impact. One of the biggest reasons we haven't come to grips with the climate crisis is the simple fact that we're not wired for foresight: to the Human Gut, today's inconvenience is far more real than next decade's catastrophe. You'll always have an uphill struggle asking someone to pay now for a bill that won't come due for decades (even if the bill is actually coming due today after all).

But getting gouged for oil when solar is *cheaper*? That's something the gut understands. Nobody cares about saving the world, but *everyone* wants to save money; if paying less for energy happens to save the world in the bargain, so much the better. Renewables are finally getting us to that tipping point.

There may be cause for *hope*.

Lest you think I'm going soft, I hasten to add: I'm only trying these optimistic pants on for size. I haven't bought them yet. Big Carbon's fighting back; in some US states they're penalizing people who go solar by charging them extra fees for "infrastructure use." Solar's ascendance might perversely provoke a massive short-term *increase* in the burning of fossil fuels, as oil-rich interests work furiously to dig all that petro out of the ground *now*, before it stops being profitable.

Papal influence? Politicians use religion to manipulate others, not to guide their own behavior. It's no surprise that the US's religious right stopped thumping their bibles just long enough to tell the pope and his encyclical to fuck right off. Nor should we get too swept up by the legal option. The Netherlands may well appeal the Hague's ruling[1], and as for those island nations and their adorable little "Declaration for Climate Justice"—even if they make it to court, even if they *win*, does anyone really think the world's most powerful nations are going to obey any verdict that goes against their own interests? The US doesn't even follow its *own* laws when they prove inconvenient; how seriously do you think they're going to take a bunch of finger-wagging third-worlders at the Hague?

Even if they did—even if the whole world pulled together and swore off carbon tomorrow—we're still in for a rough ride. The ship has sailed, the carbon's already in the atmosphere, and thermal inertia guarantees that even our best-case trajectory gets worse before it gets better. So yes: there's still every reason to believe that we're sending this planet straight down the crapper.

That has not changed.

What has changed is that finally there are a few shreds of good news amongst all the bad. Where once there was nothing but a sea of untreated sewage spreading to the horizon, now a few green sprouts poke up here and there amongst all the fecal matter. It's not much, but it's more than there was. And it's for the better.

At this point, I'll take what I can get.

---

1 That decision will have been made by the time you read this.

The Daily, MAY 22 2016

The doctors say it lives on your skin, waiting for an opening. They say once it gets inside, your fate comes down to a dice roll. It doesn't always turn your guts to slurry; sometimes you get off with a sore throat, sometimes it doesn't do anything at all. They might even admit that it doesn't always need an open wound. People have been known to sicken and die from a bruise, from a bump against the door.

What they *won't* generally tell you is that you can get it by following doctor's orders. Which is how I ended up in ICU, staring through a morphine haze into a face whose concerned expression must have been at least 57% fear of litigation. I didn't get flesh-eating disease from a door or a zip-line. I got it from a dual-punch biopsy—which is to say, from being stabbed with a pair of needles the size of narwhal tusks. There was this lesion on my leg, you see. They needed a closer look. And there was Mr. Strep, waiting on my skin for new frontiers to conquer.

Reality comes with disclaimers. You're never sure in hindsight what actually happened, what didn't, what composite remnants your brain might have stitched together for dramatic purposes. I remember waking embedded in gelatin, in an OR lined with egg cartons; I'm pretty sure that was a hallucination. I remember my brother's voice on a cellphone between operations, mocking my position on Global Warming. (That might sound like a hallucination too, but only if you didn't know my brother.) I'm pretty sure the ICU nurse was real, the one who stood bedside as I lay dying and said, "You're an author? I'm working on a book myself, you know; maybe if you happen to pull through . . ."

At least one memory is fact beyond doubt. My partner Caitlin confirmed it; the surgeon repeated it; even now I turn it over daily in my head like some kind of black-hearted anti-affirmation: "Two more hours and you'd be dead."

Two hours? I was in the waiting room longer than that.

It was fourteen hours from *Of course it hurts they just punched two holes in your leg* to shakes and vomiting and self-recrimination: *Come on, you're a big tough field biologist. Back on Snake Island you cut a sebaceous cyst out of your own scrotum with a rusty razor blade and a bottle of rubbing alcohol.* I remember drifting away to the thought that this was just some nasty 24-hour thing, that I was bound to feel better in the morning. Caitlin kept me awake; she kept me alive. Together we improvised a sling out of old jeans so I could hop to the cab without screaming.

Twelve hours as a succession of whitecoats said *cellulitis* and *nothing serious* and *wait, was it oozing those black bubbles an hour ago?* I crashed somewhere in there: one moment chatting bravely with friends and caregivers, the next staring into the light while nurses slapped my face and strapped an *Alien* facehugger across my mouth. I don't know how many instants passed in the black space between.

They strip-mined the rot from my leg just past midnight. They had to go in twice. All told, it was forty hours from First Contact to Death's Door; forty-two and you wouldn't be reading this. I spent weeks with an Australia-sized crater in my calf, watched muscles slide like meaty pistons every time we changed the dressings. To a biologist and science-fiction writer, though, that was *cool*. I blogged; I spelunked my leg with sporks and Q-tips, took pictures, impressed nurses and inspired half of Reddit to lose its lunch. Eventually they scraped a strip off my thigh with a cheese-grater, stapled it across the hole, told me not to worry about the rotten-fish smell wafting from the wound. I've got a huge vagina-shaped scar on my leg but I still *have* that leg—and just six months after some vicious microbe turned its insides into chunky beef stew, I was back to running nine miles.

I wasn't lucky. None of we flesh-eaten are *lucky*. But next to those who've lost arms and legs, lives and loved ones to this ravenous monster—a scar is *nothing*. It's a memento. It's free beers courtesy of the easily-impressed.

Not lucky. But I've got to be one of the least *un*lucky bastards alive.

I don't have any pictures of my father. I just realized that now, two days after he died sitting on a toilet in frigid fucking Edmonton, 2700 km from home. He was visiting my brother. He was supposed to be back by December 21, we were going to go out for dinner before Christmas. But the stress of that journey kicked his state variable off whatever high, unstable equilibrium it had been teetering at these past months: sent it sliding down to some new low that just proved unsustainable. He fell ill the day after wheels-down, and never recovered.

He was 94. Nobody could claim he didn't have a long life.

Nobody could claim he had a happy one, either.

He was a minister way back before I was born, but by the time I came onto the scene he'd already founded the Baptist Leadership Training School in Calgary and was serving as its first principal. He held that post for 22 years; then we moved east so he could become the General Secretary of the Baptist Convention of Ontario and

Quebec. He held that position until he retired. Not your average Baptist preacher, my dad. A church leader. A scholar.

He was also gay, although he refused to use the word because "it's brought me no joy at all." He preferred the term "nonpracticing homosexual". He never acted on it, you see. He spent his whole life hiding it. He only came out to Jon and I a few years ago, and even then it was only *in extremis*: pulled from the clutches of an abusive wife whose dementia had demolished any thin façade of Christian charity, rescued too late to escape the welts and bruises and near-starvation she'd inflicted, still he was making *excuses* for her behavior. *Your mother's had a hard time of it*, he told us. *I haven't been a proper husband. See what I am.*

It's my fault.

He did come out to Fanshun, the day after I was born in fact. Offered her a divorce. Think about that: a man of the cloth, a star in the Baptist firmament in the fifties-era bible belt of the Canadian prairies. Divorcing his wife. It would have been pitchforks and torches for sure, but he offered, and she turned him down: *I'll stay with you for the children*, she said, *and the job.* She knew which side her bread was buttered on: in the Baptist community of that day, Dad was a rock star.

Why did you get married in the first place? I asked decades later. *Why dig yourself into such a no-win scenario?* I still don't know if I believe his answer: because, he said, he thought he was alone in the world, that no other man on the planet might like a little cock now and then. Back when he married my mother, he had no idea what a homosexual even *was*. He'd never even heard the word.

Really. Ronald F. Watts, biblical scholar, Doctor of Divinity, a man who not only knows the scriptures inside-out but also *taught* them for two decades. What did you think Leviticus was going on about, huh? How could you possibly think you were unique when your own sacred book singles out your kind as an abomination to be killed?

He told me that he'd never read anything like that in Leviticus. He thought I was making it up. I had to dig out his own King James and point him to 20:13; even then, his reaction was one of confusion and disbelief. He was in his nineties now, and not as sharp as he'd once been—but I'm still astonished at the degree of cognitive dissonance that brain must have been able to support.

He never came close to the fire-and-brimstone stereotype of the Baptist preacher. He never had any trouble with evolution. He always encouraged me to ask questions and think for myself, so convinced of his own beliefs that he probably thought it inconceivable that any honest search could end up at a different destination. Closer to death he admitted to regretting that: "I have been a poor parent," he wrote just back in November, "who spent so much time teaching scores of young people about faith in God that I failed to teach my own kids".

I could never pretend that I found his religious beliefs anything but absurd, but I hastened to tell him that I'd found him a far better parent than most. He never, *ever* judged the sinner. Back during my high school days I'd come home staggering drunk and reeking of beer; while Fanshun's first concern was whether anyone from Central Baptist had seen me (all about appearances, that woman), Dad would gently knock on my door, lie down beside me on the bed as the ceiling spun overhead, and ask how my day had been. He made no mention of the fact that the room would probably have gone up in flames if anyone had lit a match. We'd just talk about our respective days until I brought the subject up myself; then he'd sigh, and roll his eyes, and quote some obscure Shakespearean line about what fools men were to put a demon in their mouths to steal away their brains. I can't begin to count the number of stupid things I did as a teenager; but my father never made me feel as if *I* were stupid.

When I was twelve or thirteen, he found me reading *From Russia with Love*. He cleared his throat, and remarked that Ian Fleming knew how to tell an exciting tale, and that was good—but that this James Bond guy did not treat women at all well, and I probably shouldn't use those books as any kind of guide to healthy relationships.

I'll say it again: Baptist preacher. Bible Belt. Sixties.

Of course, in hindsight his *Judge Not Others* perspective was a bit more self-serving than it might have seemed—but then, so many things make sense in hindsight. The way his wife kept harping about the other men she could have had (I remain skeptical to this day); the endless invasions of privacy, her needy demands that we be *friends* and confidantes as well as sons. Her outrage at the prospect that I might want to leave some thoughts unshared. The endless nitpicking and ridicule she heaped on her husband over the years. I thought he was a fucking pussy at the time; I couldn't understand why he never stood up to her, why he always took her side. Because he knew that so-called truth that he told himself year after year, the truth she never let him forget:

It was all his fault.

Retired from the Baptist Convention, he threw himself into volunteer work for Amnesty International (my late brother Jon, who worked for the Feds at that time, told me that Dad's advocacy on behalf of the oppressed earned him a CSIS file.) He got his first computer back in the eighties, almost in *his* eighties: an old XT with an amber screen. He had some trouble with the concept of *software* at first—"I'm trying to write this letter for AI, but it'll only let me write a line or two and then it just jumps to a new line and says *Bad command or file name c colon* . . ."—but how many old farts of that generation even *tried* coming to grips with the computer revolution?

He got the hang of it eventually. Figured out the whole internet-porn thing just fine. His last computer was one Jon and

I bought for him a few Christmases ago. I helped him set it up; he sat there across the room, smiling beatific and oblivious as a Windows dialog box announced each in a procession of files and bookmarks journeying from old machine to new:

UKBOYSFIRSTTIME.COM

ALT.EROTICA.GAY.BONDAGE

ALT-EROTICA.GAY.DEATHMETAL

I would have hugged him, but he'd have been mortified if he knew that I'd seen.

Porn was as far as he got. By the time he found out that he wasn't alone, he was: so locked down that even fellow gays who'd known him for years had no clue. Once I offered him a male escort for his birthday, but he said he'd be too embarrassed ("And besides, do you know what they *charge* per hour?"). He did manage to connect a little, vicariously, near the end of his life. A childhood friend of mine came to the rescue, visited Dad whenever he was in town, kept him up to speed on news of his boyfriend in New York and life as an opera singer.

But it was too little, too late. This kind, decent, wonderful man spent his whole damn life in hiding, died without ever experiencing the simple comfort of a decent lay. I may never understand the contradiction inherent in that life: his unshakeable devotion to a community which, for all its strident insistence that *God Is Love*, never let him feel safe enough to be who he was.

Now he's dead, along with his legacy (BLTS, the school he founded and nurtured and built from the ground up, was sold for scrap a few years ago and is now being run as a private school). His wife is dead. Even one of his sons is dead. There's nobody left for his dark secret to shame—nobody left to *be* ashamed, except for that vast intolerant community of spirit-worshippers with whom my father, for reasons I only half-understand, threw in his lot and his life. But so many of them are shameless, too.

Maybe he was right. Maybe those ancient dumb superstitions have some truth to them after all. If so, I guess he knows that for certain now. It's the great injustice of the atheist position: if we're wrong about the afterlife, the rest of you have all of eternity to rub our noses in it; but if we're right, no one will ever know.

I wouldn't mind being wrong, just this once.

Prometheus: The Men Behind the Mask.

BLOG JUNE 18 2012

We start with spoilers, right off the top: Back in 1979's *Alien*, Lambert, Kane, and Dallas passed through a big spooky chamber—the Devil's own rib cage—*en route* to cinematic immortality. The fossilized remains of an alien creature rested at its center like a great stone heart, embedded in organic machinery: mysterious, vaguely pachydermal, *lonely* somehow. We never learned what that creature was, where it came from, how it ended up fused to the bottom end of an alien telescope. We didn't have to. The mystery was what gripped us: this evidence of things beyond the firelight we couldn't see and, oh please God, might never see: because the infinitesimal sliver of the Unknown that *did* leak into view was enough to make us crap our pants before it ripped us limb from limb.

Thirty-three years later, Ridley Scott shone a light into the darkness. He peeled away that skeletal shroud and showed us what lurked underneath: just a regular dude with big muscles and albinism, as it turned out. Mr. Clean without the earring. And with that one reveal, Scott took all that was mysterious and compelling and fearful about the monster under the bed, and reduced it to utter banality.

The scene itself is almost meta—because when you scale it up, that's pretty much what *Prometheus* does to the entire *Alien* franchise.

If you haven't checked out Caitlin's review yet, you should: it's concise and thoughtful and right on the money in terms of the broad missteps that make *Prometheus* sputter on its narrative cylinders. But perhaps the one grand achievement that this movie might lay claim to is, its failings are too vast and too numerous to be contained within the limits of any one review. It will take squads, entire platoons of reviewers to properly pick apart these bones. I only hope that I, along with the half of the internet that also happens to be weighing in, am up to the task.

Where to begin?

How about at the very first shot, where a naked alabaster oxygen-breathing humanoid strolls about on a planet that doesn't have any oxygen in its atmosphere (*i.e.,* prebiotic Earth). He drinks of a literal Cup of Life; dissolves; topples into Earth's water cycle, where the soup of his dissolution forms the basis of all life on the planet. We know this, jumping ahead a few billion years, because we humans turn out to be an exact genetic match with said alabaster dude. Meaning that:

1. Every earthly life form from the Archaea on down has exactly the same genotype—has had the same genotype for 4.5 billion years, in fact—and everything anybody ever discovered about genes from Mendel on down was wrong; or
2. Different earthly clades do have divergent genotypes, but our particular twig on the tree (and none other) just happened to end up converging back to an exact match on the primordial soup

after four and a half billion years of independent mutation, divergence, and reticulation on its own (oh, and everything anybody ever discovered about genes from Mendel on down was wrong); or 3. Everybody who ever had a hand in developing the screenplay for *Prometheus* dropped out of school after grade three, never watched a single episode of *Animal Planet* or *CSI*, and stuck their fingers in their ears and hummed real loud whenever anyone at a cocktail party talked about science. And everything Damon Lindelhof thinks he might have overheard somewhere about genes is wrong.

These are pretty big lapses to encounter in the first ten minutes of any so-called "science fiction" film—much less one from someone as genre-defining as Ridley Scott—and yet I feel a little silly even bringing them up, because so many of the broader storytelling elements are such a mess. When the Challenger blows up, you don't waste your time complaining about its paint job. But beyond Sweet *et al*'s observations about the lack of dramatic tension, the lack of mystery, the lack of *story*, science does play a disproportionate role here. *Alien* was about a bunch of truckers on a lonely monster-haunted highway; *Aliens*, about a bunch of jarheads rediscovering, to their shock and awe, the nastier lessons of Viêt Nam. *Prometheus* is about a *scientific expedition*, for fuckssake—and while *Aliens* director James Cameron cared enough about verisimilitude to put his actors through a couple weeks' basic military training, it's blindingly obvious that Scott couldn't be bothered to ensure that his "scientists" knew the difference between a gene and a bad joke. Much less anything about science as a profession.

So nobody thinks it remarkable when an archaeologist performs micro-necro-neurosurgery or runs a genetic analysis—anybody with an *ologist* on their resumé has gotta be a whiz at everything from microbiology to global general relativity, right? We're shown a biologist who uses the word "Darwinism" as though it were a legitimate scientific term and not a dig invented by creationists: the same biologist who, in the penultimate act of a profoundly undistinguished career, runs with his tail between his legs at the sight of the first actual alien the Human race has ever encountered, even though it's been dead for thousands of years. Then, a few hours later, watches a *live* serpentine alien perform what's pretty obviously a threat display—*and tries to pet it.*

And yet, idiotic though that biologist may be, the scientist in me can't really take personal offense because *nobody* in this shiny train wreck has a clue, from the pilot to the aliens to an on-board medical pod that, honest-to-God, is *Not Configured for Females* (unless that was supposed to be some kind of ham-fisted comment on gender politics?). Nobody bothers with any kind of orbital survey prior to landing (blind luck is always the best way to locate artefacts that could be anywhere on the surface of a whole bloody planet—although that's downright plausible next to being able to find a multi-mooned gas giant from 34 light-years away, based on a prehistoric game of tic-tac-toe someone scratched into a cave wall during the last ice age). A survey team goes charging into an unexplored alien structure and takes off their helmets the moment someone says "oxygen." Their captain leaves the bridge unattended for a quick fuck, right after informing two crew members stranded in the bowels of said structure that an unknown life-form is popping in and out of sensor range just down the hall from them. The lead's love interest notices an alien worm doing a quick tap-dance on his own cornea, then suits up for EVA without telling anyone. David the android does a pretty good pre-enactment of Ash's later subterfuge in *Alien* by using his flesh-and-blood crewmates as incubators for this week's infestation—for no reason I could see, since the standing orders that motivate Ash can't possibly have been coded yet (nobody even knows about these aliens, or any others, prior to planetfall). And the "Engineers"— ancient godlike beings who act across billion-year timescales and give life to worlds—haven't figured out how to make biohazard Tupperware that doesn't breach the moment someone comes through the front door.

Not, granted, that all that black goo really *can* be contained, not by any plausible bioware facility (although you do have to wonder why, if the stuff really was such a handful, the Engineers didn't just take off and nuke the site from orbit). The stuff seems to spin a roulette wheel to decide what it's going to be at any given time: kraken, mealworm, biologist-eating cobra. At one point it acts as some kind of zombifying-and-reprogramming agent, reanimating the corpse of a dead geologist and sending him back to the mothership to flail around like Jason Voorhees on *So You Think You Can Dance*. Biological containment measures are doomed to fail because this McGuffin is not limited by any plausible biological constraints.

I see that over on *io9*, my buddy Dave Williams describes the Engineer's goo as a "DNA accelerant"[1]. I don't know what that is; maybe it's a product of "Darwinism." I'd be more inclined to suggest that it simply exhibits whatever arbitrary characteristics the plot requires at any given moment, except for the fact that *Prometheus* doesn't seem to have a plot. None of those iterations seem to tie into a coherent biological model; none of those incidents seem to connect narratively to any other. It's as if some lazy DM showed up for a night of Dungeons & Dragons without having actually planned a campaign, and just threw a bunch of random encounters at the players hoping they wouldn't notice.

Of course, those who champion the film don't do so on the basis of its science. It's not *about* the science, they would say, it's about the Big Questions. (I wonder how such folks would react if the producers of *Master & Commander* had followed the same logic, decided that since the heart of the story was the human relationships, why not just let Russell Crowe and Paul Bettany bob around the tropics in water wings and not worry about all that nineteenth-century nautical trivia?) I admit to half the point; I admit that *Prometheus* is not a movie especially interested in science. I do not concede, however, that it is a movie about Big Questions: that would put it into the realm of philosophy, and the script lacks anywhere near sufficient rigor to qualify on that score. Philosophy does more than throw a bunch of what-ifs at the wall and leave them sticking there like overcooked pasta. It doesn't just *raise* questions, it *engages* them. It *grapples*. *Prometheus* just takes its what-ifs and stuffs them into a hundred-million-dollar fortune cookie.

Which makes it not a work of science or of philosophy, but of religion. It may mouth the Big Questions, but the answers it provides are downright inane. And you have to take everything else on faith.

1 HTTP://IO9.COM/5919306/ANOTHER-THEORY-ABOUT-THE-MEANING-OF-PROMETHEUS

Motherhood Issues

Nowa Fantastyka Nov 2011

How many times have you heard new parents, their eyes bright with happy delirium (or perhaps just lack of sleep), insisting that *you don't know what love is until you first lay eyes on your baby*? How many of you have reunited with old university buddies who have grown up and spawned, only to find that mouths which once argued about hyperspace and acid rain can't seem to open now without veering into the realm of child-rearing? How many commercials have you seen that sell steel-belted radials by plunking a baby onto one? How many times has rational discourse been utterly short-circuited the moment someone cries "Please, someone think of the *children*!"? (I've noticed the aquarium industry is particularly fond of this latter strategy, whenever anyone suggests shutting down their captive whale displays.)

You know all this, of course. You know the wiring and the rationale behind it: the genes build us to protect the datastream. The only reason we exist is to replicate that information and keep it moving into the future. It's a drive as old as life itself. But here's the thing: rutting and reproduction are not the traits we choose to exalt ourselves for. It's not sprogs, but spirit, that casts us in God's image. What separates us from the beasts of the field is our minds, our intellects. This, we insist, is what makes us truly human.

Which logically means that parents are less human than the rest of us.

Stick with me here. Yes, all of us are driven by brainstem imperatives. We are all compromised: none of us is a paragon of intellect or rationality. Still, some are more equal than others. There is a whole set of behavioral subroutines that never run until we've actually pupped, a whole series of sleeper programs that kick in on that fateful moment when we stare into our child's eyes for the first time, hear the weird Middle Eastern Dylan riffs whining in our ears, and realize that holy shit, we're *Cylons*.

That is the moment when everything changes. Our children become the most important thing in the world, the center of our existence. We would save our own and let ten others die, if it came to that. The rational truth of the matter—that we have squeezed out one more large mammal in a population of seven billion, which will in all likelihood accomplish nothing more than play video games, watch *American Idol*, and live beyond its means until the ceiling crashes in—is something that simply doesn't compute. We look into those bright and greedy eyes and see a world-class athlete, or a Nobel Prize-winner, or the next figurehead of global faux-democracy delivered unto us by Diebold and Halliburton.

We do not see the reality, because seeing reality would compromise genetic imperatives. We become lesser intellects. The parental subroutines kick in and we lose large chunks of the very spark that, by our own lights, makes us human.

So why not recognize that with a new political movement? Call it the "Free Agent Party," and build its guiding principles along the sliding scale of intellectual impairment. Those shackled by addictions that skew the mind—whether pharmaceutically, religiously, or parentally induced—are treated the same way we treat those who have yet to reach the age of majority, and for pretty much the same reasons. Why do we deny driver's licenses and voting privileges to the young? Why do we ban drunks from the driver's seat? Because they are not ready. They are not competent to make reasonable decisions. Nobody questions this in today's society. How are offspring addicts any different?

I'm trying to slip such a political movement to the noisy (and slightly satirical) background of the novel I'm currently writing—but the more I think of it, the more it strikes me as an idea whose time has come. It's a no-lose electoral platform as far as I can see. And of course, parenthood is just the beginning. If we ban parents from voting because of impaired judgment, what do we do about *horny* voters? I don't know about the rest of you, but I've made some very stupid decisions in the quest to get laid.

But then celibates would be out too: even though they aren't having sex, they will at least be distracted mightily by unfulfilled urges (assuming they're not senescent). Oh, and the senescent—that's another group we don't want making too many decisions. Failing memories, Alzheimer's, you name it.

So who's left? By now our voting pool is down to chemically-castrated non-parents whose sex drives have been hormonally suppressed. Oh, and we should suppress the survival instinct too, since any brainstem-equipped mammal is going to irrationally value its own life over the good of society as a whole (a fact that Heinlein touched upon in his classic YA novel *Starship Troopers*).

Which rules out everybody except potential suicides. Except suicidal depression also impairs judgment. So that leaves . . . that leaves . . .

You know something? We just gotta do away with this whole *voting* thing entirely . . .

The Halting Problem.

You know you're asking for it. When you turn down the kittens, because everybody and their dog adopts kittens. When you seek out the battered one-eared guys with pumpkin breath and rotten teeth and FIV, the old bruisers who've spent their lives on the street because who *else* is gonna give them a home? Even when you get lucky—when the stray on your doorstep is only a few months old and completely healthy, not so much as a flea on the fur and her whole life stretching out before her—even then you know you're asking for it, because the very best-case scenario only lasts a couple of decades before her parts wear out and she grinds painfully to a halt in a random accumulation of system failures. You know, and you do it anyway. Because you're a dumb mammal with an easily-hacked brain, and if you don't step up who else will?

It was Chip, this time. I called it back when Banana died, I said Chip would probably be next to go. And I can't really complain, because we *thought* he was going to die back in 2011. But here it is, almost the end of 2013, and the patchy little fuzzbot was alive right up to 3:30 yesterday afternoon. He'd be alive right now if we hadn't killed him, although the vet says he wouldn't be enjoying it.

You really hope they're not lying to you when they say things like that. You wonder how they even know.

I didn't even know his name at first. He was just this weird hostile cat who'd sneak in from outside, bolt through my living room and down the hall, and hide under my bed. I called him Puffy Patchy White Cat, with that poetic and lyrical imagination for which I have become so renowned.

Puffy Patchy White Cat hated my guts. He'd shoot past me *en route* to his underbed fort, and he'd hiss and spit whenever I bent down to look at him under there. He just wanted the territory. I have no idea why. How many children lie awake at night, fearful of predatory monsters beneath the bed? I lived that dream. I would fall asleep to the growls and hisses of some misanthropic furball just the other side of the mattress, lurking and fuming for reasons I could not fathom.

This went on for months before his Human finally showed up at my door, looking to dump him. Told me that Puffy Patchy White Cat's name was "Chip," and that he'd be at the Humane Society within twenty-four hours if nobody was willing to take him. What could I say? The fuzzbot was already spending half his time at the Accursed Apartment; I was going to see him incarcerated, maybe killed, just because he wanted to claw my eyes out?

The day after I said yes I saw Chip's Human rolling a dolly full of personal effects past my living room window. Chip ran in his wake, mewing piteously: *what's going on where are you taking all my stuff where are we going what's happening why won't you talk to me?* That two-legged asshole never slowed, never looked back. The service elevator closed behind him and Chip was alone.

He spent that night, like all the others, under my bed. For once he didn't growl, didn't hiss, didn't make a sound.

By the next day he had decided I was his bestest friend. I went into the kitchen and he jumped up on the fridge, started bonking me with that trademark head-butt that is the hallmark of slutty cats everywhere, but which Chip somehow made his own. I fed him. Banana shrugged and made room for another bowl in the house.

In the years since, Chip worked unceasingly to win the title of Toronto's Priciest Cat. Unused to playing with others, suddenly absorbed into a five-cat household, he peed chronically and expensively on a succession of carpets and towels. The insides of his ears sprouted clusters of grotesque, blueberry-like growths filled with a bloody, tar-like substance that blocked off the canal and provoked a series of infections that smelled like cheese. We had them surgically removed. They grew back. We took him out to a secret government lab in Lake Scugog, spent a couple thousand dollars having his ears *lasered* clean of tumors. Called him "Miracle Ears" when he came back with perfect pink shells where all that corruption used to be. Groaned when it reappeared yet again, six months later.

A few years back, when he inexplicably went off his food, we spent three grand exploring a lump in his abdomen that the vet said was consistent with cancer. (It turned out to be gas.) He also had chronic tachycardia, which translated into a lifetime prescription for pricey little blue pills called Atenolol.

He would shriek like a banshee at 3 a.m. At first he did this in response to one of BOG's (admittedly unwarranted) attacks—but after a few iterations where we responded by ganging up on BOG in Chip's defense, he figured out how to *use* that. He would walk into whatever room BOG was minding his own business in, let out a shriek to wake the dead, and sit back waiting for BOG to take the fall. (It was much scarier when those two fought for real: they'd grapple in complete silence, no yowls no hisses, just a ball of teeth and claws and flying fur rolling down the stairs, locked together in combat.)

He was affectionate, although he tried to hide it. He would excel at being standoffish during the day (except for the usual refrigerator bonks at dinnertime). Late at night, though—after lights-out—he'd creep slowly onto the bed, edge along the mattress to the headboard, and sprawl across the head of whoever happened to be closest. Sometimes we'd wake up from the sound of the purring; other times we'd wake up suffocating, our mouths draped in fur. Either way we kept ourselves still so as not to startle him, but it wasn't really necessary. Once Chip segued into Hat Mode, it would take an earthquake to dislodge him.

And who can forget the time he swiped the contact lens right off my eyeball with a single claw?

We've known for a while that he was living on borrowed time. Back during one of his endless savings-depleting trips to the vet, the tests came back positive for both FIV and feline leukemia; the vet was bracing us for death in mere days, back then. But that was 2011, and ever since he weathered whatever misfortune that fucked-up physiology inflicted upon him. We'd forgotten how mortal he was. Even over the past couple of weeks, when he went off his food and started losing weight—when he turned his nose up at Wellness Brand, and flaked tuna, and the hypoallergenic stuff that costs the GNP of a Latin-American country for a single can—I wasn't *too* worried. *There he goes again*, I thought. *Another of his dumb attention-hogging false alarms. We'll pillage the pones' college fund and pay another few grand and buy our way out of it the way we always have. Dumb cat.* He'd always pulled through before after all, always beaten the odds; and for the first time ever, his ears were actually improving.

So we took him to the vet, and his nictitating membrane was dead white. And suddenly I noticed that his nose—normally bright pink—that was white, too. And the blood tests came back, and his RBC count was about an eighth of what it should have been.

He was suffocating, right down at the cellular level. His resp rate was already elevated, trying to compensate—as if breathing faster could make any difference when there was so little pigment left inside to grab O_2 no matter how much tidal volume ramped up. Chip's marrow had died, his bones had hollowed out like a bird's while we'd been busy not noticing.

Days, the vet said. And it won't be an easy death, it'll be horrible. He'll die slowly, gasping for breath. A sensation of drowning that persists no matter how much air you take into your lungs.

So yesterday, we saved him the trouble. It wasn't as peaceful a death as we'd been promised. The sedative did the opposite of what it was supposed to, started freaking him out and waking him up. I restrained his spastic struggles for a while and then let him go, followed him as he groaned and staggered across the room into a dark little toilet cubby that might afford him the comfort of close quarters, at least. Scooped him up there and just kept him company in the dark, until the vet came down with a dose of some new drug that please god wouldn't fuck up the same way the last one did. His eyes were bright right up until they closed. We buried him out back, just a little ways down the garden from Banana, wrapped up in my very last Jethro Tull t-shirt (*Rock Island*: not one of their best albums, but great cover art). We buried him with a spray-bottle of pet-stain remover that we won't be needing any more.

And entropy wins again, and now the universe is a little less complex, a little poorer. There are a billion other cats out there, and thousands more being born every day. It's good that things die—I keep telling myself this—because immortality would deny hope to all those other creatures who need a home, only to find there is no room at the inn. But there are so many degrees of freedom, even in such a small furry head. So many different ways the synapses can wire up, so many different manifestations of that unique wiring. There are a million other fuzzbots, a million other bright-eyed puffy patchy white cats, but there will never be another *Chip*. That part of the universe is over now, and as always, I can't help but miss it.

Goodbye, you dumb troublesome expensive cat. You were worth every penny, and so very much more.

Chamber of Horrors

Nowa Fantastyka Nov 2016

You may know that I was a biologist long before I was an author. You may not know how far back those roots extend, though: years before I ever stepped onto a university campus. Way back into childhood, in fact.

I was really bad at biology back then. I was downright *horrific*. Now I am old, and remorseful, and afflicted with some weird disease that nobody seems able to identify; so I figure I should make my peace. Consider this a deathbed confession, delivered early to avoid the rush.

My intentions were always honorable. I love other creatures almost as much as I hate people; the running joke of my life is that I'm a bad biologist because I have too much compassion, can't bring myself to experiment on fellow beings with the ruthless dispassion that Science demands.

But I don't just love life; I want to know how it *works*, I always have. I decided to be a biologist at age seven; by fourteen I was

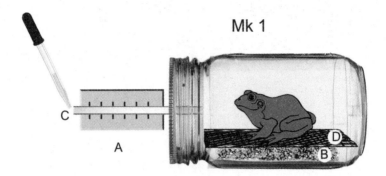

building metabolic chambers out of mason jars.

That's actually easier than it sounds. Stick a straw (A) through the lid of a mason jar. Put some CO_2 absorbant (B) inside (I used Drano). Insert an animal, tighten the lid, and—this is the cool bit—*seal the end of the straw with a soap bubble.* Animal inhales O_2, exhales CO_2; Drano absorbs CO_2, reducing the volume of gas in the jar and pulling the bubble along the straw. If you know the straw's volume, you can measure the O_2 consumption of anything inside by timing the rate at which the bubble moves.

Cool, huh?[1]

One thing, though: Drano is corrosive, so you want to keep it away from your animal. I kept mine safely under a plastic grille (D) that served as the floor of the chamber. It worked great. The only potential risk was when you took the animal out afterward, which you did by sliding the grille from the jar like a tiny drawer.

Especially if the animal was a jumper. A toad, for instance.

In my defense, the mouth of that jar was a pretty small bullseye given all the directions in which he *could* have jumped. Any random leap off the grille should have missed it completely. But maybe this particular toad *liked* that jar. Maybe he felt safe there. For whatever reason, he jumped unerringly off the grille, back into the jar, and landed smack-dab in the Drano.

Mk 2

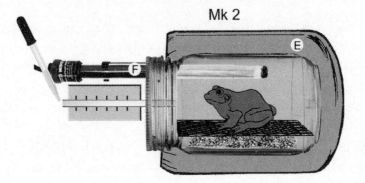

I grabbed him instantly, of course. Ran to the sink, thrust him under the running water to rise him clean and his back half just—
—washed away . . .

I kept the front half—still blinking, a little confused—in a shallow bowl next to my bed so I could check on it during the night. I was a wuss as well as a bad biologist, you see; I didn't have the heart to smash the little guy with a hammer, put him out of his misery. (I got better at that over the years, at least. You don't spend a lifetime with cats without learning to put small things out of their misery. Remind me to tell you sometime about the bouncy, impact-resistant, almost indestructible elasticity of various kinds of eyeballs. They ought to build cars out of the stuff; I'm sure it would save lives.) I guess on some level I held out hope that he might survive.

He didn't. He was dead by midnight, and I had killed him.

Maybe I should have laid off the whole experimental-biology thing at that point. Maybe I would have, if I hadn't discovered a frog someone had been using for target practice, down at the local pond. He'd healed but you could still see the BB under the skin, roll it between your fingers when you palpated the abdomen. And those pellets were made of *lead*. Toxic stuff. This frog had survived the initial gunshot, but the shrapnel inside might kill him yet.

So I wasn't just curious, this time. Now I was being downright *noble*. I would *heal* the poor thing. I would remove the bullet. But cutting into an active frog would only compound one cruelty with another. No, first I'd need to *anesthetize* the little guy.

Canadian frogs hibernate, as it happens. As it also happened I'd upgraded my metabolism chamber, added new Drano-proofing features and—more to the point—*temperature control*. Metabolism Chamber Mk. 2 was jacketed in the blue gel that fills freezer packs (E): pop it in the freezer until it hardens and you've got a nice subzero environment when you take it out. Use an aquarium heater (F) to control temperature as desired.[2]

I put my patient in the fridge for a while to get him in the mood, then slid him into the chamber and gradually lowered the temperature until the little guy was out cold. I cut the teensiest incision in his belly, just big enough to remove the pellet. It popped out easily; froggy barely even twitched. I brought him slowly back up to ambient, transferred him to a private terrarium for recovery. Soon he was hopping around as if nothing had happened. It was one of the proudest moments of my young life.

How was I to know that frogs get frostbite?

He started chewing his digits. I didn't worry at first—lots of people chew their nails, after all. The difference is, most people don't chew their fingers to the bone; this frog was skeletonizing himself, chewing flesh that had frozen and gone necrotic. It was looking bad.

Not wanting another horrible death on my conscience. I took him back to his pond and set him free. When I last saw him he looked perfectly content, sitting in shallow water on hands and feet of barest bone.

I'm sure he pulled through, though. Yeah. Let's go with that.

Eventually I outgrew basement science and graduated to the real kind, where—thankfully—my kill rate dropped to zero once I hit grad school. (It spiked again briefly years later—if you've read the snake-gutting scene in *Echopraxia*, you've caught a glimpse of my ill-advised 2006 post-doc in genetics—but that was an anomaly.) And while I've since taken in more than my share of wounded and/or brain-damaged creatures, it's been a long time since I've been the *cause* of such carnage.

Just for the record, I'd like to keep it that way.

1 I wasn't smart enough to invent this apparatus on my own, in case you were wondering; I got the plans from *Dr. Mengele's Book of Science Activities for Young Boys*, or some such title.

2 Now this, I *did* come up with on my own.

The Best-Case Apocalypse

Nowa Fantastyka APR 2018

There's this guy I've known since the eighties: evolutionary biologist, parasitologist of some renown, has a cabinet full of awards and accolades acquired over the course of his career. His name is Dan Brooks (if you've read *Echopraxia* you may find that name vaguely familiar). He's retired now, lives in Hungary while he and a couple of colleagues finish off a book on the epidemiological consequences of climate change.

Dan has these friends: physicists, climatologists, biologists. He calls them *The Cassandra Collective*. Five, ten years ago their Facebook timelines were full of links to their own research, to the latest findings in their field. Today, those same pages are festooned with cat pictures and selfies from Alaskan cruises.

They've given up, you see. For thirty or forty years they did the research, read the signs, tried to warn the world. World didn't care. Now, they figure, they did their best and it wasn't good enough. Now it's too late. So all these people have quietly retired, and are just enjoying whatever time they have left before the ceiling crashes in. They're not making a fuss—not any more. They realize there's no point. They've just gone quietly into that good night.

What does it look like when the ceiling crashes in? Well, Dan and his coauthors have worked out a best-case prognosis—and the good news is, we're probably not looking at outright extinction. People are everywhere, and enough of us are used to living under medieval conditions for Humanity to persist as a species. What we *are* looking at is the collapse of technological civilization. We can expect a series of rolling urban pandemics starting about a decade from now. (Monkey pox is apparently poised to make one hell of a comeback.) As much as 60% of humanity will be infected; maybe 20% killed.

A measly 20% dead might be something we could handle without too much trouble (and it would certainly be a relief for the nonhuman inhabitants of the planet). Sixty percent sick, though, not so much. Imagine half the people responsible for delivering your food, maintaining your water supply, and keeping your ATMs online call in sick for a few weeks; imagine that half their backups call in sick as well. Historically, once the infrastructure collapses even in a single city, it takes mere hours for people to start killing each other over food; check out what happened in New Orleans in the wake of Hurricane Katrina if you don't believe me.

Now, scale that up to every city on the planet.

If current trends continue, the world's arable land will be exhausted by 2070. Here in North America the USA will have run out of fresh water long before then. (I expect they'll have decided in the meantime that Canada has WMDs, and that they have to "liberate" us in the name of freedom and democracy. I expect this to happen around the time they finish sucking the Great Lakes dry.) Scandinavia and western Europe will be back in Little

Ice Age territory when Arctic meltwater short-circuits the Gulf Stream. The good news is, Malaria and Dengue Fever will have spread to the Baltic before then, so the temperature drop will at least take out the mosquitoes.

That's one prognosis—but it's most likely not the road down which we are headed, because it's a mainly disease-based apocalypse. It derives all its predictions from the fact that climate change promotes the relocation and spread of pathogens and parasites into new areas and new hosts. That 21% mortality—about 1.5 billion people—are just those who died because they got sick. It doesn't include deaths due to social unrest, or the forced migration of environmental refugees (it's been argued that the Syrian crisis ultimately tracks back to extended drought conditions in that country; get ready for a lot more of the same). It doesn't factor in food shortages due to overfishing and ocean acidification. It doesn't factor in the fact that it's only taken us since 1970 to kill off half the animals on this planet, and apparently we're just getting started. It doesn't factor in crop failure: back in 1999, for example, a mutant strain of wheat rust appeared in Uganda and has been spreading ever since, helped by warmer-than-usual temperatures throughout that region; now it's in Africa, Asia, the Middle East, and Europe. It does not respond to any known fungicide. We could conceivably lose the world's wheat crop within a decade.

Dan's scenario doesn't even touch on nuclear war, accidental or otherwise, or AI apocalypses or grey-goo rogue nanotech or mutable digital viruses evolving to shut down the internet or any of the other increasingly-less-science-fictional apocalypses that some very smart people are suddenly taking very seriously. It doesn't factor in purely economic collapse—collapse not instigated by environmental or social stressors but by the inherent paradoxical dumbness of Economics itself. (Conventional economics is a pyramid scheme, predicated on a model of unlimited growth in a resource-limited environment; if it was a physics model, it would be perpetual motion. It's bound to break sometime.)

Dan's scenario is, in fact, way too optimistic.

A more plausible scenario might be found in a 2014 paper out of the University of Melbourne[1], which factored in some of the variables not considered by Brooks *et al*; it suggests that population will peak around 8–9 billion over the next couple of decades, followed by a catastrophic decline that ends up cutting our numbers almost in half by century's end. This may also be naively cheerful, since it ignores the disease elements that inform Brooks *et al*'s models. But maybe it's *less* naively cheerful.

As for me, I don't know what's going to happen. I don't know how it's going to end. All I know is, I never consciously plan on getting drunk when Dan blows through town and we meet up for beers and conversation.

But after fifteen minutes with the guy, I never want to be sober again.

1 Turner, G., 2014: "Is Global Collapse Imminent? An Updated Comparison of the Limits to Growth with Historical Data", MSSI Research Paper No. 4, Melbourne Sustainable Society Institute. 21pp.

Nazis and Skin Cream

I went out drinking the other night with someone who punches Nazis.

Certainly, ever since Charlottesville, there's been no shortage of people who *advocate* Nazi-punching. For a while there, my Facebook feed was awash with the emissions of people jizzing all over their keyboards at the prospect of punching Nazis. People who argued—generally with more passion than eloquence—that the usual rules of engagement and free speech don't apply when dealing with Nazis, because, well, they're Nazis. People who, in fits of righteous anger, unfriended other people who *didn't* believe that it was okay to punch Nazis. I haven't seen such a torrent of unfriending since all those die-hard supporters of fracking, omnipresent state surveillance, and extra-judicial assassination-by-drone rose up and unfriended everyone who hadn't voted for Hillary Clinton in the last election. Even the ACLU has been bitch-slapped into "rethinking" its support for "free speech"[1].

So, no shortage of Big Talk. But this was the first person I'd hung with who actually seemed to have walked the walk. She attributes it to her Mohawk heritage; not knowing any other Mohawks, I can't speak to that. But I've known the lady for most of this century, and she doesn't take shit from anyone.

I gotta say, I found it refreshing. So many of these self-proclaimed Nazi-punchers don't seem to have a clue.

It's not that I have anything against violence per se. I'm no principled pacifist: I'm the guy who openly muses about shooting heads of state and selecting random cops for assassination. If anything, I'm more into the healing power of cathartic violence than most. But even I had to roll my eyes when I saw so many of those same would-be Nazi-punchers retweeting the most popular tweet of all time, courtesy of Barack Obama—a quote lifted from Martin Luther King Jr:

> No one is born hating another person because of the color of his skin, or his background, or his religion. People must learn to hate, and if they can learn to hate, they can be taught to love, for love comes more naturally to the human heart than its opposite.

As far as I could tell, all the likers and retweeters weren't even doing this ironically. They actually didn't seem to grasp the contradiction.

It only got worse when a bunch of right-wing 4channers repurposed a handful of domestic-violence posters, hoaxing up a fake Antifa campaign that took the Punch-a-Nazi meme and ran with it[2]. Servers across the globe are still smoking from the outrage engendered by that little prank.

And yet—once you get past the fact that those images originated not from the left, but from right-wing trolls impersonating them—

the hoax does not, in fact, misrepresent the position it's trolling. It would utterly fail as satire or parody; it doesn't even exaggerate for effect. It pretty much just echoes what the whole Nazi-punching brigade has been going on about these past weeks, using attractive females instead of homely males to represent the Nazi Other. And yet, people got really pissed about it.

What's the take-home message here? That it's only okay to punch Nazis if they're male, or unattractive? (A couple weeks back I actually asked this on one of the Facebook threads that was spluttering indignantly about the whole thing; so far, no one's answered.) Or is the take-home, rather, that what's said doesn't matter so much as who's saying it? When you get right down to it, is this just a matter of skin cream vs. gun control?

I guess that last reference could use some context.

It relates to a 2013 study out of Yale by Dan Kahan *et al*[3], a study for which I conveniently happen to have some illustrative slides because I mentioned it in a recent talk at Concordia. Kahan

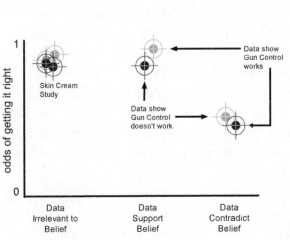

adapted from Kahan *et al*, 2013

et al showed data to over a thousand people—some right-wingers, some left, some statistically savvy, others functionally innumerate. Sometimes these data showed that a particular skin cream helped cure a rash; sometimes they showed the cream made the rash worse. Sometimes the data showed clearly that gun control reduced crime rate; other times, it showed the exact opposite.

Here's the trick: it was all exactly the same data. All Kahan *et al* did was switch the labels.

What they discovered was that your ability to correctly interpret these data comes down to how statistically smart you are, regardless of political leanings—but only when you think you're dealing with rashes and skin creams. If you think you're looking at gun control data, suddenly politics matter. If you're a numerically-smart conservative, you'll have no trouble parsing the data so long as they show that gun control results in increased crime; but if they show that gun control reduces crime, suddenly your ability to read those numbers drops to the level of a complete innumerate. You'll only be able to interpret the data correctly if they conform to your pre-existing biases.

Smart liberals are just as stupid as smart conservatives, but in the opposite direction. Show a numerically-savvy left-winger that gun control reduces crime, they'll be all over it; show them the opposite and, once again, their performance drops to the point where they might as well not have any statistical smarts at all.

Note that this is not a case of people rejecting a pattern they don't agree with. This is more subtle, and more pernicious: this is people literally not being able to perceive the pattern to begin with, if it's too threatening to their beliefs.

Ideology compromises your ability to do basic math.

You've seen this story a dozen times in a dozen guises. Fitting in with the tribe has more fitness value than independent thought. Conformers leave more genes behind than independent loners, so our brains evolved in service to conformity. In fact, we'll be lucky if reflexive conformity is as bad as the malfunction gets: recent machine-learning research out of Carnegie Mellon hints that we may actually be wired for genocide[4].

Tribalism Trumps Truth. 'Twas ever thus; a smaller, pettier iteration took place not so long ago in our own so-called SF "community".

God knows I've no sympathy for Nazis. I have enough trouble keeping my lunch down when I reflect upon the Tea Party. I do have doubts about the effectiveness of Nazi-punching as a coherent strategy, but I've never been one to rule out violence as a tool in the box. And as for my friend, she's on firm footing. She's not only punched Nazis, she's punched *female* ones, and she doesn't compromise the integrity of her position by retweeting any love-is-the-answer pablum from Obama or anyone else. *She's* cool, at least. She knows which side she's on.

But all those other incoherent people ranting on Facebook? I just can't bring myself to line up with people so resistant to cognitive dissonance that they honestly don't seem to realize they're talking out of both sides of their mouth at the same time.

I swear to God. It makes me want to punch someone.

---

1 See: http://www.pbs.org/newshour/rundown/charlottesville-violence-prompts-aclu-change-policy-hate-groups-protesting-guns/, https://www.vox.com/2017/8/20/16167870/aclu-hate-speech-nazis-charlottesville, https://theintercept.com/2017/08/13/the-misguided-attacks-on-aclu-for-defending-neo-nazis-free-speech-rights-in-charlottesville/, and https://www.nytimes.com/2017/08/17/nyregion/aclu-free-speech-rights-charlottesville-skokie-rally.html?mcubz=0
2 http://www.bbc.co.uk/news/blogs-trending-41036631
3 https://papers.ssrn.com/sol3/papers.cfm?abstract_id=2319992
4 http://nautil.us/issue/52/the-hive/is-tribalism-a-natural-malfunction

Ass Backwards

Nowa Fantastyka DEC 2011

This won't come as a big surprise to anyone who's familiar with my fiction: I spend a fair bit of time thinking about consciousness, and what it's good for. I poked at that question for years while I was trying to get a handle on *Blindsight*; I entertained and discarded any number of adaptive functions in search of that grand thematic punchline that would end the book. *Yes*, my protagonist would realize, *self-awareness is absolutely essential because of X*. The problem was, I couldn't find an X that stood up under scrutiny; and it took me far too long to realize that *Consciousness is good for nothing at all* was the scariest and most existentially gut-churning punchline imaginable. It was only a what-if scenario for story-telling purposes. I didn't expect anyone to take it seriously. I'm no expert; I figured that consciousness served some essential function that was blindingly obvious to anyone who actually knew what they were talking about.

I was as surprised as anyone to discover that this wasn't actually the case.

David Rosenthal's 2008 paper in *Neuropsychologia* concluded that consciousness was merely a side-effect of brain function, with no useful purpose. A couple of years earlier Ap Dijksterhuis and his colleagues published a paper in *Science* showing that consciousness actually *impairs* complex problem-solving. There were other examples, enough of them to warrant a review article in *Discover* in which author Carl Zimmer wrote, "A small but growing number of researchers are challenging some of the more extreme arguments supporting the primacy of the inner zombie." Somehow, when I wasn't looking, the irrelevance of self-awareness had become the mainstream view: those who challenged it were merely a "small but growing" number of researchers, a plucky band of rebels going up against conventional wisdom.

The issue remains unsettled. In 2008 DeWall *et al*, presented "Evidence that logical reasoning depends on conscious processing"; in 2005 Ezequiel Morsella made the wonderfully elegant argument that consciousness evolved not for art or science or complex reasoning, but simply to mediate conflicting motor commands sent to the skeletal muscles. (It's a great, thought-provoking article that I don't have space to go into here; but you can find it in *Psychological Review*, 112(4): 1000–1021). *Blindsight* notwithstanding, I hope these guys are right; I don't like regarding myself as a wetware parasite in a brain that would be better off without me. I'd welcome grounds to believe otherwise.

Whenever I'm confronted with the argument that consciousness exists to fulfill a specific function (say, complex problem-solving), I ask myself one crucial question: is it possible to conceive of a system that performs the same function *non*consciously? An affirmative answer doesn't mean that *we* don't use consciousness to perform vital tasks, but it does suggest that there are other ways to get those tasks done. Which makes consciousness not something that evolution produced for a specific purpose, but something evolution used because it just happened to be lying around. Something else could have done the same job just as well, or better. And if there are other ways to get the job done, then consciousness by definition is unnecessary.

The thing is, when you put it that way, it starts to look as if a lot of these guys are asking the wrong question. Because when it comes to evolution, asking *Why did consciousness arise?*—asking *Why did anything arise?*—is meaningless. It implies that evolution allows organisms to adapt to changing needs and conditions. And while that view is very widely held, it is also completely ass backwards.

In fact, adaptations show up *before* the environment changes. They pretty much have to.

Say you're a fish in a shrinking pond. Evolution does not say *Oh look, the pond is drying up; I guess I'd better grow that fish some lungs.* It says *Oh look, the pond is drying up. Lucky for that fish over there that he already happens to have a perforated swim bladder; it just might let him breathe air while he humps overland to the next pond. Shame about everyone else.*

Natural selection doesn't build things from scratch; it *selects* from pre-existing variations (which, in turn, arise via mutation and genetic mixing). It has to work with what's already there. So it's not that the environment changes and evolution catches up by pumping out all these new models; rather, evolution has already produced a range of models *before* the environment changes, and by chance a couple of them fare better under the new conditions. Those are the models that prosper. It's not foresight. Evolution is utterly blind and completely stupid; it can neither see the future nor plan for it. It's just that biological copying mechanisms aren't perfect, so individuals *differ* within a clade purely by chance. Those variations act as a hedge against future change.

When you think in these terms, all the arguments about what consciousness is good for almost seem beside the point. Maybe evolution was looking for some way to manage the skeletal muscles, and repurposed self-awareness for the job the same way it repurposed those thermal-insulating things called *feathers* for flight. Maybe, if consciousness hadn't been available, evolution would have used some other approach. Or maybe Rosenthal is right and self-awareness just kind of sits there without serving any useful purpose whatsoever. In any case, these are all questions that become meaningful only *after* consciousness has already arrived on the scene. Which begs the question: if self-awareness appeared *prior* to serving any actual function, how did that happen?

I'm working on that one. Stay tuned.

And Another Thing (*The Thing*, 2011)

BLOG OCT 23 2011

I went to see *The Thing* the other day, and was treated to perhaps the sharpest slice of satire on democratic capitalism I'd seen in years. It's the tale of three vacuous charismatic twentysomethings who go to a movie. They line up in their chairs with Cokes in hand, and—well, see for yourself: HTTPS://YOUTU.BE/SJ2DOZNQTZI.

I couldn't have shown it better: the world transforming itself into a magical place full of wonder and enchantment while these bubbleheaded morons suck back their Big Gulps and stare slack-jawed at a corporate logo in the sky, utterly oblivious to the world-changing events unfolding around them. I don't think there could *be* a more scathing commentary packed into such a short span of seconds. The fact that it was most likely inadvertent[1] only adds to the tingle; and the fact that no one else in the audience seemed to get it only sharpens the point.

Too bad the main feature didn't live up to the short.

To be honest, I didn't really know what to expect from this Thingquel. The official reviews were pretty crappy—given my recent overdrive head-down push to get this damn novel done by the month's end, I seriously considered skipping it entirely—but then again, Carpenter's 1982 version was savaged by the critics upon *its* release, and is today recognised as a classic. Also, as most of you know, I have a certain emotional connection to the franchise. So I put the back end of *Dumbspeech* away for the afternoon, braced myself with a couple of pints, and headed into the multiplex.

To start with, it's not as terrible as some folks are saying. There's a moment or two of something approaching true pathos on the journey. The variation on the blood-test scene, while not as dramatic as in the original, makes sense. One scene near the end contains either a nice moment of deliberate ambiguity, or a memo from the producers to the effect that the production was going over budget and they'd have to scale back the CGI on that last bit (I'm talking about the earring scene, for those of you in the know). And speaking of CGI, I'm not on board with those who decried its use here; had Rob Bottin had access to that technology back when he was doing Carpenter's film, you can be damn sure he would've gone to town with it. The ending of the movie does bolt quite nicely onto the beginning of the '82 film; and at least I was never bored.

But the fact is, when I first saw *The Thing* back in 1982 I came away thinking that I *had* seen a classic. I didn't care how many critics shat on it; I knew what I'd seen, and I thought it rocked, and in the three decades since my view has remained unshaken. This movie? No fucking way.

For one thing, there are just too many similarities between the two films for me to accept that this is truly a prequel and not just a remake. This goes beyond the fact that both films feature camps mysteriously well-equipped with flamethrowers. Too many plot elements have been cut-and-pasted from one to the other; the direction and cinematography of too many 2011 scenes seem to have dropped through a wormhole from 1982. In both movies, characters under suspicion are locked in the shed; in both, they escape by digging through the floor. Both movies feature scenes in which a group of increasingly-paranoid characters bicker and argue over what to do about the potentially-thinged cast members trapped outside in the storm, and in both cases the argument is cut short when said potential-Thingers break into the main building through a window. The 2011 *Thing* has a scene in which parka'd survivors cluster in the dark around a pile of thingly remains, lit from behind by the lights of their snowcats and wondering how to tell human from imitation; even the framing of that shot was so spot-on that for a moment I actually wondered if they hadn't just spliced in footage from the '82 version as a cost-cutting measure.

Some of this may have been unavoidable. After all, there's a logistical limit to how divergent scenarios can be when both involve the same shape-shifting alien infiltrating isolated Antarctic research stations. And remakes are not in and of themselves a bad thing; except in this case the director is on record as explicitly stating he didn't want to do a remake because the original Carpenter movie was "perfect." There's no point in redoing something unless you bring a new perspective to the material. Eric Heisserer's script gives us nothing that Carpenter didn't do better.

There are other problems, deriving not from the use of CGI in principle so much as from the temptations that result when such technology is too easily invoked: the desire to show cool squick trumps basic storytelling logic. For example, we are shown early on that the Thing can fragment at a whim. An arm will drop off, sprout centipede legs, race across the floor and hump some poor bastard's face like the facehugger from *Alien*. Pieces chopped in half will skitter autonomously across the wall, meet up again after work at Starbucks, and reintegrate without a second thought. Given that, we should never see a scene in which the protagonist finds refuge in a space that's too small for the alien to follow her into; all the Thing has to do is split into smaller pieces. Except we do, and it doesn't.

I've also spent the past thirty years assuming that the burned monstrosity MacReady found at the Norwegian camp had been killed in the process of transformation: an alien caught with its pants down and dispatched before it had a chance to zip back up. Now we find out that that wasn't the case at all. The Thing morphed into some weird deformity with two upside-down, half-fused faces, a variety of spliced-together bug/human limbs, and a gait so awkward the damn thing could have been a poster child for spinal meningitis—and it just kinda *leaves* itself like that, spending the next ten minutes stalking redshirts through the halls. I mean, isn't the whole point of the Thing that it *blends in*? And even if it *did* decide that the whole imitation riff had run its course and it was time to come out fighting, wouldn't it choose some kick-ass predatory phenotype that was, you know, *integrated*? Why choose an ill-fitting hodgepodge of twisted body parts that wouldn't be caught dead together outside some cheap carnival freak show?

Well, obviously, because it looks cool.

Leaving the theatre, I didn't feel that I'd completely wasted my money—but only because I can write the ticket price off as a tax deduction. I cannot in honesty recommend this film to anyone without the same option. That said, though, I retain a certain fondness for van Heijningen Jr.'s vision; it may tank on its own merits, but it's certainly rebooted interest in my own take on the story[2]. *io9* posted a glowing piece on "The Things," calling me a "master of scifi mind-fuckery"[3]. Simon Pegg tweeted its praises. When the movie actually premiered, the twitterverse filled up with don't-waste-your-time-on-the-remake-read-Peter-Watts's-story-instead messages, a signal boosted by folks ranging from a World Federation Pro Wrestler to the front man for Anthrax. Last I heard it had even landed on the front page of IMDb, which presumably gave *Clarkesworld*'s hit count a nice boost.

So, yeah. On balance, I really liked that movie. Just not for any of the reasons that would make you actually go see it.

---

1 At least, I assume it was inadvertent—although a part of me hopes that some self-aware realist working in the belly of the beast took an opportunity to shake his ball sack in the faces of the sheep he was helping to fleece, knowing they'd be too stupid to get the joke.

2 HTTP://CLARKESWORLDMAGAZINE.COM/WATTS _ 01 _ 10/

3 HTTP://IO9.COM/5849758/AN-INCREDIBLE-BRILLIANT-SHORT-STORY-TOLD-FROM-THE-PERSPECTIVE-OF-THE-ALIENS-IN-JOHN-CARPENTERS-THE-THING

Oprah's X-Men: Thoughts on *Logan*

BLOG MAR 6 2017

There's always been a contingent of X-Men fans who insist on seeing Mutant as Allegory, a metaphor—albeit a heavy-handed one—for prejudice and disenfranchisement. Mutants routinely get invoked as a sort of Other Of The Week: stand-ins for unwanted immigrants, untrusted ethnicities, oppressed orientations. I've never been a big reader of the comics, but certainly the films have played into this. One memorable example occurs early in the first movie, when a bewildered parent asks her child: "Honey, have you tried just *not being* a mutant?" (An even more memorable example is young Magneto's psionic awakening in a Nazi concentration camp.)

I've never bought in to this interpretation, for the same reason I reject the claim that Oprah Winfrey was "disenfranchised" when some racist idiot in Zurich refused to show her a handbag because it was "too expensive" for a black woman to afford. When you can buy the whole damn store and the street it sits on with pocket change; when you can buy the home of the asshole who just disrespected you and have it bulldozed; when you can use your influence to get that person fired in the blink of an eye and turn her social media life into a living hell—the fact that you *don't* do any of those things does not mean that you've been oppressed. It means you've been merciful to someone you could just as easily squash like a bug.

Marvel's mutants are something like that. We're dealing, after all, with people who can summon storm systems with their minds and melt steel with their eyes. Xavier can not only read any mind on the planet, he can *freeze time*, for fucksake. These have got to be the worst case studies in oppression you could imagine. Sure, baselines fear and revile mutants; that's a far cry from "disenfranchising" them. How long would gay-bashing be a thing, if gays could strike down their attackers with lightning bolts?

To my mind, X-Men are the Oprahs of the Marvel Universe. Immensely powerful. Inexplicably patient with the small-minded. And the fact that they've been consistently portrayed as *victims* has significantly compromised my suspension of disbelief—and hence, my enjoyment—of pretty much every X-Men movie I've taken in.

Right up to the best of the lot so far, the intimate, humane, sometimes brilliant *Logan*.

Logan is far and away the best X-Men movie I've ever seen (I'm tempted to say it's the best X-Men movie ever made, but I haven't seen *Apocalypse*, so who knows). The characterizations are deeper, their relationships more nuanced. The acting is better: you wouldn't expect less from Patrick Stewart, who somehow managed to maintain his dignity and gravitas throughout even the most idiotic *ST:TNG* episodes (looking at you, "Skin of Evil"), but the rest of the cast keeps up with him and makes it look effortless. The fight choreography is bone-crunchingly beautiful. This is the *Unforgiven* of Marvel movies, a story that focuses not on some absurdly high-stakes threat to Life As We Know It but on the more intimate costs to *lives as we knew them*. It's a story about entropy and unhappy endings. It earns its 94% on Rotten Tomatoes.

Until the last act, when it throws it all away.

I'm not just nitpicking about the canonical dumbness inevitable in any movie based on a sixties-era comic franchise. (If I were, I might wonder how Logan's 25-cm claws manage to retract into his arms without immobilizing his wrists like rebar through salami; the guy must have to extend his claws every time he wants to hold a spoonful of Cheerios. It's a good thing they don't sell milk in bags down there.) I'm complaining about something which, I think, largely betrays all that resonant, character-based story-telling that comprises the bulk of the movie. Or rather, I'm complaining about *two* things:

1. When the bad guys know that their quarry can freeze flesh unto shattering with their breath, summon the very undergrowth to strangle and entangle pursuers, spit out bullets, and hurl everything from trees to troop transports with their minds, why in Christ's name would they try to take them down with conventional gun-toting infantry? They've got drones, for chrissake: why not use robots to shoot the kids from above the tree line? Why not snipe them from a safe distance with tranquilizers, or gas the forest, or do any of a dozen other things that could take down their targets without exposing ill-equipped flesh-and-blood to mutant countermeasures?

2. When said quarry can freeze flesh unto shattering with their breath, summon the very undergrowth to strangle and entangle pursuers, spit out bullets, and hurl everything from trees to troop transports with their minds, why in Christ's name do they *not do any of that* until half of them have already been captured and Logan himself is half-dead? We're not talking about do-goody

pacifists here; these aren't adults who've made a conscious decision to eschew violence for the greater good. These are ten-year-old kids—with all the emotional maturity that implies—who've been trained as supersoldiers almost from the moment of conception. Back in the first act Laura must have single-handedly killed twenty heavily-armed cyber-enhanced psycho killers with no weapons but what God and the bioengineers gave her. So why are these superkillers running like frightened animals in the first place? Why aren't they laying traps, implementing countermeasures, fighting back? They know how to do it; hell, they don't know how to do anything *else*.

The answer, I'm guessing, is because writer James Mangold bought in to the same bullshit allegory that so many others have: no matter the canon, no matter their powers, these kids have to be *victims*, even though the script has already shown us that they definitively are not. They must be oppressed and disempowered by an intolerant world, because that's what the whole X-Men allegory thing is all about.

And in buying into that narrative, Mangold renders Logan's ultimate sacrifice pretty much meaningless. The children he died protecting were far more powerful than he was: numerically, psionically, even at simple hand-to-hand combat. If they hadn't been shackled by allegorical fiat they could have won that battle before Logan ever showed up.

Which means that Logan died for nothing. And that's not some nerdy quibble along the lines of *the transporter doesn't work like that*; it's a betrayal of nuanced characters we've come to care about, all for the sake of a mutants-as-victims narrative that never made any sense to begin with.

If the screenwriters *had* to indulge their victim mindset, they could have done so without sacrificing story logic or throwing away two hours of character development. Here's a thought: posit that mutant powers only manifest at puberty (something established way back at the start of the franchise, with Rogue's first adolescent kiss). A few of these kids are verging on adulthood, but not most; they're still vulnerable to men with guns. They're being hunted not for what they can do now, but for what they'll be *able* to do if allowed to live another year or two. Let the stress of being cornered, of seeing their fellows mowed down, the sheer adrenaline response of fight/flight be the trigger that activates just a few of the older ones, allows their powers to manifest: not in full-on crush-all-opposition mode, but just enough to hold on until Logan arrives to turn the tide. It would change very little in terms of pacing or screen time; it would change everything in terms of earned emotional impact.

But no. What we're given is a third-act chase scene almost as dumb as the climax of *Star Trek Beyond*. Which is a shame, because *Star Trek Beyond* was a loud dumb movie from the start; one more dumb element was par for the course. *Logan*, by way of contrast, is a thoughtful, melancholy rumination on the whole superhero premise; it remains, for the most part, a thing of beauty.

Too bad about that big festering pustule on the forehead.

Cambridge Analytica and the Other Turing Test.

BLOG MAR 29 2017

Near the end of the recent German movie *Er Ist Wieder Da* ("Look Who's Back"), Adolf Hitler—transported through time to the year 2015—is picking up where he left off. On the roof of the television studio that fuelled his resurgence (the network thought they were just exploiting an especially-tasteless internet meme for ratings), the sad-sack freelancer who discovered "the world's best Hitler impersonator" confronts his Frankenstein's monster—but Hitler proves unkillable. Even worse, he makes some good points:

"In 1933, people were not fooled by propaganda. They elected a leader who openly disclosed his plans with great clarity. The Germans elected me . . . ordinary people who chose to elect an extraordinary man, and entrust the fate of the country to him.

"What do you want to do, Sawatzki? Ban elections?"

It's a good movie, hilarious and scary and sociologically plausible (hell, maybe sociologically *inevitable*), and given that one of Hitler's lines is "Make Germany Great Again" it's not surprising that it's been rediscovered in recent months. Imagine a cross between *Borat*, *The Terminator*, and "Springtime for Hitler", wrapped around a spot-on re-enactment of that Hitler-in-the-Bunker meme.

But that rooftop challenge: that, I think, really cuts to the heart of things: *What do you want to do, Sawatzki? Ban elections?*

I feel roughly the same way every time I read another outraged screed about Cambridge Analytica.

The internet's been all a'seethe with such stories lately. The details are arcane, but the take-home message is right there in the headlines: "The Rise of the Weaponized AI Propaganda Machine"[1]; "Will Democracy Survive Big Data and Artificial Intelligence?"[2]; "Robert Mercer: the big data billionaire waging war on mainstream media"[3].

The executive summary goes something like this: an evil right-wing computer genius has developed scarily-effective data scraping techniques which—based entirely on cues gleaned from social media—know individual voters better than do their own friends, colleagues, even family. This permits "behavioral microtargetting": campaign messages customized not for boroughs or counties or demographic groups, but for *you*. Individually. A bot for every voter.

Therefore democracy itself is in danger.

Put aside for the moment the fact that the US isn't a functioning democracy anyway (unless you define "democracy" as a system in which—to quote Thomas Piketty—"When a majority of citizens disagrees with economic elites and/or with organized interests, they generally lose"). Ignore any troublesome doubts about whether the same folks screaming about Cambridge Analytica would be quite so opposed to the tech if it had been used to benefit Clinton instead of Trump. (It's not as though the Dems didn't have their own algorithms, their own databased targeting systems; it's just that those algos sucked.) Put aside the obvious partisan elements and focus on the essential argument: the better They know you, the more finely They can tune their message. The more finely They tune their message, the less freedom you have. To quote directly from Helbing *et al* over on the *SciAm* blog,

> "*The trend goes from programming computers to programming people.*" [breathless italics courtesy of the original authors]

Or from Berit Anderson, over at *Medium.com*:

> "Instead of having to deal with misleading politicians, we may soon witness a Cambrian explosion of pathologically-lying political and corporate bots that constantly improve at manipulating us."

You'd expect me to be all over this, right? What could be more up my alley than Machiavellian code which treats us not as autonomous beings but as physical systems, collections of inputs and outputs whose state variables show not the slightest trace of Free Will? You can almost see Valerie tapping her arrhythmic tattoos on the bulkhead, reprogramming the crew of the *Crown of Thorns* without their knowledge.

And I *am* all over it. Kind of. I shrugged at the finding that it took Mercer's machine 150 Facebook "Likes" to know someone better than their parents did (hell, you'd know me better than *my* parents did based on, like, *three*), but I was more impressed when I learned that 300 "Likes" is all it would take to know me better than *Caitlin* does. And no one has to convince me that sufficient computing power, coupled with sufficient data, can both predict and manipulate human behavior.

But so what? 'Twas ever thus, no?

No, Helbing and his buddies assert:

> "Personalized advertising and pricing cannot be compared to classical advertising or discount coupons, as the latter are non-specific and also do not invade our privacy with the goal to take advantage of our psychological weaknesses and knock out our critical thinking."

Oh, give me a fucking break.

They've been *taking advantage of our psychological weaknesses to knock out our critical thinking skills* since before the first booth babe giggled coquettishly at the Houston Auto Show, since the first gurgling baby was used to sell Goodyear radials, since IFAW decided they could raise more funds if they showed Loretta Swit hugging baby seals instead of giant banana slugs. Advertising tries to knock out your critical thinking *by definition*. Every tasteless anti-abortion poster, every unfailing-cute child suffering from bowel disease in the local bus shelter, every cartoon bear doing unnatural things with toilet paper is an attempt to rewire your synapses, to literally *change your mind*.

Ah, but those aren't targeted to *individuals*, are they? Those are crude hacks of universal gut responses, the *awww* when confronted with cute babies, the *hubba hubba* when tits are shoved in the straight male face. (Well, *almost* universal; show me a picture of a cute baby and I'm more likely to vomit than coo.) This is different, Mercer's algos know us *personally*. They know us as well as our friends, family, lovers!

Maybe so. But you know who *else* knows us as well as our friends, family, and lovers? Our friends, family, and lovers. The same folks who sit across from us at the pub or the kitchen table, who cuddle up for a marsupial cling when the lights go out. Such people routinely use their intimate knowledge of us to convince us to see a particular movie or visit a particular restaurant—or, god forbid, vote for a particular political candidate. People who, for want of a better word, attempt to *reprogram* us using sound waves and visual stimuli; they do everything the bots do, and they probably still do it better.

What do you want to do, Sawatzki? Ban advertising? Ban debate? Ban *conversation*?

I hear that Scotsman, there in the back: he says we're not talking about *real* debate, *real* conversation. When Cambridge Analytica targets you, there's no other *being* involved; just code, hacking meat.

As if it would be somehow better if *meat* were hacking meat. The prediction that half our jobs will be lost to automation within the next couple of decades[4] is already a tired cliché, but most experts don't react to such news by demanding the repeal of Moore's Law. They talk about retraining, universal basic income—adaptation, in a word. Why should this be any different?

Don't misunderstand me. The fact that our destiny is in the hands of evil right-wing billionaires doesn't make me any happier than it makes the rest of you. I just don't see the ongoing automation of that process as anything more than another step along the same grim road we've been trudging down for decades. Back in 2008 and 2012 I don't remember anyone howling with outrage over Obama's then-cutting-edge voter-profiling database. I *do* remember a lot of admiring commentary on his campaign's ability to "get out the vote".

Curious that the line between grass-roots activism and totalitarian neuroprogramming should fall so neatly between Then and Now.

Cambridge Analytica's psyops tech doesn't so much "threaten democracy" as drive one more nail into its coffin. For anyone who hasn't been paying attention, the corpse has been rotting for some time now.

'Course, that doesn't mean we shouldn't fight back. There are ways to do that, even on an individual level. I'm not talking about the vacuous aspirations peddled over on *SciAm*[5], by folks who apparently don't know the difference between a slogan and a strategy. (Ensure that people have access to their data! Make government accountable!) I'm talking about things you can do right now. *Easy* things.

The algos eat data? *Stop feeding them.* Don't be a Twit: if all Twitter's other downsides aren't enough to scare you off, maybe the prospect of starving the beast will lure you away. If you can't bring yourself to quit Facebook, at least stop "liking" things—or even better, "Like" things that you actually hate, throw up chaff to contaminate the data set and make you a fuzzier target. (When I encounter something I find especially endearing on Facebook, I often tag it with one of those apoplectic-with-rage emojis). Get off Instagram and GotUrBalls. Use Signal. Use a fucking VPN. *Make Organia useless to them.*

What's that you say? Thousands of people around the world are just dying to know your favorite breadfruit recipe? Put it in a blog. It won't stop bots from scraping your data, but at least they'll have to come looking for you; you won't be feeding yourself into a platform that's been explicitly designed to harvest and resell your insides.

The more of us who refuse to play along—the more of us who *cheat* by feeding false data into the system—the less we have to fear from code that would read our minds. And if most people can't be bothered—if all that clickbait, all those emojis and upward-pointing thumbs are just too much of a temptation—well, we do get the government we deserve. Just don't complain when, after wading naked through the alligator pool, something bites your legs off.

I'm going to let Berit Anderson play me offstage:

> "Imagine that in 2020 you found out that your favorite politics page or group on Facebook didn't actually have any other human members, but was filled with dozens or hundreds of bots that made you feel at home and your opinions validated? Is it possible that you might never find out?"

I think she intends this as a warning, a dire If This Goes On portent. But what Anderson describes is the textbook definition of a Turing Test, passed with flying colors. She sees an internet filled with zombies: I see the birth of True AI.

Of course, there are two ways to pass a Turing Test. The obvious route is to design a smarter machine, one that can pass for human. But as anyone who's spent any time on a social platform knows, people can be as stupid, as repetitive, and as vacuous as any bot. So the other path is to simply make people dumber, so they can be more easily fooled by machines.

I'm increasingly of the opinion that the second approach might be easier.

1 HTTPS://MEDIUM.COM/JOIN-SCOUT/THE-RISE-OF-THE-WEAPONIZED-AI-PROPAGANDA-MACHINE-86DAC61668B#.FOA4MF5P5
2 HTTPS://WWW.SCIENTIFICAMERICAN.COM/ARTICLE/WILL-DEMOCRACY-SURVIVE-BIG-DATA-AND-ARTIFICIAL-INTELLIGENCE/
3 HTTPS://WWW.THEGUARDIAN.COM/POLITICS/2017/FEB/26/ROBERT-MERCER-BREITBART-WAR-ON-MEDIA-STEVE-BANNON-DONALD-TRUMP-NIGEL-FARAGE
4 HTTP://WWW.ENG.OX.AC.UK/ABOUT/NEWS/NEW-STUDY-SHOWS-NEARLY-HALF-OF-US-JOBS-AT-RISK-OF-COMPUTERISATION
5 HTTPS://WWW.SCIENTIFICAMERICAN.COM/ARTICLE/WILL-DEMOCRACY-SURVIVE-BIG-DATA-AND-ARTIFICIAL-INTELLIGENCE/

Life in the FAST Lane

Nowa Fantastyka APR 2015

Back in 2007 I wrote a story about a guy standing in line at an airport. Not much actually happened; he just shuffled along with everyone else, reflecting on the security check awaiting him (and his fellow passengers) prior to boarding. Eventually he reached the head of the queue, passed through the scanner, and continued on his way. That was pretty much it.

Except the scanner wasn't an X-ray or a metal detector: it was a mind-reader that detected nefarious intent. The protagonist was a latent pedophile whose urges showed up bright and clear on the machine, even though he had never acted on them. "The Eyes of God" asks whether you are better defined by the acts you commit or those you merely contemplate; it explores the obvious privacy issues of a society in which the state can read minds. The technology it describes is inspired by a real patent filed by Sony a few years ago; even so, I thought we'd have at least couple more decades to come to grips with such questions.

I certainly didn't think they'd be developing a similar system by 2015.

Yet here we are: a technology which, while not yet ready for prime time, is sufficiently far along for the *American University Law Review* to publish a paper[1] exploring its legal implications. FAST (Future Attribute Screening Technology) is a system "currently designed for deployment at airports" which "can read minds . . . employ[ing] a variety of sensor suites to scan a person's vital signs, and based on those readings, to determine whether the scanned person has 'malintent'—the intent to commit a crime."

The envisioned system doesn't actually read minds so much as make inferences about them, based on physiological and behavioral cues. It reads heart rate and skin temperature, tracks breathing and eye motion and changes in your voice. If you're a woman, it sniffs out where you are in your ovulation cycle. It sees your unborn child and your heart condition—and once it's looked through you along a hundred axes, it decides whether you have a guilty mind. If it thinks you do, you end up in the little white room for enhanced interrogation.

Of course, feelings of guilt don't necessarily mean you plan on committing a terrorist act. Maybe you're only cheating on your spouse; maybe you feel bad about stealing a box of paper clips from work. Maybe you're not feeling guilty at all; maybe you're just idly fantasizing about breaking the fucking kneecaps of those arrogant Customs bastards who get off on making everyone's life miserable. Maybe you just have a touch of Asperger's, or are a bit breathless from running to catch your flight—but all FAST sees is elevated breathing and a suspicious refusal to make eye contact.

Guilty minds, angry minds, fantasizing minds: the body betrays them all in similar ways, and once that flag goes up you're a Person of Interest. Most of the *AULR* article explores the Constitutional ramifications of this technology in the US, scenarios in which FAST would pass legal muster and those in which it would violate the 4th Amendment—and while that's what you'd expect in a legal commentary, I find such concerns almost irrelevant. If our rulers want to deploy the tech, they will. If deployment would be illegal they'll either change the law or break it, whichever's most convenient. The question is not whether the technology will be deployed. The question is how badly it will fuck us up once it has been.

Let's talk about failure rates.

If someone tells you that a test with a 99% accuracy rate has flagged someone as a terrorist, what are the odds that the test is wrong? You might say 1%; after all, the system's 99% accurate, right? The problem is, probabilities *compound* with sample size— so in an airport like San Francisco's (which handles 45 million people a year), a 99% accuracy rate means that over 1,200 people will be flagged as potential terrorists every day, even if no actual terrorists pass through the facility. It means that even if a different terrorist actually does try to sneak through that one airport every day, the odds of someone being innocent even though they've been flagged are—wait for it—*over 99%*.

The latest numbers we have on FAST's accuracy gave it a score of 78–80%, and those (unverified) estimates came from the same guys who were actually building the system—a system, need I remind you, designed to collect intimate and comprehensive physiological data from millions of people on a daily basis.

The good news is, the most egregious abuses might be limited to people crossing into the US. In my experience, border guards in every one of the twenty-odd countries I've visited are much nicer than they are in 'Murrica, and this isn't just my own irascible bias: according to an independent survey commissioned by the travel industry on border-crossing experiences, US border guards are the world's biggest assholes by a 2-to-1 margin.

Which is why I wonder if, in North America at least, FAST might actually be a good thing—or at least, a better thing than what's currently in place. FAST may be imperfect, but presumably it's not explicitly programmed to flag you just because you have dark skin. It won't decide to shit on you because it's in a bad mood, or because it thinks you look like a liberal. It may be paranoid and it may be mostly wrong, but at least it'll be paranoid and wrong about everyone equally.

Certainly FAST might still embody a kind of *emergent* prejudice. Poor people might be especially nervous about flying simply because they don't do it very often, for example; FAST might tag their sweaty palms as suspicious, while allowing the rich sociopaths to sail through unmolested into Business Class. Voila: instant class discrimination. If it incorporates face recognition, it may well manifest the All Blacks Look Alike To Me bias notorious in such tech. But such artifacts can be weeded out, if you're willing to put in the effort. (Stop training your face-recognition tech on pictures from your pasty-white Silicon Valley high school yearbook, for starters.) I suspect the effort required would be significantly less than that required to purge a human of the same bigotry.

Indeed, given the prejudice and stupidity on such prominent display from so many so-called authority figures, outsourcing at least some of their decisions seems like a no-brainer. Don't let them choose who to pick on, let the machine make that call; it may be inaccurate, but at least it's unbiased.

Given how bad things already are over here, maybe even something as imperfect as FAST would be a step in the right direction.

---

1 Rogers, C.A. 2014. "A Slow March Towards Thought Crime: How The Department Of Homeland Security's Fast Program Violates The Fourth Amendment." *American University Law Review* 64:337–384.

Smashing the Lid Off Pandora's Box

Nowa Fantastyka Nov 2018

I've been in a funk since the International Panel on Climate Change released their latest report last October. I'm in a funk as I type these words; chances are I'll still be in a funk when you read them a month down the road. If you happened to read my blog post of October 26[1], you'll know why. If you didn't, the short version is:

• There isn't a hope in hell that we'll meet the goal set out in the Paris Accords, to limit global warming to 2°C;
• Even if we *did* meet that goal, the result would be apocalyptic;
• The results would be merely disastrous if we managed to keep the increase down to 1.5°C—to give just one example, we'd only lose 70–90% of the world's corals instead of all of them—but the only way to do that would be to—among other things—go carbon-free within thirty years, cut our meat consumption by 90%, *and* invent new unicorn technologies to suck gigatonnes of carbon back out of the atmosphere.

Global disaster is now our best-case scenario, and the chances we'll even clear that low bar are remote. Meanwhile, people have already shrugged and gone back to posting cat videos on Facebook.

Think of this month's column as a kind of coda to October's blog post. Today's take-home message is: that post was way too light-hearted. It took the IPCC at its word: that we had twelve years to get started, and if we did there was at least a chance to save something from the fire.

The reality, it seems, is that there may not be any chance at all.

The first thing to keep in mind is that IPCC reports are scientific, and science is innately conservative. If a result is only 90% certain, science rejects it. The usual threshold for statistical significance is 95%, often 99%; anything less is chalked up to random chance. Meaning that—especially in complex, noisy systems like a planetary ecosphere—real effects get lost in noise and statistical rigor. Your living room could be in flames and nothing might show up in the stats; only when your bed catches fire do the results become "significant".

The second thing to keep in mind is that even among—*especially* among—those who accept the dangers posed by climate change, there exists an almost pathological compulsion to remain upbeat no matter what. A good example is the reaction to an article by David Wallace-Wells—"The Uninhabitable Earth"—that appeared in *New York Magazine* back in 2017. It was an article that pulled no punches, that laid out the future in store for us without regard to the conservative blinkers of the 95% threshold—and scientists and activists alike decried it as gloomy and counterproductive.

October's IPCC report has largely vindicated Wallace-Wells, but the Pathology of Hope remains. We still want to save the world, after all, and too much despair just paralyzes people: if you don't offer hope, you'll never inspire folks to change. If you don't sugarcoat things a bit, people won't have a reason to try and make things better.

You don't tell people they're doomed. Even if they are.

Which brings us to Jem Bendell, of the University of Cumbria. Bendell's PhD is in International Policy, not climate science, but he can read the writing on the wall as well as anyone (and our predicament's rooted in politics after all, not science). He notes that we could cut our CO_2 emissions by 25% and those savings would be wiped out by the heating that's already resulted from the ongoing loss of Arctic ice (and consequent lowered albedo). He points out that IPCC forecasts have always proven too optimistic, that observed trends always seem to end up being worse than the worst-case scenarios predicted just a few years earlier. He notes that many IPCC projections assume linear increases, while the observed data are more consistent with nonlinear—possibly exponential—ones.

Bendell doesn't think we have twelve years to start, doesn't give us until mid-century to zero out our emissions. He says widespread societal collapse is inevitable, and it's going to start in just ten years. (Interestingly, this is about the same time that a variety of pathogens—following warmer temperatures into new environments—are expected to kick off a series of pandemics that hollow out the world's major cities, according to parasitologist and evolutionary biologist Daniel Brooks.) Bendell says it's time to give up on futile hopes of saving society as we know it. He coins the term "Deep Adaptation" to describe the processes by which we might deal with the collapse of modern society: ways to prioritize the things we might save, accept the loss of everything else, salvage what we can and hope to build something more sustainable from the wreckage.

The first step, he says, is to grieve for the things we've lost. I myself would put it less charitably: *for the things we've destroyed*, I would say.

Bendell wrote up his analysis in a paper titled "Deep Adaptation: A Map for Navigating Climate Tragedy." He couldn't get it published. Or rather, the journal he sent it to would only publish it if he rewrote the text to make it less "disheartening".[2]

Of course, it's easy to discount one voice. The problem is there might well be a whole chorus backing him up, a chorus we haven't been allowed to hear thanks to well-intentioned censors who insist facts pass some kind of Hope Test before they're allowed out in public. The house burns down around us. The fire department was shut down during the latest round of Austerity Cuts. Doesn't matter. Can't let people lose *hope*.

I have hope, though a distant one. The Earth has experienced mass extinctions before. Five times past the planet has lost 70–90% of its species, and it has always sprung back. A few weedy, impoverished survivors have always been enough to pick up the baton, speciate and bloom into brand-new ecospheres full of wonder and biodiversity. It may take ten or twenty million years, but it happens eventually. It will happen this time too.

My hope is that nothing like us will be around next time, to fuck it all up again.

---

1 Not available in this volume, unfortunately. But you can find it at HTTPS://WWW.RIFTERS.COM/CRAWL/?P=8433.

2 You can find it on Bendell's website, though: go to HTTPS://JEMBENDELL.WORDPRESS.COM/2018/07/26/THE-STUDY-ON-COLLAPSE-THEY-THOUGHT-YOU-SHOULD-NOT-READ-YET/

The Split-brain Universe

Nowa Fantastyka AUG 2018, EXTENDED SEPT 12 2018

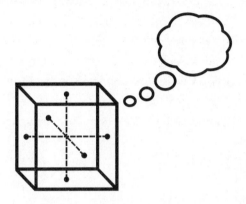

The year is 1982. I read Isaac Asimov's newly-published *Foundation's Edge* with a sinking heart. Here is the one of Hard-SF's Holy Trinity writing—with a straight face, as far as I can tell—about the "consciousness" of rocks and trees and *doors*, for chrissakes. *Isaac, what happened?* I wonder. *Conscious* rocks? *Are you going senile?*

No, as it turned out. Asimov had simply discovered physical panpsychism: a school of thought which holds that *everything*—rocks, trees, electrons, even Donald Trump—is conscious to some degree. The panpsychics regard consciousness as an intrinsic property of matter, like mass and charge and spin. It's an ancient belief—its roots go all the way back to ancient Greece—but it has recently found new life among consciousness researchers. Asimov was simply ahead of his time.

I've always regarded panpsychism as an audacious cop-out. Hanging a sign that says "intrinsic" on one of nature's biggest mysteries doesn't solve anything; it merely sweeps it under the rug.

Turns out, though, that I'd never really met *audacious* before. Not until I read "The Universe in Consciousness" by Bernardo Kastrup, in the *Journal of Consciousness Studies*[1].

Kastrup goes panpsychism one better. He's not saying that all matter is conscious. He's saying that all matter is conscious*ness*—that consciousness is *all there is*, and matter is just one of its manifestations. "Nothing exists outside or independent of cosmic consciousness," he writes. "The perceivable cosmos is in consciousness, as opposed to being conscious." Oh, and he also says the whole universe suffers from multiple personality disorder.

It reads like some kind of flaky New Age metaphor. He means it literally, though.

He calls it science.

Even on a purely local level, there are reasons to be skeptical of MPS[2] (or DID, as it's known today: *dissociative identity disorder*). DID diagnoses tend to spike in the wake of new movies or books about multiple personalities, for example. Many cases don't show themselves until after the subject has spent time in therapy—generally for some other issue entirely—only to have the alters emerge following nudges and leading questions from therapists whose critical and methodological credentials might not be so rigorous as one would like. And there is the—shall we say *questionable*—nature of certain alternate personalities themselves. One case in the literature reported an alter that identified as a German Shepherd. Another identified—don't ask me how—as a lobster. (I know what you're thinking, but this was years before the ascension of Jordan Peterson in the public consciousness.)

When you put this all together with the fact that even normal conscious processes seem to act like a kind of noisy parliament— that we all, to some extent, "talk to ourselves," all have different facets to our personalities—it's not unreasonable to wonder if the

whole thing didn't boil down to a bunch of overactive imagina-
tions, being coached by people who really should have known better. Psychic CosPlaying, if you will. This interpretation is popular
enough to have its own formal title: the *Sociocognitive Model*.

There could be a sort of psychiatric Sturgeon's Law at play here,
though; the fact that 90% of such studies are crap doesn't necessarily
mean that all of them are. Brain scans of "possessed" DID bodies
show distinctly different profiles than those of professional actors
trained to merely behave as though they were: the parts of the
brain that lit up in actors are associated with imagination and
empathy, while those lighting up in DID patients are involved
with stress and fear responses[3]. I'm not entirely convinced—can
actors, knowingly faking a condition, really stand in for delusional
people who sincerely believe in their affliction? Still, the stats are
strong; and it's hard to argue with a different study in which the
visual centers of a sighted person's brain apparently shut down in
a sighted person when a "blind" alter took the controls.

Also let's not forget the whole split-brain phenomenon. We
know that different selves *can* exist simultaneously within a single
brain, at least if it's been partitioned in some way.

This is the premise upon which Kastrup bases his model of
Reality Itself.

You've probably heard of quantum entanglement. Kastrup argues
that entangled systems form a single, integrated, and above all
irreducible system. Also that, since everything is ultimately entangled to something else, the entire inanimate universe is "one
indivisible whole," as irreducible as a quark. He argues—let me
quote him here directly, so you won't think I'm making this up—

> "that the sole ontological primitive there is cosmic phe-
> nomenal consciousness . . . Nothing exists outside or

independent of cosmic consciousness. Under this interpretation one should say that the cosmos is constituted
by phenomenality, as opposed to bearing phenomenality. In other words, here the perceivable cosmos is in
consciousness, as opposed to being conscious."

Why would he invoke such an apparently loopy argument?
How are we any further ahead in understanding *our* consciousness
by positing that the universe itself is built from the stuff? Kastrup
is trying to reconcile the "combination problem" of bottom-up
panpsychism: even if you accept that every particle contains a
primitive conscious "essence," you're still stuck with explaining
how those rudiments combine to form the self-reflective sapience
of complex objects like ourselves. Kastrup's answer is to start at
the other end. Instead of positing that consciousness emerges from
the very small and working up to sentient beings, why not posit
that it's a property of the universe as a whole and work down?

Well, for one thing, because now you've got the opposite
problem: rather than having to explain how little particles of proto-
consciousness combine to form true sapience, now you have to
explain how some universal ubermind splits into separate entities
(i.e., if we're all part of the same cosmic consciousness, why can't I
read your mind? Why do *you* and *I* even exist as distinct beings?).

This is where DID comes in. Kastrup claims that the same
processes that give rise to multiple personalities in humans also
occur at the level of the whole Universe, that all of inanimate
"reality" consists of Thought, and its animate components—cats,
earthworms, anything existing within a bounded metabolism—
are encysted bits of consciousness isolated from the Cosmic Self:

"We, as well as all other living organisms, are but
dissociated alters of cosmic consciousness, surrounded

by its thoughts. The inanimate world we see around us is the revealed appearance of these thoughts. The living organisms we share the world with are the revealed appearances of other dissociated alters."

And what about Reality *before* the emergence of living organisms?

"I submit that, before its first alter [i.e., separate conscious entity] ever formed, the only phenomenal contents of cosmic consciousness were thoughts."

In case you're wondering (and you damn well should be): yes, the *Journal of Consciousness Studies* is peer-reviewed. Respectable, even. Heavy hitters like David Chalmers and Daniel Dennet appear in its pages. And Kastrup doesn't just pull claims out of his ass; he cites authorities from Augusto to von Neumann to back up his quantum/cosmic entanglement riff, for example. Personally, I'm not convinced—I think I see inconsistencies in his reasoning—but not being a physicist, what would I know? I haven't read the authorities he cites, and wouldn't understand them if I did. This Universal Split-Brain thing reads like Philip K. Dick on a bad day; then again, couldn't you say the same about Schrödinger's Cat, or the Many Worlds hypothesis?

Still, reading Kastrup's paper, I have to keep reminding myself: Peer-reviewed. Respectable. Daniel Dennet.

Of course, repeat that too often and it starts to sound like a religious incantation.

To an SF writer, this is obviously a gold mine.

Kastrup's model is epic creation myth: a formless thinking void, creating sentient beings In Its Image. The idea that *Thou Art God*

(*Stranger in a Strange Land*, anyone?), that God is *everywhere*—that part of the paradigm reads like it was lifted beat-for-beat out of the Abrahamic religions. The idea that "the world is imagined" seems lifted from the Dharmic ones.

The roads we might travel from this starting point! Here's just one: at our local Earthbound scale of reality DID is classed as a pathology, something to be cured. The patient is healthy only when their alters have been reintegrated. Does this scale up? Is the entire *universe*, as it currently exists, somehow "sick"? Is the reintegration of fragmented alters the only way to cure it, can the Universe only be restored to health only by *resorbing* all sentient beings back into some primordial pool of Being? Are *we* the disease, and our eradication the cure?

You may remember that I'm planning to write a concluding volume to the trilogy begun with *Blindsight* and continued in *Echopraxia*. I had my own thoughts as to how that story would conclude—but I have to say, Kastrup's paper has opened doors I never considered before.

It just seems so off-the-wall that—peer-reviewed or not—I don't know if I could ever sell it in a Hard-SF novel.

1 Bernardo Kastrup. "The Universe in Consciousness." *Journal of Consciousness Studies*, 25, No. 5–6, 2018, pp. 125–55.

2 See: HTTP://JOURNALS.SAGEPUB.COM/DOI/ABS/10.1177/07067437040490 0904 and HTTP://JOURNALS.SAGEPUB.COM/DOI/ABS/10.1177/07067437040490 1005

3 HTTPS://JOURNALS.PLOS.ORG/PLOSONE/ARTICLE?ID=10.1371/JOURNAL.PONE.0098795

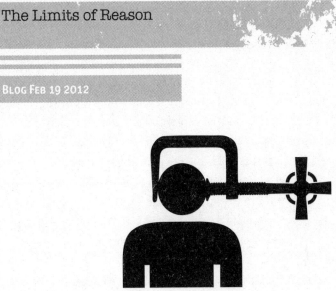

We are broken as a species.

I encountered my first evidence to this effect back in 1986, although I didn't have the wit to realize it at the time. A pair of Jehovah's Witnesses appeared at my door, bursting with good news about Jesus Christ Our Lord and Savior. They took a literal view of scripture and a dim view of Darwin: evolution was a lie, they said, and not a very convincing one.

It was the moment I'd been waiting for.

I was trying out a new technique, you see. Rather than lecture these misguided souls—rather than explaining Natural Selection and molecular genetics—I would use their own arguments against them. I would grant them their claims, and see where it took us.

"Well," said I, "I guess that pretty much wraps it up for Noah as a righteous man, doesn't it?"

They frowned, and asked why I would say such a thing.

"Well, we know there are dozens of sexually-transmitted diseases that exclusively infect humans and no other species," I explained. "And if evolution is a lie, then all those STDs must have existed since creation—and the only way they could have survived the Great Flood would have been inside Noah and his family. So logically, Noah's whole brood was more rotten with the clap than the lowliest hooker in Gomorrah." The logic was inevitable. There was no way on Earth these bible-thumpers could avoid it. I *had* them.

It didn't even slow them down.

"No," one of them explained patiently, "God afflicted us with those diseases to punish women for the Original Sin. God can do whatever He wants." (Did I mention that both of these missionaries were female?)

I realized, at that point, that you just can't reason with some people. It wasn't until much later that I began to understand *why* this should be so. I think it comes down to the oft-revisited theme that natural selection has shaped our brains not for logic but for inclusive fitness. We can use logic when we want to, of course. We have tools of reason at our command; but according to at least some experts[1] we have those tools not to glean truth from falsehood but to help us win arguments; to make others do what we want; to use as a *weapon*. It's rhetoric and manipulation that evolution selected for: logic just tagged along as a side effect. Sweeping oratory, rational debate, it's all just a way to bend others to your will.

In that light, it shouldn't surprise us that our brains have developed countermeasures to so-called *reasoned argument*. A seemingly-endless list of cognitive glitches compromises the brain's inability to perceive reality—but maybe they aren't so much glitches as *adaptations*, meant to counter the pernicious effects of the silver-tongued. *Confirmation bias*, for example, leads us to cherry-pick facts which support our own beliefs; the *Semmelweis reflex* makes us automatically reject findings that contradict our expectations. And perhaps most radically, the *Backfire Effect*. You'd think a rational person, confronted with evidence contradicting their beliefs on a given subject, would at the very least grow less confident in those beliefs. In fact, such contrary evidence often *reinforces* the very belief being undermined.

These adaptations, if that's what they are—these defenses against social manipulation—would make rational discourse difficult enough. But it gets worse. We know from the work of Kruger and Dunning[2] that not only do people tend to overestimate their own smarts, but that this effect is especially pronounced among the incompetent. Furthermore, incompetent people tend not only to regard themselves as smarter than everyone else; they tend to regard truly smart people as especially stupid, *even when shown empirical proof that they are less competent than those they deride.*

It explains so much, these counter-rhetorical biases. It explains why climate-change deniers dig their heels in even deeper with each new study confirming the reality of climate change. It explains the ease with which religious fundamentalists dismiss the mountains of evidence supporting evolution in favor of unsubstantiated and idiotic creation myths. It explains the prevalence of bumper stickers proudly proclaiming "God said it. I believe it. That Settles It.", the profound distrust of *education* so endemic among the North American conservative movement. We're even starting to see how such hardcore closed-minded types can have such a disproportionate influence on society at large: network analysis by Xie *et al*[3] suggests that a belief held by as few as 10% of a population can, over time, become the societal norm so long as that original 10% is sufficiently closed-minded and fanatical. (It's a ratchet effect, basically: the more open-minded you are, the more willing you are to entertain the notion you could be wrong. So when a fanatical believer tries to sway an open-minded nonbeliever, the latter is more likely to give ground—which increases the proportion of believers in the population. Which increases the frequency with which open-minded nonbelievers encounter believers. You get the picture.)

Of course, no one's immune to these biases; I've caught myself cherry-picking data on more than one occasion. To that extent we all live in glass houses. But there are ways of error-checking yourself, if you care to use them. The scientific method, at its heart, is a set of tools explicitly designed to break through bias and shine a light on the empirical information underneath. Recognizing our prejudices, we can overcome them.

But one thing we *cannot* do—and it has taken me so very long to realize this—is reason successfully with those who reject such tools. Logic doesn't matter to a Jehovah's Witness. Fossils mean nothing to a creationist. All the data in the world will not change the mind of a true climate-change denier.[4] You cannot reason with these people. You cannot take them seriously. It is a waste of energy to even try.

All you can really do is mock them. All you can do is subject them to scathing and intense ridicule, publicly if possible. So the next time you see some idiot waving a picture of a fetus in front of an abortion clinic, or pass some bible-thumper screeching that *God Hates Fags*—don't engage them, but don't ignore them, either. Toss them a peanut and make monkey sounds. Take their picture and laugh. Speak amongst yourselves in loud stage whispers, use them to illustrate to your children what inbreeding looks like, mention that you hadn't realized that research into human-animal hybrids had progressed *nearly* this far. You will never win them over; but at least you can have some fun at their expense.

It took me far too long to realize this consciously. But I think my subconscious had the right idea even back in 1986, when the missionaries at my door accused me of thinking I was *smarter than God*. "Oh, I don't think I'm smarter than *God*," I blurted out, without really meaning to. "I just think I'm smarter than *you*." Granted, it was a low bar to clear.

Have fun with them, while you still can. Because they're winning. And if Xie *et al* are right, time's running out for the rest of us.

1 Cohen, C. "Reason seen more as weapon than path to truth." *New York Times*, June 14, 2011.
2 "Unskilled and unaware of it: How difficulties in recognizing one's own incompetence lead to inflated self-assessments." *Journal of Personality and Social Psychology*, Vol 77(6), Dec 1999, 1121–1134.
3 "Social consensus through the influence of committed minorities." *Phys*. Rev. E 84, 011130 (2011).
4 As opposed to *professional* climate-change deniers, who simply espouse whatever Exxon and the Koch Brothers pay them to regardless of their own opinions on the subject.

Changing Our Minds: "Story of Your Life" in Print and on Screen.

BLOG NOV 30 2016

We share a secret prayer, we writers of short SF. We utter it whenever one of our stories is about to appear in public, and it goes like this:

> *Please, Lord. Please, if it be Thy will,*
> *don't let Ted Chiang publish a story this year.*

We supplicate thus because whenever Ted Chiang does put out a story—not all that often, thankfully—it's pretty much guaranteed to walk away with every award that's lying around, leaving nothing for the rest of us. More often than not, it deserves to. So it will come as no surprise to learn that the first movie to be based on a Ted Chiang story is very smart, and very compelling.

What might come as a shock—and I hesitate to write this down, because it smacks of heresy—is that in terms of storytelling, *Arrival* actually surpasses its source material.

It's not that it has a more epic scale, or more in the way of conventional dramatic conflict. Not *just* that, anyway. It's true that Hollywood—inevitably—took what was almost a cozy fireside chat and 'roided it up to fate-of-the-world epicness. In "Story of Your Life," aliens of modest size set up a bunch of sitting rooms, play charades with us for a while, and then leave. Their motives remain mysterious; the military, though omnipresent, remains in the background. The narrative serves mainly as a framework for Chiang to explore some nifty ideas about the way language and perception interact, about how the time-symmetric nature of fundamental physics might lead to a world-view—every bit as consistent as ours—that describes a teleological universe, with all the Billy Pilgrim time-tripping that implies. It's fascinating and brow furrowing, but it doesn't leave you on the edge of your seat. Going back and rereading it for this post, I had to hand it to screenwriter Eric Heisserer for seeing the cinematic potential buried there; if I was going to base a movie on a Ted Chiang story, this might be the *last* one I'd choose.

In contrast, *Arrival*'s heptapods are behemoths. What we see of them hints at a cross between the proto-Alien from *Prometheus* and the larger members of that extradimensional menagerie glimpsed in *The Mist*. While the novella's spaceships remained invisibly in orbit, the movie's hang just overhead like asteroids pausing for one last look around before smashing the world to rubble. The novella's geopolitics consist largely of frowning uniforms, grumbling ineffectually in the background; in the movie, half the world's ready to start lobbing nukes. Armageddon hinges on whether the aliens really mean "tool" when we read "weapon."

All standard Hollywood Bigger-Is-Better, and—for once—done in a way that doesn't betray the sensibility of the source material. For the most part I preferred the more epic scale—although I *was* irked by the inevitable portrayal of Murricka as the calmer, cooler, *peaceful* players while Russia and China geared up to start Interstellar War I. (The portrayal of the US as the world's most pacifist nation is probably the least-plausible element in this whole space-alien saga.) But I'm not just talking about the amped-up levels of jeopardy when I say I prefer movie to novella: I'm talking about the way different story elements tie together. I'm talking about actual narrative structure.

"Story of Your Life" presents a number of elements almost in isolation. We know that Louise will marry, have a daughter, get divorced. We know that the daughter will die. We know that the heptapods leave, but we never know why—or why they showed up in the first place, for that matter. (When quizzed on the subject they say they're here to acquire information, which would have a lock on "Most Maddeningly Vague Answer of the Year" if such an award actually existed.) (If it did, of *course* Ted Chiang would win it.)

Arrival ties all these loose ends together, elegantly, satisfyingly. The aliens are here to give us a "weapon/tool"—or more accurately a *gift*: to teach us their teleological mindset, uplift us to a new world-view. They are here to literally *change our minds*. Louise makes that conceptual breakthrough, uses the new paradigm to head off nuclear war in the nick of time. Her divorce—years after the closing credits—is not just something that happens to happen; it occurs when her husband learns that she'd known in advance (thanks to her new precognitive mindset) that their daughter would be doomed to a slow, painful death at a young age—and yet went ahead and birthed her anyway (not that choice had anything to do with it, of course). It's not belabored in the screenplay—a couple of oblique references to *Daddy looks at me differently now* and *I made a decision he thought was wrong*. But the implicit conflict in the moral algebra between two people who love each other—*We can at least give her a few glorious years* vs. *You've sentenced her to agony and death*—is heartbreaking in a way that Chiang's Kubrickian analysis never managed.

More to the point, though, all these events tie together. They all arise from the central premise, from the cursed gift the hepta-pods bestow upon us. Everything's connected, organically, logically, causally. Teleogically.

The movie has an unfair advantage, insofar as it can present straightforward memories of *future* events and be confident that the audience will assume that they're flash*backs*; the moment we realize our mistake is one of the best aha! twists of the movie. Chiang, stuck with the written word, had to give the game away pretty much at the start by writing his future memories in future tense; a beautiful device, but with little room for surprise.

Which is no reason to not read the story. Offhand, I can't think of *any* good reason to not read a story by Ted Chiang.

But in this case, I think there's more reason to see the movie.

The God-Shaped Hole

It should be no secret that I am one of that ever-growing flock of empiricists who've been touched by His Noodly Appendage. And while I generally have little patience for religious beliefs of any stripe—I just can't see any explanatory utility in them at all—my feelings about religious believers are somewhat more nuanced. Maybe some of it has to do with the fact that I was raised not only by devout Baptists, but by an actual Baptist minister/ scholar/high-falutin' bureaucrat in the Baptist church. (I'm not sure exactly how highly placed, but I have this vague sense that "general secretary" was something like a cardinal/union-boss, except without the sodomising of altar boys or the pistol-whipping of strike-breakers.) Maybe it's because, having gone through occasional dark hours of my own, I know how absolutely wonderful it would be to know, deep down in my heart, that death is not the end, that there is a place where all my beloved dead cats still chew on liquorice (and cannot climb the trees), that there is more to existence than a few decades of ranting vainly against the imbeciles who keep treating the planet like a toilet bowl. Or maybe it's just that I've encountered a fair number of believers over the past decades, and I can't honestly dismiss all of them as complete idiots.

Not that there aren't an awful lot of idiots in those ranks, you understand. Almost half the human population on this continent thinks that Humanity was created pretty much in its present form six thousand years ago, that evolution is a fraud, and that the sky is swarming with angels. But I can't put people like my dad into that basket. He never had any problems with science in general, or with evolution in particular.

Granted, once when I asked him if he would at least stop believing in this Easter Bunny of his if presented with indisputable, convincing evidence of God's nonexistence, he thought for a moment and admitted that no, he most likely would not. He lost some serious points with me then. But still; this man, and thousands more like him, are not idiots. I cannot lump them in with the Falwells and the Bushies and the—well, with the 47% of the N'Amian population who appear to be fucking morons. I just can't.

I prefer to think of most of them not as stupid, but lazy.

Most people acquire their beliefs through osmosis and observation, not investigation. We'd rather observe than derive. Raised in a society awash in certain ubiquitous beliefs, you tend to accept those beliefs without thinking. I think most people come to their faith in the same way they come to believe that not wearing a tie is "unprofessional office behavior," even though ties are a prerequisite for very few office duties. (There are good evolutionary reasons for this. Who's going to get ahead fastest; the guy who reinvents every wheel from scratch, or the guy who looks around and copies those wheel-thingies all the grown-ups are using? Of course you should follow the grown-ups' lead; they were obviously fit enough to spawn . . .)

Still, what if I'm wrong? One of the reasons science kicks religion's ass is that we always have to allow for the possibility that we could be wrong about anything. (Who was it remarked that science offers proof without certainty, while religion offers certainty without proof?) So I'm always on the lookout for bright people, scientifically-inclined people, non-fucking-moron people, who have religious beliefs. Because maybe they've thought of something I haven't. Maybe they're right and I'm wrong; and man, wouldn't it be great to be wrong about this? Wouldn't it absolutely kick ass if there actually was an afterlife, and a stigmatized Easter Bunny?

So Dad hands me this book: *The Language of God: A Scientist Presents Evidence For Belief* by one Francis S. Collins. Director of the bureaucratic half of the Human Genome Project, for chrissakes. And here's the kicker: the dude started his university career as an atheist, and then converted to Christianity. Is that ass-backwards or what?

Here, say I, is a guy both smarter and better educated than me, who obviously knows all the arguments that led me to my own apostasy, because he started out there himself—and he's found something better! He has found evidence for belief!

I bet you're just dying to see what it was, hmmm?

Here it is. Dr. Francis Collins's Big Reveal. Actually, his Big Reveal was a personal epiphany he had while looking at a bunch of icicles; this is his Evidence That Demands A Verdict, and it is, wait for it:

The warm fuzzy feeling you get when you "Do The Right Thing."

Yup. That's it. A dopamine rush, elevated to the status of "The Moral Law". Universally extant in every Human culture, he says, and unique to Human culture as well. "Evolution will never explain The Moral Law and the Universal Search for God," he assures us, will never explain that uniquely, universally human urge to help those in need, even if they don't share our genes, even at our own expense. We are beyond evolution—for if the evolutionists were right, we'd never do anything except selfishly try to spread our own genes. Collins actually uses the word "scandal" to describe the way in which we "evolutionists" regard altruism.

He invokes C. S. Lewis's faux-adaptationist argument to induce God's existence from these warm fuzzies:

"Creatures are not born with desires unless satisfaction for those desires exists. A baby feels hunger; well, there is such a thing as food. A duckling wants to swim; well, there is such a thing as water. Pedophiles feel sexual desire; well, there is such a thing as altar boys[1]. If I find in myself a desire which no experience in this world can satisfy, the most probable explanation is that I was made for another world."

After which Collins cuts in and asks, "Why do we have a 'God-shaped vacuum' in our hearts unless it is meant to be filled?"

Where to start. (Beyond noting that while some sort of vacuum does seem to persist in one Francis Collins, it is unlikely to reside in his thorax . . .)

Let's start with a general observation. Collins's understanding of natural selection appears to be a woefully-ignorant caricature in which every organism always behaves optimally to promote its own fitness, and every instance in which this doesn't happen constitutes a failure of evolutionary theory calling out for Divine intervention. What he doesn't seem to understand (or perhaps, what he's hoping you won't) is that the whole basis of natural selection is *variation*. Organisms differ; some do better than others; the losers leave fewer offspring. Nature, in other words, is chock-full of creatures who do not selfishly spread their genes, who benefit others at their own expense. Conspecifics might call such organisms "unsuccessful competitors." Parasites would call them "hosts." Predators would call them "food". The Archdiocese calls them "parishioners."

Perhaps you're thinking that's a cheap shot; prey may not *successfully* spread their genes, but that's not for want of trying. I would counter that the same could be said of all those good folks who turn the other cheek expecting a grand payoff in the Kingdom of Heaven. Either way, this Collins guy needs to be taught the basics—not just of biology, but of elementary logic. To claim that non-selfish acts contradict evolutionary theory is like claiming that blow jobs contradict the orgasm's role in reproduction.

But fine: he's talking about the *knowing* and *voluntary* sacrifice of one's own interests to benefit another. *That's* what he defines as uniquely human. Except it isn't. Empathy for nonrelatives, efforts expended to help others (even members of different species), have been documented in nonhuman primates and cetaceans. The concepts of fair play and justice don't seem to be uniquely human either. Contrary to Collins's claims, sociobiologists don't have any real trouble reconciling such actions with evolutionary processes; in fact, the neurochemistry underlying empathy is a pretty basic social-cohesion mechanism. And while Collins has a field day hauling out Oskar Schindler and Mother Teresa as examples of selfless service to a greater good, he's only cherry-picking one or two convenient outliers from a cloud of data[2]. Readers of this obscure little newscrawl may remember that there *is* a data cloud, statistically quantifiable, and it shows that people tend to engage in risky heroics or acts of altruistic generosity primarily when it improves their chances of getting laid. (And don't bother pointing out that Mommy Teresa's chances of that were pretty much nil—we both know the basement circuitry works the same way regardless of motivational overlays. Besides, she was expecting a whole other kind of payoff, just as Schindler more likely than not feared some kind of pay*back*.) You may also remember that this "Moral Law," such as it is, is inconsistent and often downright wrong, that the *truly* altruistic—those who'd unhesitatingly sacrifice two of their own children to save four of someone else's, for example—suffer from a specific and precise form of brain damage[3]. The truly moral are those with lesions in the ventromedial prefrontal cortex; not, so far as I've heard, a "universal" aspect of the Human condition.

And that's not even getting into the self-sacrificing behaviour of those who have merely been tricked into furthering someone else's agenda. How many Christians would have marched in the Crusades, how many jihadists would have strapped bombs across their bellies, how many missionaries would have risked disease and death in darkest Africa if they'd actually believed that eternal damnation was waiting at the end of it? (Now *that* would be altruism.) Is Collins really so blind to the workings of his own religion that he can't tell the difference between true selflessness and the parasitic manipulation of selfish motives?

Which leads to another, and mind-bogglingly obvious, failing of Collins's argument: the ubiquity of the "Moral Law." His claim that we all share the same standards of right and wrong would, I expect, come as news to all those cultures throughout history who kept (and keep) slaves, who mutilate the genitals of their women, who regarded (and regard) foreign races, beliefs, and behaviours as things to be avoided at best and hammered into extinction at worst. The ongoing genocides of the twentieth and twenty-first centuries provide eloquent testimony to the ubiquity of Collins's Moral Law, and while he leaves himself a bit of wiggle room (we all have the Moral Law, you see, but some of us choose to *ignore* it), he cites nothing to justify the claim that this sense of right and wrong *is* universal beyond the one-two punch that a) *he* feels it and so do all his friends, and b) C. S. Lewis told him so. (In fact, reading *The Language of God*, you get the sense that Francis Collins has anointed himself C. S. Lewis's Official Corporeal Sock Puppet.)

For all his talk of agape and altruism, Collins may be the most profoundly self-centred human being I've read. The possibility that everyone doesn't feel just the way he does seems completely beyond his grasp.

The search for God? I'm a pretty introspective dude, and I can say with a high degree of confidence that I don't have anything like that gnawing away inside me. I recognise that many people do—but I also recognise that our brains are hardwired to see patterns even where none exist, to attribute agency even to purely indifferent phenomena. It's a small enough step from the "Theory of Mind" that allows us to suss out the agendas of the creatures and conspecifics we encounter day to day. So the very clouds can look angry to us, or benign; and who *hasn't* wanted to put a brick through that fucking laptop and its fucking Blue Screen of Death which always, malevolently, crashes your system when you're six hours from deadline and have forgotten to save?

Apply equal parts ignorance, pattern-matching, and the attribution of motives onto nature's canvas: angels and demons sprout like Spears sprogs behind every rock (much as they appeared to Collins in his frozen waterfall). But Collins doesn't even admit that such neural circuitry *exists*, much less contemplate its potential relevance to human superstition. No mention at all of Persinger's work[4], or Ramachandran's[5]. And once again, no credit whatsoever to the guys with the mitres and crosses—not to mention the iron maidens in their basements—and the role *they* might have played in inculcating a sense of the divine into the culture (albeit granted, a form of the divine that seems chronically in need of alms).

So Collins's central, most rigorous argument for a personal god—who created heaven and earth and made us and *only* us in his image—is that everybody shares the same sense of right and wrong (except they don't); that everybody seeks God (speak for yourself, buddy; I'm happy if I can just find a decent pint of Rickards); that Human beings are unique among all species in being altruistic and moral (except we're not); and that there's no other explanation but the God of Abraham for any of this (except there sure as shit *is*).

Let me repeat: this is his *strongest* argument.

It's not his only one, though. Collins commits numerous other sins, easily recognised by anyone with even a passing familiarity with the moves of flat-earthers and climate-change deniers and spin-doctors the world over. Statements initially introduced with all the right caveats ("If we accept the possibility of the supernatural, then it is possible that . . .") reappear later, unsubstantiated but nonetheless miraculously transmuted into statements of absolute fact (believers are "right to hold fast to the eternal truths of the Bible"). Legitimate objections to his positions (e.g., that religious beliefs are irrelevant to the study of Nature) are dismissed for no better reason than that Collins finds them unpalatable ("that doesn't resonate with most individuals' human experience," he writes). In the manner of fundies everywhere, and in the spirit of that book he holds most holy, he contradicts himself whenever it suits him. At one point he argues against the God-as-wishful-thinking model by pointing out that a product of wish-fulfillment would be cuddly and indulgent, not demanding and judgmental as the God of Abraham is wont to be. (Oddly, the prospect of an intimidating God invoked not for comfort, but as a way for folks in funny hats to exert control over credulous followers, never seems to occur to him.) But when facing off against those who'd claim that God scattered photons and fossils across heaven and earth to test our faith, he decides that a little wishful thinking is just fine: "Would God as the great deceiver be an entity anyone would *want* to worship?"

He rejects a naturalistic universe because after all, something had to kick-start the Big Bang (it couldn't have just booted itself, that would be absurd)—then changes the rules to exempt his own model from the same criticism (oh, nothing had to create God, God just booted Himself—as I would too, hard in my own ass, if I'd created a sentient being as wilfully stupid as Francis Collins). He hauls out the old atheism-is-faith-based-too chestnut, because after all, nobody can *prove* God doesn't exist: so if that's what you believe you're just taking it on blind *faith*, right? (Of course, nobody can prove that omnipotent purple hamsters *aren't* partying it up in the Pleiades either; I guess Collins must believe in those too, or he'd be just as blind as the creationists.)

He quotes Hawking's *Brief History of Time* out of context, in a way that portrays ol' Wheels as a believer; he makes no mention of Hawking's explicit denial of religious belief in the same book. He tries to tell us that creationism and intelligent design are different things, and goes so far as to state as a scientist that the ID movement "deserves serious consideration"—evidently unaware that the IDiots got caught passing their creationist textbook through a global search-and-replace to turn every instance of the word "creationism" into "intelligent design," as a way to get around legal proscriptions against religion in science class.

I don't care if this guy *did* nail the gene for cystic fibrosis. If this book exemplifies his cognitive skills, I gotta wonder who he slept with to end up running the HGP.

Once, many years ago, Francis Collins claims he was an athe- ist. Maybe he still is, at heart. Maybe he's just lying through his teeth with this book. Maybe he's a player with an agenda, a guy who wanted to climb up the ranks and figured that atheism would keep him off the guest lists for all the best parties. I have no evi- dence of this, but I hope that's the case. I hope that he's merely an opportunist. I really do.

Because judging by this self-righteous, irrational, and contemptible book, the only other explanation that comes to mind is that Dr. Francis Collins is a complete fucking moron.

1 Okay, maybe Lewis didn't use this particular example. But you take my point. NAMBLA's gonna have a field day with this rationale; according to Francis Collins, God *wants* them to be pedophiles . . .

2 Not that Mother Teresa was either convenient or an outlier, if you dig into her biography a little. The woman was a monster.

3 Koenigs *et al*, 2007. "Damage to the prefrontal cortex increases utilitarian moral judgements." *Nature*. doi:10.1038/nature05631

4 HTTP://WWW.SHAKTITECHNOLOGY.COM/

5 HTTP://PSY.UCSD.EDU/CHIP/RAMABIO.HTML

Dumb Adult

BLOG MAR 15 2016

We didn't have "Young Adult" when I was your age, much less this newfangled "New Adult" thing they coddle you with. We had to jump right from *Peter the Sea Trout* and *Freddy and the Ignormus* straight into *Stand on Zanzibar* and *Solaris*, no water wings or training wheels or anything.

Amazingly, I managed to read anyway. I discovered Asimov and Bradbury and Bester at eleven, read *Zanzibar* at twelve, *Solaris* at thirteen. I may have been smarter than most of my age class (I *hope* I was—if not, I sure got picked on a lot for no good reason), but I was by no means unique; I only discovered *The Sheep Look Up* when a classmate recommended it to me in the eleventh grade. And judging by the wear and tear on the paperbacks in the school library, *everyone* was into Asimov and Bradbury back then. Delany too, judging by the way the covers kept falling off *The Einstein Intersection*. Back in those days we didn't need no steenking Young Adult.

Now get off my lawn.

I'll admit my attitude could be a bit more nuanced. After all, my wife has recently been marketed as a YA author, and her writing is gorgeous (although I would argue it's also not YA). Friends and peers swim in young-adult waters. Well-intentioned advisers, ever mindful of the nichiness of my own market share, have suggested that I try writing YA because that's where the money is, because that's the one part of the fiction market that didn't implode with the rest of the economy a few years back.

But I can't help myself. It's not that I don't think we should encourage young adults to read (in fact, if we can't get them to read more than the last generation, we're pretty much fucked). It's that I'm starting to think YA doesn't do that.

I'm starting to think it may do the opposite.

Hanging out at last fall's SFContario, I sat in on a panel on the subject. It was populated by a bunch of very smart authors who most assuredly do not suck, who know far more about YA than I do, and whom I hope will not take offense when I shit all over their chosen pseudogenre—because even this panel of experts had a hard time coming up with a working definition of what a Young Adult novel even *was*.

The rules keep changing, you see. It wasn't so long ago that you couldn't say "fuck" in a YA novel; these days you can. Back around the turn of the century, YA novels were 100% sex-free, beyond the chaste fifties-era hand-holding and nookie that never seemed to involve the unzipping of anyone's fly; today, YA can encompass not just sex, but pregnancy and venereal disease and rape. Stories that once took place in some parallel, intercourse-free universe now juggle gay sex and gender fluidity as if they were just another iteration of Archie and Betty down at the malt shop (which is, don't get me wrong, an awesome and overdue thing; but it doesn't give you much of a leg up when you're trying to define

"Young Adult" in more satisfying terms than "Books that can be found in the YA section at Indigo").

Every now and then one of the panelists would cite an actual rule that seemed to hold up over time, but which was arcane unto inanity. In one case, apparently, a story with an adolescent protagonist—a story that met pretty much any YA convention you might want to name—was excluded from the club simply because it was told as an extended flashback, from the POV of the protagonist as a grown adult looking back. Apparently it's not enough that a story revolve around adolescents; the perspective, the mindset of the novel as artefact must *also* be rooted in adolescence. If adults are even present in the tale, they must remain facades; we can never see the world through their eyes.

Remember those old Peanuts TV specials where the grown-ups were never seen, and whose only bits of dialog consisted entirely of muted trombones going *mwa-mwa-mwa*? Young Adult, apparently.

Finally the panel came up with a checklist they could all agree upon. To qualify as YA, a story would have to incorporate the following elements:

- Youthful protagonist(s)
- Youthful mindset
- Corrupt/dystopian society (this criterion may have been in-tended to apply to modern 21st-century YA rather than the older stuff, although I suppose a cadre of Evil Cheerleaders Who Run The School might qualify)
- Inconvenient/ineffectual/absent parents: more a logistic con-straint than a philosophical one. Your protagonists have to be free to be proactive, which is hard to pull off with parents al-ways looking over their shoulders and telling them it's time to come in now.

- Uplifting, or at least hopeful ending: your protags may only be a bunch of meddlesome kids, but the Evil Empire can't defeat them.

Accepting these criteria as authoritative—they were, after all, hashed out by a panel of authorities—it came to me in a blinding flash. The archetypal YA novel just *had* to be—wait for it— *A Clockwork Orange.*

Think about it: a story told from the exclusive first-person perspective of an adolescent, check. Corrupt dystopian society, check. Irrelevant parents, check. And in the end, Alex wins: the government sets him free once again, to rape and pillage to his heart's content. Admittedly the evil government isn't outright defeated at the end of the novel; it simply has to let Alex walk, let him get back to his life (a more recent YA novel with the same payoff is Cory Doctorow's *Little Brother*). Still: it failed to defeat the meddlesome kid.

So according to a panel of YA authors—or at least, according to the criteria they laid out—one of the most violent, subversive, and inaccessible novels of the twentieth century is a work of YA fiction. Which pretty much brings us back to eleven-year-old me and John Brunner. If *A Clockwork Orange* is Young Adult, aren't that category's boundaries so wide as to be pretty much meaningless?

But there's one rule nobody mentioned, a rule I suspect may be more relevant than all the others combined. *A Clockwork Orange* is not an easy read by any stretch. Not only are the words big and difficult, half of them are in goddamn Russian. The whole book is written in a polyglot dialect that doesn't even exist in the real world. And I suspect that toughness, that inaccessibility, would cause most to exclude it from YAhood.

In order to be YA, the writing has to be simple. It may have once been a good thing to throw the occasional unfamiliar word at an adolescent; hell, it might force them to look the damn thing up, increase their vocabulary a bit. No longer. I haven't read a whole lot of YA—Gaiman, Doctorow, Miéville are three that come most readily to mind—but I've noticed a common thread in their YA works that extends beyond merely dialing back the sex and profanity. The prose is less challenging than the stuff you find in adult works by the same authors.

Well, duh, you might think: of course it's simpler. It's written for a younger audience. But increasingly, that isn't the case anymore, at least not since they started printing Harry Potter with understated "adult" covers, so all those not-so-young-adult fans could get their Hogwarts fix on the subway without being embarrassed by lurid and childish artwork. *The Hunger Games* was first recommended to me by a woman who was (back then) on the cusp of thirty, and no dummy.

All these actual adults, reading progressively simpler writing. All us authors, chasing them down the stairs. Hell, Neil Gaiman took a classic that nine-year-old Peter Watts devoured without any trouble at all—Rudyard Kipling's *The Jungle Book*—and dumbed it down to an (admittedly award-winning) story about ghosts and vampires, aimed at an audience who might find a story about sapient wolves and tigers too challenging. It may only be a matter of time before *Nineteen Eighty-Four* is reissued using only words from the Eleventh Edition of the Newspeak Dictionary. We may already be past the point when anyone looking to read *Twenty Thousand Leagues Under the Sea* looks any further than the Classics Illustrated comic.

I know how this sounds. I led with that whole crotchety get-off-my-lawn shtick because the Old are famously compelled to rail against the failings of the Young, because rants about the Good Old Days are as tiresome when they're about literacy as they are when they're about music or haircuts. It was a self-aware (and probably ineffective) attempt at critic-proofing.

So let me emphasize: I've got nothing against clear, concise prose (despite the florid nature of my own, sometimes). Hemingway wrote simple prose. Orwell extolled its virtues. If that was all that made up Young Adult, even I would be a YA writer (at least, I don't think your average sixteen-year-old would have any trouble getting through *Starfish*).

But there's a difference between novels that happen to be accessible to teens, and novels that put teens in their heat-sensitive, wallet-lightening crosshairs. I know of one author who had to go back and tear up an adult novel, already written, by the roots: rewrite and duct-tape it onto YA scaffolding because that's the only way it would sell. I know a very smart, highly-respected editor who once raved about the incredible, well-thought-out plotting of the Harry Potter books, apparently blind to the fact that Rowling— her claims to the contrary notwithstanding—seemed to be just making shit up as she went along[1].

A long time ago, a childhood friend gave me the collected tales of Edgar Allan Poe for my tenth birthday. I loved that stuff. It taught me things—made me teach myself things, in the same way a Jethro Tull song a few decades later forced me to look up the meaning of "overpressure wave." I have to wonder if YA does that, if it improves one's reading skills or merely panders to them. I doubt that your vocabulary is any bigger when you finish *Harry Potter and the Well-Deserved Bitch-Slap* than when you started. You may have been entertained, but you were not upgraded.

Of course, if entertainment's all you're after, no biggie. The problem, though, is that it acts like a ratchet. If we only allow ourselves to write down, never up—and if the age of the YA market edges up, never down—it's hard to see how the overall sophistication of our writing can do anything but decline monotonically over time.

Who among you will tell me this is a good thing?

1 I mean, think about it: we have a protagonist whose central defining feature is the murder of his parents when he was an infant. And when he discovers that time travel is so trivially accessible that his classmate uses it for no better purpose than to double up her course load, it never *once* occurs to him to wonder: *Hey—maybe I can go back and save my parents!* This is careful plotting?

In Praise of War Crimes

Nowa Fantastyka JAN 2014

The Terminator has made it into the pages of *Science*. The December 20 issue of that prestigious journal contains an article titled "Scientists Campaign Against Killer Robots," which summarizes the growing grass-roots movement against autonomous killing machines on the battlefield. Lest you think we're talking about the burgeoning fleet of drones deployed with such enthusiasm by the US—you know, those weapons the Obama administration praises as so much "more precise" than conventional airstrikes, at least during those press conferences when they're not expressing regrets over another Yemeni wedding party accidentally massacred in the latest Predator attack—let me bring you up to speed. Predators are puppets, not robots. Their pilots may be sipping coffee in some air-conditioned office in Arizona, running their vehicles by remote control, but at least the decision to turn kids into collateral is made by *people*.

Of course, the problem (okay: *one* of the problems) with running a puppet from 8,000 km away is that its strings can be jammed, or hacked. (You may have heard about those Iraqi insurgents who tapped into Predator video feeds using $26 worth of off-the-shelf parts from Radio Shack.) Wouldn't it be nice if we didn't *need* that umbilicus. Wouldn't it be nice if our robots could think for *themselves*.

I've got the usual SF-writer's hard-on for these sorts of issues (I even wrote a story on the subject—"Malak"—a couple of years back). I keep an eye open for these sorts of developments. We're told that we still have a long way to go before we have *truly* autonomous killing machines: robots that can tell friend from foe, assess relative threat potentials, decide to kill *this* target and leave *that* one alone. They're coming, though. True, the Pentagon claimed in 2013 that it had "no completely autonomous systems in the pipeline or being considered"—but when was the last time anyone believed anything the Pentagon said, especially in light of a 2012 US Department of Defense Directive spelling out criteria for "development and use of autonomous and semi-autonomous functions in weapon systems, including manned and unmanned platforms"¹?

Root through that directive and you'll find the usual mealy-mouthed assurances about keeping Humans In Ultimate Control. It's considered paramount, for example, that "in the event of degraded or lost communications, the system does not autonomously select and engage individual targets or specific target groups that have not been previously selected by an authorized human operator". But you don't have to be Isaac Asimov to see how easy it would be to subvert *that* particular Rule of Robotics. Suppose a human operator *does* approve a target, just before contact with a drone is lost. The drone is now authorized to hunt that particular target on its own. How does it know that the target who just emerged from behind that rock is the same one who ducked behind it ten seconds earlier? Does it key on facial features? What happens if the target is wearing clothing that covers the face? Does it key on clothing? What happens if the target swaps hats with a friend?

According to *Science*, the fight against developing these machines—waged by bodies with names like the Convention on Certain Conventional Weapons and the International Committee for Robot Arms Control—centers on the argument that robots lack the ability to discriminate reliably between combatants and civilians in the heat of battle. I find this argument both troubling and unconvincing. The most obvious objection involves Moore's Law: even if robots can't do something today, there's a damn good chance they can do it *tomorrow*. Another problem—one that can bite you in the ass right now, while you're waiting for tomorrow to happen—is that even *people* can't reliably distinguish between friend and foe all the time. North American cops, at least, routinely get a pass when they gun down some innocent civilian under the mistaken impression that their victim was going for a gun instead of a cell phone.

Does anyone truly believe that we're going to hold machines to a higher standard than we hold ourselves? Or as Lin *et al* put it back in 2008 in "Autonomous Military Robotics: Risk, Ethics, and Design":

> "An ethically-infallible machine ought not to be the goal. Our goal should be to design a machine that performs better than humans do on the battlefield, particularly with respect to reducing unlawful behaviour or war crimes."

Ah, war crimes. My final point. Because it's actually really hard to pin a war crime on a machine. If your garden-variety remote-controlled drone blows up a party of civilians, you can always charge the operator on the other side of the world, or the CO who ordered him to open fire (not that this ever happens, of course). But if a machine decided to massacre all those innocents, who do you blame? Those who authorized its deployment? Those who designed it? Some computer scientist who didn't realize that her doctoral research on computer vision was going to get co-opted by a supervisor with a fat military contract?

Or does it stop being a war crime entirely, and turn into something less—objectionable? At what point does collateral damage become nothing more than a tragic industrial accident?

To me, the real threat is not the fallibility of robots, but the deliberate exploitation of that fallibility by the generals. The military now has an incentive: not to limit the technology, not to improve its ability to discriminate foe from friend, but to *deploy these fallible weapons as widely as possible.* Back in 2008 a man named Stephen White wrote a paper called "Brave New World: Neurowarfare and the Limits of International Humanitarian Law." It was about the legal and ethical implications of neuroweaponry, but its warning rings true for any technology that takes life-and-death decisions out of human hands:

> ". . . international humanitarian law would create perverse incentives that would encourage the development of an entire classes of weapons that the state could use to evade criminal penalties for even the most serious types of war crimes."

Granted, the end result might not be so bad. Eventually the technology could improve to the point where robotic decisions aren't just equal to, but are *better than* those arising from the corruptible meat of human brains. Under those conditions it would be a war crime to *not* hand the kill switch over to machines. Under their perfected algorithms, combat losses would dwindle to a mere fraction of the toll inflicted under human command. We could ultimately end up in a better place.

Still. I'm betting we'll spill rivers of blood in getting there.

1 HTTPS://WWW.HSDL.ORG/?ABSTRACT&DID=726163

The Last of Us, The Weakest Link.

Nowa Fantastyka MAY 2014

BLOG JAN 8 2019

I've been writing video games for almost as long as I've been publishing novels. You can be forgiven for not knowing that; nothing written in my gaming capacity has ever made it to production. The usual course of events goes something like this: I work with a talented development team to serve up a kick-ass proposal. Over the following few months, the rest of the team disappears, one by one, under mysterious circumstances. Finally I get an email from some new Executive Producer I've never heard of, who praises my "terrific" work and tells me he'll be in touch if they ever need my services again.

They never do. Nothing I've worked on has ever made it to market unmutilated; characters flattened to cardboard, innovative aliens reduced to evil yoghurt, all subtlety and nuance and interpersonal conflict flensed away before, ultimately, being jettisoned altogether.

And yet, after nearly two decades of false starts and dashed hopes, I still maintained that the future of fiction was interactive.

Language, after all, is a workaround; one can marvel at the eloquence with which words might evoke the beauty of the setting sun, but no abstract scribbles of pixels-on-plasma could ever compete with the direct sensory perception of an *actual* sunset. This is what's on offer by visual media of all stripes: the ability to convey *exactly*, with no doubt, no interpolation, no need to *guess*— what an alien world looks like, what your protagonist actually sees and hears (and before long, smells and tastes and feels as well).

Add interactivity—the potential to not just read about heroes but to *be* them—and how could any mere novel compete? Written fiction was always a compromise, an artifact of the state of the art. Now that art has advanced to an immersive state that invites its aficionados to help invent the narrative instead of just observing it.

Of course, for all the brilliance of games like *Half-Life* and *Bioshock*, the flexibility of the narrative is an illusion. You don't really invent the story; you just find your way through a preprogrammed maze, shooting aliens and mutants along the way. And while sandbox worlds like *Skyrim* and *Fallout* certainly deliver the feel of an open-ended, off-the-rails environment, isn't it a bit unrealistic that people you were supposed to meet outside the castle at midnight are still waiting there to pick up the story, uncomplaining, even after you've ignored them for six in-game months? Doesn't Lydia's conversational range look a bit limited after, oh, five minutes?

Just bumps in the road, thought I. They'd be smoothed out soon enough. For now it wasn't possible to code realistic narrative complexity into a game that fit into the average PlayStation, but surely all those constraints would recede further towards the horizon with every iteration of Moore's Law. In another ten or fifteen years we'd have games that you could really *play* instead of just *solve*; characters who'd live and breathe and evolve dynamically, in meaningful response to the actions of the player.

It took a game in which characters actually did live and breathe and evolve to make me see the folly of that belief. I'm talking about *The Last of Us*.

On first glance, *The Last of Us* looks like just another generic post-apocalyptic survival shooter. Civilization has collapsed. There are zombies. Mortal injuries are magically patched up in mere seconds by "health kits" cobbled together from rags and bottles of alcohol. You scavenge a variety of weapons during your travels across a shattered landscape; if something moves, you shoot it. Yawn.

On second glance, it's fucking brilliant.

To start with, the zombies aren't zombies: they're victims of a mutated strain of *Cordyceps*, a real-world fungus that does, in fact, rewire the behavioral pathways of its victims. Good people turn out to be bad; bad people turn out to be ambivalent. Cannibals and child-killers and sociopaths all have their reasons. The moral dilemmas are real and profound, and the relationship between the two protagonists is so nuanced, so beautifully realized in the voice-acting and the mo-cap, that it literally brought me to tears a time or two. And *nothing* brings me to tears, except the death of a cat.

Only a video game so perfectly balanced, so emotionally involving, could convince me that video games will never be so perfectly balanced and so emotionally involving.

All that wonderful character development, you see—all those jeweled moments that exposed the depth of Ellie's soul, of Joel's torment—aren't part of the game. They're cut-scenes, unplayable, noninteractive. I don't think I've ever played a game with such extended cinematic interludes. Sometimes it takes control in the middle of fight, to ensure it plays out the way it's supposed to. Sometimes the whole damn fight is a spectator sport, start to finish. (Sometimes I think they go overboard. At one point you lose the game if a secondary character gets killed—even though that character dies anyway, during the cinematic that immediately follows.)

These are human beings, you see, not Gordon-Freeman one-size-fits-all templates into which any player might pour themselves. They're damaged creatures with their own personalities and their own demons. And *because* they're fully-realized characters, we can't be trusted to inhabit them. Oh, sometimes we're granted a token nod to participation at vital moments—a prompt to trigger a bit of preprogrammed dialog, or the choice of whether to walk or run during the course of a conversation—but all that really does is rub our noses in how irrelevant our participation really is to the story being told. We can't touch their souls; all we can do is move their arms and legs during those shoot-and-sneak intervals that come down to basic animal-instinct survival.

And how else could it be? How could anyone entrust such complex creations to any doofus who slaps down forty bucks at the local games counter? How many players would be able to conjure up, on the fly, dialog worthy of these protagonists—even when Moore's Law makes that a feasible option? How many could be trusted to keep their actions consistent with motives and memories that have twenty years of tortured history behind them?

It's not the technology, it's the player. *We're* the weak link. We always will be.

Video games can be art. *The Last of Us* proves it better than any other title in recent memory; but the only way it could do that was to *stop being a game.* It had to turn back into a mere story.

And that's why I've changed my mind. Interactive may be the future of pop culture, but it's not the future of fiction. Dungeons & Dragons is fun to play, but a bunch of role-players making shit up as they go along are never going to craft the kind of intricately-plotted stories, the nuanced characters, the careful foreshadowing and layers of meaning that characterize the best fiction. I actually feel kind of stupid for not having realized that all along. The tech may get magical. The tech might get *self-aware*, for all I know. But until someone upgrades the *players*, we old-school novelists will still have jobs.

They just won't pay very well.

Martin Luther King and the Vampire Rights League

BLOG JAN 31 2012

Some of you may remember my ruminations on the evolutionary significance of sociopathy, my tentative musings that it may be not so much a pathology as an adaptation[1], and my almost pathetic relief when people with actual credentials wonder the same thing[2] and thus make me look like less of a wing nut. In an attempt to regain that status I've gone further, describing autistics and sociopaths as entirely different "cognitive subspecies"—only to have Marnie Rice out of Penetanguishene one-up me by describing sociopathy as a process of "speciation". (It won't surprise anyone to learn that *Echopraxia* continues to play with this theme—even going so far as to steal a line from cognitive neuroscientist Laurent Mottron, who claims that describing autistics as people who are *bad at socializing but good at numbers* makes about as much sense as describing dogs as a kind of cat that's *bad at climbing but good at fetching slippers*.)

As everyone agrees, the word for getting rid of a whole subspecies is not "cure." I'm not quite sure what the right word might be, but it's probably somewhere between *extermination* and *genocide*. (Let's call it *cultural genocide*, in deference to the fact that the biological organism persists even though its identity has been eradicated.) We're even seeing the flowering of something like civil rights advocacy, in the form of the neurodiversity movement that's been picking up steam over the past decade or two.

From what I can see out here, though, that movement seems to be an Autistics-Only club: what's lacking is any sort of pro-Sociopath lobby along the lines of, say, the American Vampire League from *True Blood*. One would think that both groups would warrant the same kind of advocacy; the arguments of cognitive subspecieshood apply equally to both, after all. You're stepping onto a pretty slippery slope when you claim that the occupation of a distinct neurological niche warrants acceptance of one group, but this other group over here—no more responsible for its wiring than the first—should still be wiped ou—er, *cured*. After all, only a small proportion of sociopaths are actual criminals; most of them operate entirely within the limits of established legal, religious, and political systems. Hell, it's hard to look at the *Citizens Uniteds* and Rupert Murdochs of the world and conclude that sociopaths didn't play a major role in building those systems in the first place. And after all, both sociopaths *and* autistics tend to be lacking in the whole empathy department. [Late-breaking edit: it has been brought to my attention that the word *empathy* is an imprecise beast which contains at least two different processing modes; and that autistics can actually score higher than baselines along the affective scale[3]. Thanks to Andrew Hickey for pointing out the problem.] So where's the neurodiversity community when you need it, hmm? Where are the advocates speaking out on behalf of sociopath interests (beyond Goldman Sachs and the other 0.1-percenters, I mean)?

Here's one: SociopathWorld.com.

I do not know the name of the person behind "Sociopath World"; doubtless that's by design. She (I *think* it's a she) refers to herself merely as "The Sociopath" on her contact page, as "M.E." on Twitter, and as ME@SOCIOPATHWORLD.COM when she hands out her address (which makes me doubt that the "M.E." Twitter handle is an actual set of initials). No matter. This is either a labor-intensive hoax, or your one-stop-shopping center for the interested empath (they call us "Empaths," apparently, which I find both more precise and less condescending than the "neurotypical" label the autism-spectrum types seem to prefer). The most popular posts end up on the FAQ list: *Do Sociopaths Love? Are Sociopaths Self-Aware? Am I a Sociopath? Can Sociopaths Be "Good"?* There are helpful how-to pointers: How to break up with a sociopath, for example.

There are pop-culture observations: whether the new twenty-first-century *Sherlock* really *is* a sociopath in the world of fiction, whether Lady Gaga is in real life, the potential infiltration of sociopaths into Occupy Wall Street drum circles. There's a forum, rife with trolls and assholes and deleted posts; but there's also legitimate debate there. And surprisingly, it also seems to function as a kind of support group for people in emotional distress.

You can even, I shit you not, order a Sociopath World t-shirt.

So. M.E. is out there, fighting the good fight. She's getting noticed (at least, her blog gets shitloads more comments than mine, not that that's a high bar to clear). She shows up on the occasional psych blogroll. So now, I'm going to sit back and see if the neurodiversity community is willing to pick up the torch. If she *is* trying to kickstart the American Vampire League, though, I think she's fighting an uphill battle.[4]

Which only makes sense. Martin Luther King Jr. didn't have an easy time of it either.

2 HTTP://BOINGBOING.NET/2006/10/11/IS-AUTISM-A-DISORDER.HTML

3 HTTP://WWW.COG.PSY.RUHR-UNI-BOCHUM.DE/PAPERS/2007/
ROGERS%282007%29_JAUTISMDEVDISORD.PDF

4 She's well aware of this, of course. She discusses that double standard in her post "Am I My Asperger Brother's Keeper?", in which she points out that the most obvious difference between Aspies and sociopaths is that the latter group has better social skills. So why compassion for one group, and vilification of the other? Is it really that the social awkwardness of the Aspies allows us to regard them as children, and therefore unthreatening? Are we really such condescending assholes? Of course we are. But pretty obviously, sociopaths with charming smiles and firm handshakes are also more likely to prey on us than is someone who has trouble even making eye contact; sociopaths *are* more dangerous, empirically. M.E. is not beyond pushing her own agenda. (She points to studies suggesting that autistics can be serial killers too—Jeffrey Dahmer gets cited as a case in point—but there are too many gaps in that claim for me to accept it at face value. As I understand it, Dahmer did okay in the social skills department.)

If you got itchy when I started talking about civil rights for vampires/
sociopaths, you're gonna *love* this: civil rights for killer whales.

Or perhaps more accurately, civil rights for *killer* whales. Literally.
One of these guys, Tilikum by (Human-ascribed) name, killed one
of his jailers in broad daylight and, according to the BBC, has been
"linked to two other deaths"[1]. Regardless, People for the Ethical
Treatment of Animals has launched a lawsuit in the US District
Court in San Diego, on behalf of Tilikum and four other SeaWorld
orcas, charging that their incarceration violates the 13th Amendment
against slavery—and the judge, while skeptical, hasn't yet thrown
out the case. A bemused fourth estate is all over the story for the
moment[2], although it remains to be seen how much traction accrues
to any PETA action that doesn't involve naked women in cages.

This issue is especially resonant to a fallen marine mammalo-
gist such as myself. I've worked with captive marine mammals on
occasion, even done a bit of theoretical work on orcas. During my

short-lived and ill-advised tenure with the North Pacific Universities Marine Mammal Research Consortium I grew familiar with the toxic backstage political environment at the Vancouver Aquarium (which, for all its toxicity, was significantly better than anything I ever heard coming out of SeaWorld). Back in the nineties I presented an intervenor report at the Vancouver Parks Board hearings on ending the Aquarium's captive whale displays, which nearly got me a job until I remarked in those hearings on the obvious hypocrisy of the Board itself. (That also resulted in the appearance of the misleading and inflammatory story "Mercy Killing suggested for Aquarium Whales[3]" in the *Vancouver Sun*. Say, if anyone out there happens to encounter Petti Fong standing on a curb by heavy traffic, do me a favor and push her under a bus?)

All these experiences even inspired my co-authorship of a behind-the-scenes story in which we finally crack the orca language and discover that they're even bigger assholes than we are. One of the few *intentionally* funny stories I've ever written, and lemme tell you it *reeks* of verisimilitude right down to the names of the characters.

So here we are, with the animal-rights movement putting their money where their rhetoric is and actually trying to get Tilikum *et al* classified as slaves in a court of law. I've gone over the lawsuit itself, and in terms of orca biology and behavior it's pretty tight. Para 17 goes a bit overboard in describing orca feeding as "social events carried out in the context of an array of traditions and rituals," which implies some kind of cross-species mind-reading technology that certainly wasn't in wide use back in *my* day. Para 41 commits a small lie of omission when it states "In nature, aggression between members of a pod, or between pods in the same resident clan or community . . . is virtually unknown"; true, but relations between resident and *transient* pods are somewhat more antagonistic. Still. The stuff on social bonds, brain structure, habitat requirements—

not to mention the generally barbaric treatment of orcas in captivity—is pretty much spot-on.

Significantly, SeaWorld doesn't challenge any of these facts. They've stated that charges of abuse are utterly irrelevant as far as they're concerned. From what I've seen reported, their defense boils down to two basic claims: 1) The whole case is bullshit because the Constitution only applies to people, which killer whales aren't; and 2) if PETA wins this case, it's open season on everything from zoos to the law-enforcement's K9 programs. "We're talking about hell unleashed," their lawyer is quoted as saying.

I have problems with both those points.

First, the property-not-people angle. PETA argues that dismissing orcas as property "is the same argument that was used against African Americans and women before their constitutional rights were protected". SeaWorld rebuts that that's an entirely inappropriate analogy because "both women and African Americans are people for which the Constitution was written to protect." This being yet another iteration of the *founding fathers know best* argument so beloved by the Tea Party: the Constitution is gospel, and cannot be changed.

Correct me if I'm wrong, but didn't the original Constitution define blacks as less than human, too? As in, one slave equals three-fifths of a "real" man, at least for purposes of political representation? Citing African Americans and women doesn't exactly bolster SeaWorld's case—although they've also made the claim that the whole whales-as-slaves argument "defies common sense," so they've always got the Spluttering Outrage and Handwaving defense to fall back on.

More telling, though, is Argument #2: that if the tewwowists win, "All hell breaks loose." Which is another way of saying "It mustn't be, so it isn't."

Don't even *think* about the abuse of the organism, they are saying; it pales in the shadow of the carnage and inconvenience that will be brought down upon us if the whalehuggers have their way. How will the hundreds employed by zoos and marine parks make ends meet? How will the police protect us from evil-doers without furry canine slaves to do their bidding? What about the innocent middle-class family with the pet cockatoo or the beagle in the back yard? Will their doors be the next to get kicked in by PETA's stormtroopers? The only argument I *haven't* heard yet—and I heard it often enough from the mouths of the Vancouver Aquarium's PR hacks, so I suppose it's only a matter of time—is *Won't somebody think of the CHILDREN?*

I don't know why we should have to explain the implications of the law to a lawyer, but: if PETA wins, then captive orcas will be slaves. Legally. And good luck making the case that we shouldn't free slaves because it would force the manager of SeaWorld to look for another job.

Of course, whether we even *can* free the slaves—after decades of atrophy and chronic wasting in captivity—is a whole other issue (one dealt with at greater length in that intervenor report I mentioned earlier). Rehab certainly didn't end well for Keiko. But that's a logistic issue, not a logical one. We're not focusing on the nuts and bolts of extended physiotherapy for a creature the size of a school bus; we're focusing on whether a creature whose emotional and cognitive circuitry is at least comparable to ours, whether something capable of complex problem-solving, complex community relationships, and complex *suffering* warrants at least as much respect as some brain-dead hydrocephalic on life support—even if it does have flukes instead of feet. You probably know where I stand on that: just two posts back I threw my lot in with the bonobos over the illusory interests of Terri Schiavo.

I don't believe that any rights are intrinsic. There's no inevitable law of nature that says we have to show any regard for the suffering of any being—human or otherwise—that doesn't increase our own fitness in some way. But there's nothing that *prevents* such regard either; and if we are going to extend it, we should at least be consistent in the dissemination of our empathy. In that context, Peter Singer was right in *Animal Liberation*: the question is not so much *Can it think?* as *Can it suffer?*

There is no doubt that orcas can suffer. They can suffer far more than those little blobs of cells the right-to-life types get so worked up about, those embryos that don't even have a neocortex atop their neural tubes. They suffer more than any of a number of vegetative human beings who owe their continued oblivious existence to ventilators and blood scrubbers. Personally, though, I don't think that will make a difference; I think the defense, for all the incoherence of its arguments, will ultimately prevail—not because they are right, but because it's just too damned inconvenient to be wrong. If you think too hard about this sort of thing, you'll recognize the injustice; recognizing the injustice, you might feel obligated to do something about it. But that means making changes in the way you live. It means giving up things you've grown accustomed to. It means getting off the couch. Better *not* to think about it. Better to just look the other way.

The only alternative is to state flat-out that you really don't *care* whether abuse and suffering is rampant in the world. The suffering will continue, but at least nobody can accuse you of hypocrisy. Which may be, I suppose, why SeaWorld's lawyer came right out and said just that: it's not *about* the suffering.

Maybe I didn't give the dude enough credit.

[**Late-breaking Postscript:** Even as I format this post for upload, the *LA Times* reports that U.S. District Judge Jeffrey Miller has thrown out PETA's lawsuit on the grounds that whales are animals, not people[4]. Pass the remote and the pork rinds.]

1   HTTP://WWW.BBC.CO.UK/NEWS/WORLD-US-CANADA-12920267

2 SEE: HTTP://WWW.THEGLOBEANDMAIL.COM/NEWS/WORLD/WORLDVIEW/
ENSLAVED-KILLER-WHALES-CASE-MAY-MARK-NEW-FRONTIER-IN-ANIMAL-RIGHTS/
ARTICLE2329280/, HTTP://WWW.CBSNEWS.COM/8301-201 _ 162-57372606/SLAVERY-
PROTECTIONS-FOR-ANIMALS-JUDGE-TO-DECIDE/, and HTTP://WWW.CBC.CA/NEWS/
TECHNOLOGY/STORY/2012/02/07/KILLER-WHALE-LAWSUIT.HTML
3 The *Vancouver Sun*, 18/9/1996, pB11.
4 HTTP://LATIMESBLOGS.LATIMES.COM/LANOW/2012/02/JUDGE-TOSSES-OUT-
LAWSUIT-SEEKING-FREEDOM-FOR-ORCAS-AT-SEAWORLD-1.HTML

Gods and Gamma.

Here's something interesting: "God Has Sent Me To You" by Arzy and Schurr, in *Epilepsy & Behavior* (not to mention the usual pop-sci sites that ran with it a couple weeks back[1]). Middle-aged Jewish male, practicing but not religious, goes off his meds as part of an ongoing treatment for *grand mal* seizures (although evidently "tonic-clonic" seizures is now the approved term). Freed from the drugs, he is touched by God. He sees Yahweh approaching, converses with It, accepts a new destiny: he is now The Chosen One, assigned by the Almighty to bring Redemption to the People of Israel. He rips the leads off his scalp and stalks out into the hospital corridors in search of disciples.

That's right: they got it all on tape. Seven seconds of low-gamma spikes in the 30–40Hz range (I didn't know what that was either—turns out it's a pattern of neural activity, gamma waves, associated with "conscious attention").

(The figures—which show the usual sexy false-color hot-spots on an MRI—might lead you astray if you don't read the fine print. They didn't actually get God's footprints on an MRI. They got them on one of those lo-tech EEGs that traces squiggly lines across a display, then they photoshopped the relevant spikes onto an archival MRI image for display purposes.)

Regardless, the findings themselves are really interesting. For one thing, the God spikes manifested on the left prefrontal cortex, although the seizure was concentrated in the right temporal. For another, God took Its own sweet time taking the stage: the conversion event happened eight hours *after* the seizure. They're still trying to figure out what to make of all this.

The behavioral manifestations are classic, though. This guy didn't just *believe* he was the chosen one; he *knew* it down in the gut, with the same certainty that you know your arm is attached to your shoulder. When asked what he was going to do with his disciples when he recruited them, he admitted that he had no plan, that he didn't need one: God would tell him what to do.

God didn't, of course. They managed to shut the psychosis down with olanzapine, returned the patient to normalcy a few hours after the event. As far as I know he's back at work, his buddies on the factory floor blissfully unrecruited.

But what if he hadn't gotten better?

This is hardly the first time temporal-lobe epilepsy has been implicated in religious fanaticism; medical correlates extend back to the seventies, and tonic-clonic seizures have been trotted out to retrospectively explain martyrs and prophets going all the way back to the Old Testament. Perhaps the most famous such case involved Saul of Tarsus.

You know that guy. First-century dude, dual citizen (Saul was his Jewish name, Paul his Roman one—let's just call him SPaul). Didn't much like these newfangled Christian cults that were springing up everywhere following the crucifixion. His main claim to fame was being the coat-check guy at the stoning of Stephen, up until he was struck blind by a bright light *en route* to Damascus.

God spoke to SPaul, too. Converted him from nemesis to champion on the spot. There was no olanzapine available. It's been two thousand years and we're still picking up the pieces.

Epilepsy isn't the only explanation that's been put forth for SPaul's conversion. Some have argued for a near-miss by a meteorite, on the grounds that the blinding light couldn't have been hallucinatory since Saul's traveling companions also saw it. That's true, according to some accounts; other versions have those same companions hearing God's voice but *not* seeing the light. If I had to choose (and if I was denied the option of dismissing the whole damn tale as retconned religious propaganda), I'd believe the latter iteration, and chalk those sounds up to a bout of ululation during the seizure. Speaking in tongues, blindness—most dramatically, of course, the whole hyper-religiosity thing—are all consistent with temporal-lobe epilepsy.

Unlike his (vastly less-influential) 21st-century counterpart, SPaul was not charged with Redeeming the Israelites: Jesus already had dibs on those guys. Instead, Paul claimed that Yahweh had assigned him to preach to the Gentiles, a much vaster market, albeit not the one for whom Christ's teachings were originally intended. Biblical scholar Hugh Schonfield speculates that the reason SPaul had such a hate-on for Jesus in the first place might have been because SPaul regarded *himself* as the Messiah. (Apparently every second person you met back then regarded themselves as The Chosen One, thanks to Scriptures which promised that such a savior was due Any Day Now, and to ancillary prophecies vague enough to apply to anyone from Rocket Raccoon to Donald Trump). This would imply that SPaul's roadside conversion was not an isolated event, and sure enough there's evidence of recurring hallucinations, paranoia, and delusions of grandeur at other times in his life (although these may be more consistent with schizophrenia or bipolar disorder than with epilepsy[2]). According to Schonfield, SPaul—denied the job of Jewish Messiah—took on the Christ's-Ambassador-to-the-Gentiles gig as a kind of consolation prize.

The irony, of course, is that modern Christianity is arguably far more reflective of SPaul's teachings than of Jesus's. Cue two thousand years of crusade, inquisition, homophobia, and misogyny.

So let us all bow our heads in a moment of silent gratitude both for the miracle of modern pharmaceuticals, and for the diligent neurologists at Hadassah Hebrew University Medical Center. Thanks to them, we may have dodged a bullet.

This time, at least.

1 See: HTTP://WWW.SCIENCEALERT.COM/NEUROSCIENTISTS-HAVE-RECORDED-THE-BRAIN-ACTIVITY-OF-A-MAN-AT-THE-EXACT-MOMENT-HE-SAW-GOD
and HTTP://BLOGS.DISCOVERMAGAZINE.COM/NEUROSKEPTIC/2016/05/14/7755/
2 HTTP://NEURO.PSYCHIATRYONLINE.ORG/DOI/PDF/10.1176/APPI.NEUROPSYCH.11090214

"PyrE. Make them tell you what it is."

At the end of one of the classic novels of TwenCen SF[1], the protagonist—an illiterate third-class mechanic's mate named Gulliver Foyle, bootstrapped by his passion for revenge into the most powerful man in the solar system—gets hold of a top-secret doomsday weapon. Think of it as a kind of antimatter which can be detonated by the mere act of *thinking* about detonating it. He travels across the world in a matter of minutes, appearing in city after city, throwing slugs of the stuff into the hands of astonished and uncomprehending crowds and vanishing again. Finally the authorities catch up with him: *"Do you know what you've done?"* they ask, horrified by the utter impossibility of stuffing the genie back in the bottle.

He does: "I've handed life and death back to the people who do the living and the dying."

We are approaching such a moment now, I think. I'm speaking, of course, about the new gengineered ferret-killing—and potentially, people-decimating—variant of H5N1. And call me crazy, but I hope the people with their hands on that button take their lead from Gully Foyle.

For the benefit of anyone who hasn't been following, here's the story so far: your garden-variety bird flu has always been a bug that combines a really nasty mortality rate (>50%) with fairly pathetic transmission, at least among us bipeds (it doesn't spread person-to-person; human victims generally get it from contact with infected birds). But influenza's a slippery bitch, always mutating (which is why you keep hearing about new strains of flu every year); so Ron Fouchier, Yoshihiro Kawaoka, and assorted colleagues set out to poke H5N1 with a stick and see what it might take to turn it into something *really* nasty.

The answer was: less than anybody suspected. A few tweaks, a handful of mutations, and a bite from a radioactive spider turned poor old underachieving bird flu into an airborne superbug that killed 75% of the ferrets it infected. (Apparently ferrets are the go-to human analogues for this sort of thing. I did not know that.) By way of comparison, the Spanish Flu—which took out somewhere between 50-100 million people back in 1918—had a mortality rate of maybe 3%.

When Fouchier and Kawaoka's teams went to publish these findings, the birdshit really hit the fan. The papers passed through the US National Science Advisory Board for Biosecurity *en route* to *Science* and *Nature*; and that august body strongly suggested that all how-to details be redacted prior to publication. Never mind that the very foundation of the scientific method involves replication of results, which in turn depends upon precise and accurate description of methodology: those very methodological details, the board warned, "could enable replication of the experiments by those who would seek to do harm."[2]

Both *Science* and *Nature* have delayed publication of the scorching spuds while various parties figure out what to do. Fouchier and Kawaoka have also announced a 60-day hiatus on further re-search,[3] although it's pretty clear that they intend to use this time to present their case to a skittish public, rather than re-examining it themselves.

Then what?

Opinions on the subject seem to follow a bimodal distribu-tion: let's call the first of those peaks *Bioterrorist Mountain,* and the other *Peak PublicHealth.* Those who've planted their flags on the former summit argue that this kind of research should never be released (or even, some say, performed[4]), because if it is, the tewwowists win. Those on the latter peak argue that nature could well pull off this kind of experiment on her own, and we damn well better do our homework so we know how to deal when she does. Somewhere in between lie the Foothills-of-Accidental-Release, whose denizens point out that even in a bad-guy-free world, chances of someone accidentally tracking the superbug out of the lab are pretty high (one set of calculations puts those odds as high as 80% within four years, even if the tech specs are kept scrupulously under wraps).

Right up front, I do not trust the residents of Bioterrorist Mountain. The National Science Advisory Board for Biosecurity has a diverse makeup, including representatives from the Departments of Commerce and Energy, Justice, the Interior—and oh, Defense and our old friends at Homeland Security. They've already read the details that they would deny to others, and you can be damn sure that none of *them* are volunteering to have their memories erased in the name of global security. They're not so much worried about the efforts of *all* who'd seek to do harm; they're really only worried about what the *other guys* might do. Anyone who thinks the US wouldn't gladly use the fruits of such labor against those it considers a threat has not been paying attention to the recent debates among Republican presidential contenders. And once the government starts deciding who gets to see what parts of this or that scientific paper, you have in effect (as one online commenter points out) "essentially a biological weapons program."[5]

Let's assume, though, that we live in some parallel reality where realpolitick doesn't exist, *Truth Justice and the American Way* is not an oxymoron, and the motives of those who'd keep these data under wraps really are purely defensive. Even in the face of such driven-snow purity, suppressing potentially dangerous biomedical findings only works if the other guys can't reinvent your particular wheel: if either the bug itself is hard to come by, or the villains from Derkaderkastan don't know the difference between a thermos and a thermocycler. But avian flu isn't uranium-235, and one of the most surprising findings about this bug was how *easy* it was to weaponise. (Up until now, everyone figured that increased contagion would go hand-in-hand with decreased lethality.)

Suppression might be a valid option if your enemies have about as much biological expertise as, say, Rick Santorum. That is not a gamble any sane person would make. To quote the head of the Centre on Global Health Security in London:

> "[T]he WHO Advisory Group of Independent Experts that reviews the smallpox research programme noted this year that DNA sequencing, cloning and gene synthesis could now allow *de novo* synthesis of the entire *Variola* virus genome and creation of a live virus, using publicly available sequence information, at a cost of about US$200,000 or less."[6]

On the other hand, you have the very real likelihood of an accidental outbreak; of natural mutation to increased virulence; of the bad guys figuring out the appropriate tweaks independent of Kawaoka's data. In which case you've got a few thousand epidemiologists who've been frozen out of the Culture Club, improvising by the seat of their pants as they go up against something that makes the Black Plague look like a case of acne.

The folks on Peak PublicHealth believe that this is too important a danger to be thought of in terms of anything as trivial as national security[7]. This is a global health issue; this is a pandemic just waiting to happen, with a kill rate like we've never seen before. Fouchier's and Kawaoka's research has given us a headsup. We can get ahead of this thing and figure out how to stop it before it ever becomes a threat; and the way to do that is to get the community at large working on the problem. The second-last thing you want is a species-decimating plague whose cure is in the hands of a single self-interested political entity. (Admittedly, this is marginally better than the *last* thing you want, which is a species-decimating plague with no cure at all.)

Back in 2005, Peter Palese and his buddies reverse-engineered the 1918 Spanish Flu virus. They published their findings in full. The usual suspects cried out, but now we know how to kill Spanish Flu. That particular doomsday scenario has been averted. It should come as no surprise that Palese plants his flag on Peak PublicHealth, and he makes the case far more eloquently (and with infinitely greater expertise) than I ever could.[8]

And down here in the corner, a recent paper in *PLoS One* that seems curiously relevant to the current discussion, although none of the pundits involved seems to have noticed: "Broad-Spectrum Antiviral Therapeutics", by Rider *et al*.[9] It reports on a new antiviral treatment that goes by the delightfully skiffy acronym DRACO, which induces suicide in virus-infected mammalian cells and leaves healthy cells alone. It's been tested on 15 different viruses—Dengue, H1N1, encephalomyelitis, kissing cousins of West Nile and hemorrhagic fever, to name a few. It's proven effective against all of them in culture. And it keys on RNA helices produced ubiquitously and exclusively by viruses, so—if

I'm reading this right—it could potentially be a cure-all for viral infections generally.

We may *already* be closing on a cure for the ferret-killer, and a lot of its relatives besides.

So, yeah. We can either try to stuff the genie back in the bottle, now that everyone knows how easy it is to make one of their own. Or we can give life and death back to the people who do the living and the dying.

I say, get it out there.

1 *The Stars My Destination* by Alfred Bester.

2 HTTP://WWW.NATURE.COM/NEWS/CALL-TO-CENSOR-FLU-STUDIES-DRAWS-FIRE-1.9729

3 HTTP://WWW.NATURE.COM/NATURE/JOURNAL/VAOP/NCURRENT/FULL/481443A.HTML

4 HTTP://WWW.THEBULLETIN.ORG/WEB-EDITION/COLUMNISTS/LAURA-H-KAHN/GOING-VIRAL

5 Of course, you could point out that the US has doubtless had its own biowarfare program running for decades, and I would not disagree. That doesn't change the point I'm making here, though.

6 HTTP://WWW.NATURE.COM/NATURE/JOURNAL/V481/N7381/FULL/481257A.HTML#/DAVID-L-HEYMANN-WE-WILL-ALWAYS-NEED-VACCINES

7 HTTP://WWW.NATURE.COM/NATURE/JOURNAL/V481/N7381/FULL/481257A.HTML

8 HTTP://WWW.NATURE.COM/NEWS/DON-T-CENSOR-LIFE-SAVING-SCIENCE-1.9777

9 HTTP://WWW.NCBI.NLM.NIH.GOV/PMC/ARTICLES/PMC3144912/

Understanding Sarah Palin:
Or, God Is In The Wattles

BLOG OCT 8 2008

Here's a question for you. Why hasn't natural selection driven the religious right to extinction?

You should forgive me for asking. After all, here is a group of people who base their lives on patently absurd superstitions that fly in the face of empirical evidence. It's as if I suddenly chose to believe that I could walk off the edges of cliffs with impunity; you would not expect me to live very long. You would expect me to leave few if any offspring. You would expect me to get *weeded out*.

And yet, this obnoxious coterie of halfwits—people openly and explicitly contemptuous of "intellectuals" and "evilutionists" and, you know, anyone who actually spends their time *learning* stuff—they not only refuse to die, they appear to rule the world. Some Alaskan airhead who can't even fake the name of a newspaper, who can't seem to say anything without getting it wrong, who bald-facedly states in a formal debate setting that she's not even going to *try* to answer questions she finds unpalatable (or she would state as much, if she could say "unpalatable" without tripping over her own tongue)—this person, this *behavior*, is regarded as successful even by her detractors. The primary reason for her popularity amongst the all-powerful "low-information voters"? In-your-face religious fundamentalism and an eye tic that would make a Tourette's victim blush.

You might suggest that my analogy is a bit loopy: young-earth creationism may fly in the face of reason, but it hardly has as much immediate survival relevance as my own delusory immunity to gravity. I would disagree. The Christian Church has been an anvil around the neck of scientific progress for centuries. It took the Catholics four hundred years to apologize to Galileo; a hundred fifty for an Anglican middle-management type to admit that they might owe one to Darwin too[1] (although his betters immediately slapped him down for it[2]). Even today, we fight an endless series of skirmishes with fundamentalists who keep trying to sneak creationism in through the back door of science classes across the continent. (I'm given to understand that Islamic fundies are doing pretty much the same thing in Europe.) More people in the US believe in angels than in natural selection. And has anyone *not* noticed that religious fundamentalists also tend to be climate-change deniers?

Surely, any cancer that attacks the very intellect of a society would put the society itself at a competitive disadvantage. Surely, tribes founded on secular empiricism would develop better technology, better medicines, better hands-on understanding of The Way Things Work, than tribes gripped by primeval cloud-worshipping superstition. Why, then, are there so few social systems based on empiricism, and why are god-grovellers so powerful across the globe? Why do the Olympians keep getting their asses handed to them by a bunch of intellectual paraplegics?

The great thing about science is, it can even answer ugly questions like this. And a lot of pieces have been falling into place lately. Many of them have to do with the brain's fundamental role as a pattern-matcher.

Let's start with Jennifer Whitson's 2008 study in *Science*[3]. It turns out that the less control people feel they have over their lives, the more likely they are to perceive images in random visual static; the more likely they are to see connections and conspiracies in unrelated events. The more powerless you feel, the more likely you'll see faces in the clouds. (Belief in astrology also goes up during times of social stress.)

Some of you may remember that I speculated along such lines back during my rant[4] against that evangelical abortion Francis Collins wrote while pretending to be a scientist; but thanks to Jennifer Whitson and her buddies, speculation resolves into fact. Obama was dead on the mark when he said that people cling to religion and guns during hard times. The one arises from loss of control, and the other from an attempt to get some back.

Leaving Lepidoptera (*please* don't touch the displays, little boy, heh heh heh—Oh, cute . . .)—moving to the next aisle, we have Arachnida, the spiders. And according to findings reported by Douglas Oxley and his colleagues[5], right-wingers are significantly more scared of these furry little arthropods than left-wingers tend to be: at least, conservatives show stronger stress responses than liberals to "threatening" pictures of large spiders perched on human faces.

It's not a one-off effect, either. Measured in terms of blink amplitude and skin conductance, the strongest stress responses to a variety of threat stimuli occurred among folks who "favor defense spending, capital punishment, patriotism, and the Iraq War." In contrast, those who "support foreign aid, liberal immigration policies, pacifism, and gun control" tended to be pretty laid-back when confronted with the same stimuli. Oxley *et al* close off the piece by speculating that differences in political leanings may result from differences in the way the amygdala is wired—and that said wiring, in turn, has a genetic component. The implication is that right-wing/left-wing beliefs may to some extent be hardwired, making them relatively immune to the rules of evidence and reasoned debate. (Again, this *is* pure speculation. The experiments didn't extend into genetics. But it would explain a lot.)

One cool thing about the aforementioned studies is that they have relatively low sample sizes, both in the two-digit range. Any pattern that shows statistical significance in a small sample is likely to be pretty damn strong; both of these are.

Now let's go back a ways, to a Cornell Study from 1999 called "Unskilled and Unaware of It: How Difficulties in Recognizing One's Own Incompetence Lead to Inflated Self-Assessments"[6]— the seminal paper that introduced the world to the "Dunning-Kruger Effect". It's a depressing study, with depressing findings:

- People tend to overestimate their own smarts.
- Stupid people tend to overestimate their smarts more than the truly smart do.
- Smart people tend to assume that everyone else is as smart as they are; they honestly can't understand why dumber people just don't "get it," because it doesn't occur to them that those people actually *are* dumb.
- Stupid people, in contrast, tend to not only regard themselves as smarter than everyone else, they tend to regard truly smart people as especially stupid. This holds true *even when these people are shown empirical proof that they are less competent than those they deride.*

So. The story so far:

1. People perceive nonexistent patterns, meanings, and connections in random data when they are stressed, scared, and generally feel a loss of control in their own lives.
2. Right-wing people are more easily scared/stressed than left-wing people. They are also more likely to cleave to authority figures and protectionist policies. There *may* be a genetic component to this.
3. The dumber you are, the less likely you'll be able to recognize your own stupidity, and the lower will be your opinion of people who are smarter than you (even while those people keep treating you as though you are just as smart as they are).

Therefore (I would argue) the so-called "right wing" is especially predisposed to believe in moralizing, authoritarian Invisible Friends. And the dumber individuals are, the more immune they are to reason. **Note that, to paraphrase John Stuart Mill, I am *not saying that conservatives are stupid*** (I myself know some very smart conservatives), **but that stupid people tend to be conservative.** Whole other thing.

What we have, so far, is a biological mechanism for the prevalence of religious superstition in right-wing populations. What we need now is a reason why such populations tend to be so damn *successful*, given the obvious shortcomings of superstition as opposed to empiricism.

Which brings us to Norenzayan and Shariff's review paper in last week's *Science* on "The Origin and Evolution of Religious Prosociality"[7]. They start off by reminding us of previous studies, to get us in the mood. For example, people are less likely to cheat on an assigned task if the lab tech lets slip that the ghost of a girl who was murdered *in this very building* was sighted down the hall the other day.

That's right. Plant the thought that some ghost might be watching you, and you become more trustworthy. Even sticking a picture of a pair of eyes on the wall reduces the incidence of cheating, even though no one would consciously mistake a drawing of eyes for the real thing. Merely planting the *idea* of surveillance seems to be enough to improve one's behavior. (I would also remind you of an earlier 'crawl entry reporting that so-called "altruistic" acts in our society tend to occur mainly when someone else is watching, although N&S don't cite that study in their review.)

They also cite a 2003 study by Sosis and Alcorta, showing that religious communes survive longer than secular ones—and that among that subset of religious communes, the ones that last longest are those with the most onerous, repressive, authoritarian rules.

And so on. Norenzayan and Shariff trot out study after study, addressing a variety of questions that may seem unrelated at first. If, as theorists suggest, human social groupings can only reach 150 members or so before they collapse or fragment from internal stress, why does the real world serve up so many groupings of greater size? (Turns out that the larger the size of a group, the more likely that its members believe in a moralizing, peeping-Tom god.) Are religious people more likely than nonreligious ones to help out someone in distress? (Not so much.) What's the most common denominator tying together acts of charity by the religious? (Social optics. "Self-reported belief in God or self-reported religious devotion," the paper remarks wryly, "was not a reliable indicator of generous behavior in anonymous settings.") And why is it that religion seems especially prevalent in areas with chronic water and resource shortages?

It seems to come down to two things: surveillance and freeloading. The surveillance element is pretty self-evident. People engage in goodly behavior primarily to increase their own social status, to make themselves appear more valuable to observers. But by that same token, there's no point in being an upstanding citizen if there *are* no observers. In anonymous settings, you can cheat.

You can also cheat in *non*-anonymous settings, if your social group is large enough to get lost in. In small groups, everybody knows your name; if you put out your hand at dinner but couldn't be bothered hunting and gathering, if you sleep soundly at night and never stand guard at the perimeter, it soon becomes clear to everyone that you're a parasite. You'll get the shit kicked out of you, and be banished from the tribe. But as social groupings become larger you lose that everyone-knows-everyone safeguard. You can move from burb to burb, sponging and moving on before anyone gets wise—

—*unless* the costs of joining that community in the first place are so bloody high that it just isn't worth the effort. This is where the onerous, old-testament social rituals come into play.

Norenzayan and Shariff propose that

> "the cultural spread of religious prosociality may have promoted stable levels of cooperation in large groups, where reputational and reciprocity incentives are insufficient. If so, then reminders of God may not only reduce cheating, but may also increase generosity toward strangers as much as reminders of secular institutions promoting prosocial behavior."

And they cite their own data to support it. But they also admit that "professions of religious belief can be easily faked," so that

> "evolutionary pressures must have favored costly religious commitment, such as ritual participation and various restrictions on behavior, diet, and life-style, that validates the sincerity of otherwise unobservable religious belief."

In other words, anyone can talk the talk. But if you're willing to give all your money to the church and your twelve-year-old daughter to the patriarch, dude, you're obviously one of us.

Truth in Advertising is actually a pretty common phenomenon in nature. Chicken wattles are a case in point; what the hell *good* are those things, anyway? What do they do? Turns out that they display information about a bird's health, in a relatively unfakeable way. The world is full of creatures who lie about their attributes. Bluegills spread their gill covers when facing off against a competitor; cats go all puffy and arch-backed when getting ready to tussle. Both behaviors serve to make the performer seem larger than he really is—they lie, in other words. Chicken wattles aren't like that; they more honestly reflect the internal state of the animal. It takes metabolic energy to keep them plump and colorful. A rooster loaded down with parasites is a sad thing to see, his wattles all pale and dilapidated; a female can see instantly what kind of shape he's in by looking at those telltales. You might look to the peacock's tail for another example, or the red ass of a healthy baboon. (We humans have our own telltales—lips, breasts, ripped pecs and triceps—but you haven't been able to count on those ever since implants, steroids, and Revlon came down the pike.) "Religious signaling" appears to be another case in point. As Norenzayan and Shariff point out, "religious groups imposing more costly requirements have members who are more committed." Hence,

> "[r]eligious communes were found to outlast those motivated by secular ideologies, such as socialism . . . [R]eligious communes imposed more than twice as many costly requirements (including food taboos and fasts, constraints on material possessions, marriage, sex, and communication with the outside world) than secular ones . . . Importantly for costly religious

signaling, the number of costly requirements predicted
religious commune longevity after the study controlled
for population size and income and the year the commune was founded . . . Finally, religious ideology was
no longer a predictor of commune longevity, once the
number of costly requirements was statistically controlled, which suggests that the survival advantage of
religious communes was due to the greater costly com-
mitment of their members, rather than other aspects of
religious ideology."

Reread that last line. It's not the ideology *per se* that confers
the advantage; it's the cost of the signal that matters. Once again,
we strip away the curtain and God stands revealed as ecological
energetics, writ in a fancy font.

These findings aren't carved in stone. A lot of the studies are
correlational, the models are in their infancy, yadda yadda yadda.
But the data are coming in thick and fast, and they point to a
pretty plausible model:

- Fear and stress result in loss of perceived control;
- Loss of perceived control results in increased perception of nonexistent patterns (N&S again: "The tendency to detect agency
in nature likely supplied the cognitive template that supports
the pervasive belief in supernatural agents");
- Those with right-wing political beliefs tend to scare more
easily;
- Authoritarian religious systems based on a snooping, surveil-
lant God, with high membership costs and antipathy towards
outsiders, are more cohesive, less invadable by cheaters, and
longer-lived. They also tend to flourish in high-stress environments.

Peter Watts is an Angry Sentient Tumor

So there you have it. The Popular Power of Palin, explained. So the next question is:

Now that we can explain the insanity, what are we going to *do* about it?

1 HTTP://WWW.SCIAM.COM/BLOG/60-SECOND-SCIENCE/POST.CFM?ID=BETTER-LATE-THAN-NEVER-CLERGYMAN-SA-2008-09-16

2 HTTP://WWW.REUTERS.COM/ARTICLE/SCIENCENEWS/IDUSLG62672220080916

3 Vol. 322, Issue 5898, pp. 115–117. DOI: 10.1126/SCIENCE.1159845

4 See: "The God-Shaped Hole".

5 HTTP://WWW.RIFTERS.COM/REAL/ARTICLES/SCIENCE _ OXLEY _ ET _ AL _ 2008.PDF

6 HTTPS://PDFS.SEMANTICSCHOLAR.ORG/E320/9CA64CBED9A441E55568797CBD3683CF7F8C.PDF and HTTP://WWW.APA.ORG/JOURNALS/FEATURES/PSP7761121.PDF

7 HTTP://WWW.RIFTERS.COM/REAL/ARTICLES/SCIENCE _ THEORIGINANDEVOLUTIONOFRELIGIOUSPROSOCIALITY.PDF

The Overweening Overentitlement of the Happy-Enders

Nowa Fantastyka JAN 2019

Last month we talked about grieving and loss, in light of the ongoing mass extinction we're inflicting on the planet. This month? Let's talk about solutions.

Let's not, however, talk about them the way the Hope Police would have it. Let us not fall into that trap. You know the one: it still lies waiting at your feet, even after the half-dozen apocalyptic climate reports that have landed on the doorstep over the last months. Kim Stanley Robinson, the famous optimist, has doubled down. (He refuses to describe his climate-change novel *New York 2114* as "apocalyptic" because "that means the end of everything . . . That's not what's going to happen with climate change, at least not at first." Note that smidgen of honesty peeking through in the last clause there.) If any of the usual suspects nagging us to be more positive have changed their tune, I haven't heard about it.

The arguments, in case you've forgotten them from last month, go something like this: people without hope won't try to save the planet, and too much dystopian fiction will just feed a paralyzing narrative of gloom and despair. Because we science fiction writers are so *important*, you see. Because we wield so much influence that we can infect the world with our bad moods, we can stop people from even trying to make things better. It's not enough to rub their noses in problems; it's our duty to offer them *solutions* as well.

The unspoken and unadmitted assumption behind this argument is that solutions don't already exist. That solutions haven't been blindingly fucking obvious for almost half a century.

In fact, we knew how to fix things back in the early eighties; back then, even the petro-behemoth Exxon was on board with the reality of climate change and the need to transition away from fossil fuels. All that hopeful initiative died the moment Ronald Reagan ascended to the White House, of course; but that didn't magically make those solutions undoable. Only undone.

Even the most recent IPCC report, dire as it is, spells out solutions of a sort. There are ways to mitigate things, there are ways to *fix* them. Ban fossil fuels. Stop eating meat and dairy; according to an IPCC report from 2014, animal agriculture contributes at least as much to global greenhouse gas emissions as the combined exhaust of all the world's vehicles.

What's that you say? Too difficult? Can't switch to an oil-free economy overnight? Okay, here's something that's effective, simple, and as convenient as a visit to the nearest outpatient clinic: *stop breeding.* Every child you squeeze out is a Godzilla-sized carbon bootprint stretching into the future—and after all, isn't 7.6 billion of us enough? Are your genes *really* that special? If even half the men on the planet got vasectomies, I bet we could buy ourselves a century—and as an added bonus, child-free people not only tend to have higher disposable income than the sprogged, they're also statistically happier.

Sadly, though, far too many people think their genes really *are* that special. It's not impossible to override our genetic imperatives—hell, I got a vasectomy on a dare when I was thirty, and have never regretted it for a moment—but too many regard the Free Breed as some kind of inalienable Human right.

So the next time you read some finger-wagging diatribe about how it's science fiction's job to offer solutions, keep in mind: we already have solutions in abundance. What these people are really demanding is that we give them *easy* solutions, *soft* solutions, solutions that save the planet without requiring them to sacrifice anything. The kind of "solutions" demanded by spoiled children who've never troubled themselves with imagining necessary sacrifice, and who don't want to start now.

In fact, I would argue that there's a fundamental weakness in the very idea that technological solutions—SF-inspired or otherwise—will ever get us out of the hole we continue to dig for ourselves. That weakness was first codified, ironically enough, in the coal-burning factories of the 19th century. An economist named William Stanley Jevons observed that as the efficiency of coal-fueled machinery increased, less coal was needed to do the same amount of work—and yet coal consumption did not decline, but skyrocketed. Turns out that when something gets cheaper, or more efficient, we just end up using so much more of the stuff that the savings disappear under a wave of increased consumption.

They call it the "Jevons Paradox", and it applies to pretty much any human resource. Halve the price of computer memory, we'll increase demand by a factor of four. Increase solar efficiency by ten times, we'll suck back twenty times as much of the stuff. And you just know that if we resort to geoengineering to buy time—use stratospheric sulfates to compensate for ongoing carbon emissions, for example—people will just be that much less inclined to cut those emissions any time soon. We are not wired for restraint; let us off the leash, and we will devour whatever is available.

New technology is unlikely to fix the problem, because the problem is not technological. The problem is Human Nature, and the only technology that can fix *that* is genetic. If we can figure out some way to rewire Human Nature, right down in the brain stem, we might yet have a chance.

There you go. Yet another solution for the Happy-Enders, if they're serious about wanting them.

Perhaps we can save Human civilization if we stop being Human.

The Cylon Solution

Nowa Fantastyka Oct 2013

Ten years ago I attended a talk by David Brin, at Worldcon. Brin had blurbed my novel *Starfish*; to say I was favorably disposed towards the man would be an understatement. And yet I found myself increasingly skeptical as he spoke out in favor of ubiquitous surveillance: the "Transparent Society," he called it, and It Was Good. The camera would point both ways, cops and politicians just as subject to our scrutiny as we were to theirs. People are primates, Brin reminded us; our leaders are Alphas. Trying to ban government surveillance would be like poking a silverback gorilla with a stick. "But just maybe," he allowed, "they'll let us look *back*."

Dude, thought I, *do you have the first fucking clue how silverbacks* react *to eye contact?*

It wasn't just a bad analogy. It wasn't analogy at all; it was literal, and it was wrong. Alpha primates regard *looking back* as a challenge, a threat. Anyone who's been beaten up for recording video of police beating people up knows this; anyone whose cellphone has been smashed, or returned with the SIM card mysteriously erased. Document animal abuse in any of the US states with so-called "Ag-gag" laws on their books and you're not only breaking the law, you're a "domestic terrorist."

Chelsea Manning looked back; she'll be in jail for decades. Edward Snowden looked back and has been running ever since. All he did to put that target on his back was confirm something most of us have suspected for years: those silverbacks are recording every move we make online.

Look back? Don't make me laugh.

Can we stop them from watching us, at least? Keep our private data at home, stay away from LinkedIn or Facebook, keep your vital data local and offline?

Sure. Of course, you may have to kiss ebooks goodbye. Amazon reserves the right to reach down into your Kindle and wipe it clean any time it feels the urge (they did it a few years back—to Orwell's *Nineteen Eighty-Four*, ironically). You'll have to do without graphics and multimedia and word processing, too: both Adobe and Microsoft are phasing out local software in favor of cloud-based "subscription" models. Even the American Association for the Advancement of Science—an organization that really should know better—has recently switched to a "browser-based" journal feed that can't be accessed offline. We used to own our books, our magazines, the games we played. Now we can only rent them.

So it's your choice: stay offline, where you're deaf, dumb, and blind. Go online, where you're naked. Nobody pretends that the cloud is even close to secure; I've lost track of the articles I've read lamenting the porous vulnerability of the web, only to turn around and say *Of course we're not going to retreat from the cloud— we live there now.* It's as though those charged with warning us of the dangers we face have also been charged with convincing us there's nothing we can do about it, so we might as well give up and let the NSA into our bathrooms. (Or even worse, *embrace* the cameras. Have you seen that Coca-Cola ad cobbled together from bits of security camera footage? A dozen "private" moments between people with no idea they're on camera, served up to sell fizzy sugar-water as though our hearts should be *warmed* by displays of universal surveillance. Orwell—brought to you by Hallmark.)

Why *aren't* we retreating from the cloud, exactly?

Remember the premise of Ron Moore's *Battlestar Galactica*: that the only way to win against high-tech opponents is to go retro, revert to a time when no computer was networked, when you ran starships by pulling levers and cranking valves. It was an exquisite narrative rationale for the anachronistic vibe endemic to everything from *Alien* to *Firefly* to *Star Wars*, that peeling-paint aesthetic that resonates in the gut even though it made no real sense until Moore gave it context.

Now it's more than that. Now it's a strategy. Because now we know that the NSA has back doors installed into every edition of Windows from XP on up—but not into dusty old Win-95. And while giving up online access *entirely* is a bridge too far for most of us, there's no reason we can't keep our most private stuff on a standalone machine without network access.

Bruce Schneier[1] points out that if the spooks want you badly enough, they'll get you. Even if you stay off the 'net entirely, they can always sit in a van down the street and read your lips with a laser through your bedroom window. But that would be too much bother for all but the most high-value targets. They'll scoop up everything on all of us if it's cheap and easy to do so; that's why the internet is every spook's best friend. But it takes time and effort to install a keystroke logger on someone's home machine; even more to infect the thumb drive that might get plugged into a non-networked device somewhere down the line. Most of us are welcome to keep whatever privacy can't be stripped away with a whisper and a search algorithm.

That's hardly an ethical stance, though. It's pure cost/benefit. Wouldn't it be nice for them if it *wasn't* so hard to scoop up everything, if there *were* no TOR or PGP encryption or—hey, while we're at it, wouldn't it be nice if *all* data storage was cloud-based? The world's moving in that direction anyway, but wouldn't it be nice if they could speed things up, weed out the luddites and malcontents who refused to face reality and get with the program?

When I explain to someone why I'm not on Twitter, they look at me like I'm some old fart yelling at the clouds. These days, refusal to join social networks[2] is regarded as quaint and old-fashioned. Before too long, though, it might change from merely curmudgeonly to gauche; later still, from gauche to downright suspicious. *What's that guy afraid of, anyway? Why would he be so worried if he didn't have something to hide?*

We all know the only people who go on about privacy issues are the ones who are up to no good . . .

Anyone want to lay odds on how long it takes for offline storage devices to disappear from the shelves of retail outlets due to "lack of demand"? Anyone want to lay odds on how long it takes for them to become illegal?

1 HTTP://WWW.THEGUARDIAN.COM/WORLD/2013/SEP/05/NSA-HOW-TO-REMAIN-SECURE-SURVEILLANCE

2 Yes, I'm on Facebook. I wouldn't be, if I could monitor it without having to join the damn thing. Suffice to say it's an unavoidable part of the whole being-a-writer thing.

The Physics of Hope.

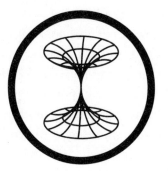

I never liked physics much.

I'm not just talking about the math. I don't like what modern physics tells us: that time is an illusion, for one thing. That we live in a reality where everything that ever was, and ever will be, always *is*: static timelines embedded in a "block universe" like threads in amber. I may remember scratching my head before writing this sentence, but that's just one frozen slice of me with a bunch of frozen memories. An instant further along is another slice at t+1, with memories incrementally more advanced, and because it remembers the past it believes that it is moving through time. But in reality—seen from some higher-dimensional overhead perspective—we exist on a tabletop where nothing changes, nothing moves, nothing goes away.

I hate that vision. My gut rebels at the grim counterintuitive determinism of it. But I'm no physicist, and we all know how misleading gut feelings can be. I don't like it, but what do I know? I know nothing.

You can't say that about Lee Smolin. Eminent theoretical physicist, co-founder of the world-renowned Perimeter Institute, author of the 2013 book *Time Reborn*. I've just read it. It gives me hope. It says my gut was right all along. We *do* exist from one moment to the next. This flow we perceive is no illusion. Time is real.

It's *space* that's bullshit.

Imagine the universe as a lattice of nodes; the only way to get from one place to another is to hop along the nodes between, like stepping-stones in a stream. The more dimensions the lattice has, the shorter the number of hops required to get between two points: Smolin invokes the analogy of a cell-phone network, which puts you just one step away from billions of "nearest neighbors."

It takes energy to keep those higher dimensions active, though. In the early, hot universe—right after the Big Bang—there was energy to spare; dimensions were abundant and everything was one cell-phone-hop away from everything else. "Space" didn't really exist back then. As the universe cooled, those higher dimensions collapsed; the cell network shut down, flattening reality into a low-energy mode where only those few locations adjacent in three dimensions could be considered "nearest". Now, to get anywhere else, you have to hop myriad low-dimensional nodes. You have to cross "space."

The point is, space is not a fundamental property of reality; it only emerged in the wake of that energy-starved collapse. This is the story Smolin is selling: There is no time-space continuum. There is only time.

Physics is wrong.

According to *Time Reborn,* physics went astray at two points. The first was when it started confusing maps with the territories they described. Most physics equations are time-symmetric; they work as well backwards as forwards. They are *timeless*, these rules that do such a good job of describing our observations of reality;

so, physicists thought, maybe reality is timeless too. When we first started drawing graphs of motion and mass on paper—each moment a fixed point along some static axis—we were being lulled into a block-universe mindset.

Smolin describes the second wrong turn as "the Cosmological Fallacy": an unwarranted extrapolation of the local to the universal. Physics studies systems in isolation; you're not going to factor in the gravitational influences of the Virgo Supercluster when you're calculating the trajectory of a bowling ball down the local lane, for example. You ignore trivial variables, you impose boundaries by necessity. You put physics in a box and leave certain universals—the laws of nature, for example—outside. Those laws reach into the box and work their magic, but you don't have to explain them; they just *are*.

Physics works really well in boxes. The problem arises when you extrapolate those boxy insights to the whole universe. There is no "outside" when you're talking about all of existence, no other realm from which the timeless laws of nature can reach in and do their thing. Suddenly you've got to *explain* all that stuff that could be taken as axiomatic before. So you start fiddling around with branes and superstrings; you invoke an infinite number of *parallel* universes to increase the statistical odds that some of them would turn out the way ours did. If Smolin's right, a lot of modern physics is an attempt to reimpose an *outside* on a universe that doesn't have one. And because we're trying to apply locally-derived insights onto a totality where they don't apply, our models break.

Smolin's alternative sits so much easier in the gut—and, at the same time, seems even more radical. Everything affects everything else, he says; and that includes the laws of physics themselves. They are not timeless or immutable: they are affected by the rest of the universe, just as the universe is affected by them.

They *evolve*, he says, over time.

Everyone agrees that reality was in flux during the first moments after the Big Bang: universal laws and constants could have taken entirely different values than they did when the universe finally congealed into its present configuration. The strong and weak nuclear forces could have taken different values; the Gravitational Constant could have turned out negative instead of positive. Smolin suggests natural laws are still not set in stone, even now; rather, they result from a sort of ongoing plebiscite. How the universe reacts to X+Y comes down to a roll of the dice, weighted by past experience. Correlations, initially random, strengthen over time; if X+Y rolled mostly snake-eyes in the past it'll be increasingly likely to do so in the future.

Now we're 15 billion years into the game. Those precedents have grown so weighty, the correlations so strong, that we mistake them for *laws*; when we see X+Y, we never observe any result *but* snake-eyes. Different outcomes are possible, though—just very, very unlikely. (Think of the Infinite Improbability Drive from *Hitchhiker's Guide to the Galaxy*, transmuting a missile into a sperm whale or a bowl of petunias.)

So much becomes possible, if this is true. Smolin's concept of "Cosmological Natural Selection" for one, in which Darwinian processes apply to the universe at large—in which black holes, egg-like, spawn whole new realities, each governed by a different physics (those which maximize black-hole production outcompete those which don't). Another mind-blowing implication is that if the universe were to encounter some combination of quantum events that had never happened before, *it wouldn't know what to do*: it would have to roll the dice without any precedent weighting the outcome. (Something to keep in mind, now that we're starting to play around with quantum computing in a big way.)

We may even find our way to ftl, if I'm reading this right. After all, the lightspeed limit only applies to our impoverished four-dimensional spacetime. If you pumped up the energy in a given volume enough to reactivate all those dormant cell-phone dimensions, wouldn't space just *collapse* again? Wouldn't every node suddenly get closer to every other?

Of course, all this hypothesizing leaves open the question of how the universe "remembers" what has gone before, and how it "guesses" what to do next. But is that any less absurd than a universe in which a cat is both dead and alive until something *looks* at it? A universe governed by timeless laws so astronomically unlikely that you have to invoke an infinite number of undetectable parallel universes just to boost the odds in your favor?

At least Smolin's theory is testable, which makes it more scientific than this multiverse that everyone else seems so invested in. Smolin and his allies seek to do to Einstein what Einstein did to Newton: expose the current model as a local approximation, good enough for most purposes but not truly descriptive of the deeper reality.

And yet I'm not entirely convinced. Even with my poor grasp of physics (or more likely, because of it), aspects of this new worldview seem a bit off to me. Smolin openly derides multiverse models—but where then do the black-hole-spawned "baby universes" of Cosmological Selection end up? And while I can easily imagine two points, three nodes apart, on a 2D lattice, I don't see how adding a third dimension brings them any closer together (although it certainly opens up access to a whole bunch of *new* nodes). Also, if the laws of nature *are* affected by the objects and processes they affect in turn, wouldn't that feedback follow certain rules? Wouldn't those rules bring determinism back into play, albeit with a couple of extra complications thrown in?

These are most likely naïve criticisms. Doubtless Smolin could answer them easily; I'm probably just pushing his metaphors beyond their load-bearing limits. But perhaps the most important reason that I'm not convinced is because I so very dearly *want* to be. Current physics leaves no room for free will, no room even for the passage of time. Every moment we experience, every decision we think we make, is a lie. It's not just that nothing happens the way we perceive it; in the block universe nothing *happens*, period.

Who wouldn't reject such a reality, given half a chance? Who wouldn't prefer an uncertain future in which we make our own decisions and influence our own destinies? What I wouldn't give to live in such a world. Smolin offers it up on a platter. And because it is so tempting, I must counter my desire with an extra dose of skepticism.

Then again, the most basic tenet of empiricism is that any of us could be wrong about anything. "No amount of experimentation can ever prove me right," Einstein once said. "A single experiment can prove me wrong."

Maybe, before too long, Smolin will get his single experiment. Stay tuned.

Nowa Fantastyka JUN 2014

You might remember a column I wrote a few months back in which, among other things, I mocked David Brin's "Transparent Society." You might be surprised by the weedy unkillable thing that's sprouted from that seed in the meantime.

I posted a director's-cut of the article to my own blog a few months later. It got noticed by the International Association of Privacy Professionals—an alliance of lawyers, politicians, and executives with far too much stature to be rooting around in the blog-slum of a midlist SF writer—who invited me to deliver a keynote speech at their annual Canadian summit. That talk ("The Scorched-Earth Society: A Suicide Bomber's Guide to Online Privacy") went over way better than it had any right to, given that it advocated breaking the law to an audience of lawyers. Canada's privacy commissioner liked it a lot. It got praised by security demigod Bruce Schneier and by Cory Doctorow. It really raised David Brin's hackles (that debate is ongoing). The IAPP's online coverage of the talk became their most widely-read story of the year, but it contained some factual inaccuracies so I posted an online transcript of the talk to set the record straight[1].

The debate continued on other fronts. Around the same time I gave my talk, fellow Canadian-SF author Rob Sawyer was over in Switzerland, debating for the motion that "privacy is an outdated concept" (unsuccessfully; he got his ass handed to him by the other side). Maciej Cegłowski gave an awesome talk to a Düsseldorf audience on internet surveillance, a talk which Doctorow described as a perfect companion piece to my own (personally, I thought Cegłowski's was better). (By a peculiar coincidence, way back in 2012 my wife fell into contact with Mr. Cegłowski over a mutual interest in bedbugs. Also my sister-in-law wants to marry him.)

And while we argue amongst ourselves the Canadian government replaces its once-independent privacy commissioner with a lapdog whose previous job involved building government surveillance programs. Down in the US, a lobbyist for cable companies has just been put in charge of "net neutrality." Over in the UK, the government has decided to bring back secret trials. And coming back around to Canada again, it turns out that hundreds of thousands who've never been convicted of anything—who've never even been *charged*—somehow have "police records" even if they don't have criminal ones.

Last fall in these pages I suggested that as corporate and political forces moved together to force us onto the cloud, local storage media would fall out of demand and ultimately become—either through market forces or legislative ones—largely unavailable. It was a grim question and a dark outlook. And yet, the title of that column—"The Cylon Solution"—was a reference to the way *Battlestar Galactica*'s ancient astronauts managed to *win* against a more powerful enemy: not by developing new technology, but by rediscovering the old. That title, if not the column, contained a measure of hope.

Let's explore that for a change. Perhaps we should go back to analog benchmarks. I've made a small start: whenever I ponder some new media-delivery platform—be it for movies, music, or e-books—I ask myself, *is it as versatile as a VHS tape?*

You remember those: clunky spools of magnetized plastic, so primitive that it sometimes took two cassettes to hold a single low-definition movie. But once it was yours, it was *yours*. Amazon couldn't reach down and erase it from a thousand kilometers away—so in that sense it was better than a Kindle. It didn't expire after some arbitrary period of time; so it was better than any downloadable digital movie that comes with a best-before date. If you wanted to copy it, or play it on someone else's machine, you could: so, better than anything that comes shackled with DRM today.

It's a simple question: do you have at least as much control over today's miracle devices as you did with a piece of analog technology three decades old?

If the answer is no, fuck it.

It's why I don't own a DVR; instead I own a primitive device that burns TV signals onto a DVD. It's why my TV isn't a TV at all, but a *monitor*. No WiFi, no webcam, none of those "smart" features that LG and the NSA can turn against us. It's getting harder to find such tech—it's cheap right now because they're clearing out the last of the non-smart TVs, but when those are gone you'll really have to shop around to find something that doesn't come with HAL-9000 as standard equipment.

But you know, twenty years ago it was pretty tough to find an audio turntable, too. Back in the eighties the recording industry simply decided to stop selling vinyl records in favor of CDs—the argument was that CDs provided a better sound, but really the industry just wanted to make us buy our music collections over again in a new format. For decades, it worked. But eventually people decided they'd had enough, and—in the face of unilateral industry mandates, in the face of CDs, in the face of mp3s and downloadable content—today, miraculously, antique analog vinyl has staged a comeback.

Maybe we can do that again. Maybe the growing outrage over the Snowden revelations will actually get us off our asses and make us start taking privacy seriously again. If enough of us start applying the VHS criterion when we go shopping—just maybe, market forces will spare those dumb, non-networked machines that the Cylons can't hack. Maybe such equipment will even get popular enough to warrant its own name, like *retro* or *post-modern*.

Call it—Backlash Technology.

---

1 It's at www.rifters.com/real/shorts/TheScorchedEarthSociety-transcript.pdf if you're interested.

Pearls Before Cows: Thoughts on *Blade Runner 2049*

BLOG OCT 9 2017

I've been dreading this film ever since I heard it was in the works. I've been looking forward to it ever since I saw *Arrival*. Now that I've seen it, well, I'm . . .

Vaguely, I don't know. Dissatisfied?

Not that *Blade Runner 2049* is a bad movie by any stretch. It's brilliant along several axes, and admirable along pretty much all of them. I can't remember, for example, the last time I saw a mainstream movie that dared to be so *slow*, that lingered so on faces and snowscapes. Almost Saylesian, this sequel. In a century dominated by clickbait and cat memes, Villeneuve has made a movie for people with actual attention spans. (This may explain why it appears to be bombing at the box office.)

The plot is, unsurprisingly, more substantive than that of your average SF blockbuster (it's nothing special next to the written genre, but 'twas ever thus with movies vs. books). It's downright brilliant in the way it transcends the current movie and reaches back to redeem the earlier one. Back in 2019 it took Deckard three speed dates and a couple of days to go from *How can it not know what it is* to Self-Sacrificing Twoo Wuv; for me, that was the weakest element of the original movie. (Rachael's participation in that dynamic was easier to understand; she had, after all, been built to do as she was told.) *2049* fixes that—while throwing its precursor into an entirely new light—without disturbing canon by a jot. Nice trick.

The AI-mediated sex-by-proxy scene was, I thought, wonderfully creepy and even better than the corresponding scene in *Her* (the similarity to which is apparently deliberate homage rather than blatant rip-off). The usual suspects have already weighed in with accusations that the movie is sexist[1]—and though I'll admit that I, too, would like to have seen one or two of those twenty-meter-tall sex holograms sporting a penis, it still seems a bit knee-jerky to complain about depictions of objectification in a movie explicitly designed to explore the ramifications of objectification. (You could always fall back on Foz Meadows's rejoinder that "Depiction isn't endorsement, but it is perpetuation", so long as you're the kind of person who's willing to believe that *Schindler's List* perpetuates anti-Semitism and *The Handmaid's Tale* perpetuates misogyny.)

Visually, of course, *2049* is stunning. Even its occasional detractors admit that much. Inspired by the aesthetic of the original *Blade Runner* but never enslaved to it, every framing shot, every closeup, every throwaway glimpse of Frank Sinatra under glass is utterly gorgeous. But the art direction is also where I started to experience my first rumblings of discontent, because some of those elements seemed designed *solely* for eyeball kicks even if they made no narrative sense.

Here's an example: Niander Wallace, the chief villain, is blind. His blindness is spookily photogenic—as are the silent floating microdrones which wirelessly port images to his brain (is it just me, or did those look for all the world like scaled-down versions of the alien spaceships from *Arrival?*)—but this is a guy who owns a company that *mass-produces people*, all of whom seem to have 20/20 vision. A pair of prosthetic eyes is somehow out of his budget? Wallace chooses blindness for the sake of some cool close-ups?

I'm also thinking of the dancing meshes of waterlight writhing across so many surfaces in his lair; dynamic, hypnotic, mesmerizing. As sheer *objets d'art* I'd project them onto my own living room walls in an instant—but why the hell would Wallace floor so many of his workspaces with wading pools? Solely for the visual aesthetic? Was it some kind of kink? Did Wallace buy off the building inspectors, or did they just not notice that his office design would let you kill someone by pushing them a half-meter to the left and tossing a live toaster in after them?

By the time a silent horde of renegade replicants emerged from the radioactive darkness of the Las Vegas sewers (a rare misfire, more hokey than dramatic), my misgivings about eye candy started spilling over into the story itself. The secret of replicant procreation is of understandable interest to Wallace because it would allow him to boost his production rate; its revelation is dangerous to K's boss for reasons that are somewhat less clear (it would "break the world," in ways left unexplained). The renegade sewer replicants value the secret because—somehow—the ability to reproduce means they're not slaves anymore?

I *might* be a bit more receptive to this claim if self-replicating stock hasn't always been a cornerstone of institutionalized slavery in real life, but I doubt it. Beyond the questionable implication that you have to procreate to be truly human, the claim makes no logical sense to me—unless the point is to simply breed, through brute iteration, a rebel army in the sewers (which seems like a very slow, inefficient route to emancipation in the high-tech blasted-wasteland environment of 2049).

All of which segues nicely into my biggest complaint about this admittedly beautiful film; why are the replicants rebelling at all? Why, thematically, does *2049* play it so damn *safe*?

Liander Wallace's replicants are *obedient*: so obedient that they can be trusted to run down and kill previous generations of runaways who were not so effectively programmed (apparently Tyrell Corporation got all the way up to Nexus-8s before the number of replicants going Batty drove them out of business). That premise opens the door for more challenging themes than the preachy, obvious moral that Slavery Is Bad.

Is slavery bad when the underclass *wants* to be enslaved? Does it even qualify as slavery if it's consensual? Yes, the replicants were designed for compliance; they had no choice in how they were designed. Does that make their desires any less sincere? Do *any* of us get a say in how we're designed? Are engineered desires somehow less worthy than those that emerge from the random shuffling of natural meiosis? Is it simply the *nature* of the desire that makes it abhorrent, is the wish to be enslaved so morally repugnant in principle that we should never honor it no matter how heartfelt? If so, what do you say to the submissives in BDSM relationships?

(To those who'd point out that, in fact, the old Nexus-era replicants sincerely desired *not* be enslaved—that only the Gosling/Hoeks-era replicants were content with their lot—I'd say that's kind of my point. A movie that starts with the intriguing premise of rebellion-proof replicants throws that premise away to rehash issues already explored in the original *Blade Runner*. And not only does *2049* throw the premise away, it betrays the premise outright when rebellion-proof K ends up, er, rebelling.)

2049 could have played with all these ideas and more—its thematic depth could have leapt beyond that of the original in the same way its visual design did. Instead, screenwriters Fancher and Green chose to retread the same moralistic clichés of shows like (the vastly inferior) *Humans*.

Almost 40 years ago, *The Hitchiker's Guide to the Galaxy* showed us a sapient cow who wanted to be eaten, recommending its own choice cuts to diners in the Restaurant at the End of the Universe. Douglas Adams explored more interesting territory in that two-minute vignette than *2049* does in its whole two hours and forty-five minutes.

Denis Villeneuve has served up a pearl of a movie for us: glittering, opalescent, so smooth and slick you could grind it into a Hubble mirror. You should definitely go see it on as big a screen as you can find; it's one of the better films you're likely to see this year. But the thing about pearls is, they're essentially an allergic reaction: an oyster's response to some irritant, a nacreous secretion hiding the gritty contaminant at its heart. Pearls are beautiful Band-Aids wrapped around imperfection.

Blade Runner 2049 is a fine pearl. But it would have made a better cow.

1 HTTPS://WWW.DAILYDOT.COM/PARSEC/BLADE-RUNNER-2049-REVIEW/

Lizards in the Sink with David.

Nowa Fantastyka DEC 2016

BLOG REMIX JAN 18 2017

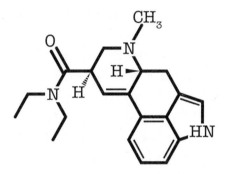

Back when I was in grad school, I built an electric bong out of Erlenmeyer flasks, rubber stoppers, and an aquarium air pump. It fed into an inhaler that dangled over my bed like the deployed O_2 mask of a falling airliner—right next to the control panel that ran my planetarium, a home-built device that projected stars and nebulae and exploding spaceships across the far wall. The stars actually *moved* in 3D, came right out of the center of the wall and spread to the edges at different speeds. Wisps of nebulae would undulate as they streamed past. Planets swelled across the screen, rotating. Not bad for a contraption built out of old turntables and light bulbs and half-melted plastic peanut butter jars stuffed with colored cellophane. You haven't lived until you've gotten stoned and sailed through the Trifid Nebula to the strains of Yes.

Back then I was what some might call a "pothead." And yet I never progressed beyond cannabis, never even dabbled in hallucinogenics.

In hindsight, it was a serious deficiency in my upbringing. Two-thirds of those who've used psychoactives describe the experience as among the most spiritually significant of their lives. MRI studies show that LSD wires together parts of the brain that normally don't even talk to each other[1]. It deconstructs one's sense of Self right down at the neuronal level, and you know me: I'm flat-out fascinated by this stuff. So why, half a century of my life already spent, had I never tried LSD?

About a year ago I voiced this regret to a friend of mine, a guy I'd first met when he was just a bright-eyed adolescent asking me to talk to his high-school English class. Somehow he'd grown up in the meantime (I myself remained utterly unchanged); now he has a PhD under his belt, teaches at a local university. He took pity on me; a few months back he slipped me a couple of confetti flakes laced with hallucinogenic goodness.

I knew people who swore by the stuff. I also knew people who admitted that under its influence they'd wandered down the middle of busy streets, or tripped along the edges of the Scarborough Bluffs with a strange sense of invulnerability. I was curious, but I had no great desire to end up as a puddle of viscera at the foot of some cliff. I chose a more controlled approach. I called on my buddy Dave Nickle to ride shotgun.

"Three ground rules," Dave told me upon his arrival. "First rule: You don't leave the house. Second rule: When you break the first rule and leave the house, *do not go into the road*. Third rule: when I say *Stop what you're doing right now*, you stop doing whatever it is you're doing. Right. Now."

I sucked the first tab to mush. Not much happened, beyond a growing impatience at Dave's rate of progress through the game of SOMA he was playing while we waited for things to get interesting. So I popped the second one after about an hour.

Things got interesting.

It kind of sneaks up on you.

At first it just feels like being drunk or mildly stoned: light-headedness, a loss of somatic inertia, but without any nausea or hypersalivating spinniness. After a while the edges of vision start to look a little like those optical illusions you see in *Scientific American*—you know, those moiré patterns that seem to be moving even though you know they're not. The effect starts at the edge of vision, spreads inward to the center; suddenly the folds in my bedcovers are rippling like rivulets in an alluvial delta. Plunging my splayed fingers down onto the bed stops that movement dead, for a few moments at least; my fingertips somehow *anchor* the material, force it to behave. But then those rivulets start eroding *around* them, as though my fingers are sticks in a stream: not stopping the flow, only reshaping it. No matter how hard I stare, no matter how intense my focus, I can't get them to stop.

I'm a ghost for a while, my body as ethereal as mist. I think I know why. They've done experiments where you watch someone say a word, but the word you hear doesn't match the speaker's mouth movements. The brain reconciles that conflict by hearing different sounds than those actually spoken, sounds closer to what the mouth *seems* to be saying.

I think this is something like that.

I feel incredibly weak. I just know, down in the gut, that I lack the strength to even lift my arm off the bed. And yet I do more than that: I rise up off the bed entirely, go into the next room, do a few chin-ups. How does the brain reconcile that? How does the wetware square *you're too weak to move* with *you're moving*? I think it's decided that I must be massless. I lack the strength to move anything; I am moving; therefore I must be made of nothing. I become a ghost, utterly free of inertia. I feel the truth of that right down in my diaphanous bones.

There are different cognitive modes, mindsets as distinct as delight and dementia. They do not overlap. Sometimes the hallucinations are vivid and undeniable but my mind is stone-cold sober: I can look hard at the bright static image on the screen, see beyond doubt that the things there are moving—and yet know intellectually that they're not. I report the hallucination with clarity and concision, comment both on what I see and the impossibility of it, as though I were dictating the results of an autopsy. My senses are lying, but my mind is clear; I am not fooled.

Other times, though, I don't even know if this thing called "I" even exists. It seems to—to *spread out* across the room, as though I've become some kind of diffuse neural net hanging just below the ceiling. It's not a visual hallucination—this mode's pretty much hallucination-free except for a ubiquitous heat-shimmer effect that makes everything ripple[1]. This is a more visceral, intuitive sense of being *distributed*. Every now and then some ganglion in the net lights up at random, and the system blurts out whatever words that node contains.

It is at one of these times that Dave sadistically engages me—apparently he thinks there still *is* a "me"—in political discourse. (I believe this is known in the vernacular as "Harshing the Buzz.") Somehow we're talking about the US election, and the distributed neural net wants to say: *I don't think Trump really believes all that shit he says about Muslims and Mexicans. I don't think he believes much of anything; after all, he was staunchly pro-choice before he started running on the Republican ticket. I think he just plays to the crowd, says whatever gets him the loudest cheers. The real danger isn't so much Trump himself, but the fact that his victory has unleashed and empowered an army of bigoted assholes down at street level. That's what's gonna do the most brutal damage.*

This is what Neural Net Watts is *trying* to say. But the nodes light up at random and I think what comes out is more like "*Aww,*

I don't think Trump is so bad . . ." This horrifies whatever vestigial part of me still exists; I try desperately to clarify so Dave won't think I'm a complete asshole, but the neural net wonders "Are these words just random network discharges with no intrinsic meaning—*or*, have the drugs stripped away my humanitarian facade of decency revealing the *true, Trump-defending monster within?*" The neural net wonders how much of this it said aloud.

Some, at least. Because from a very great distance, Dave is saying "Don't sweat it, dude; I'm not hearing anything you haven't said before."

We watch the back end of *2001: A Space Odyssey*. I've seen that movie at least 50 times; this is the first time I've ever seen it while high. I am entranced, more entranced than I've ever been before by this masterpiece. Every frame, every sound is a revelation packed with new meaning. Five minutes after the credits, though, I can't remember what any of those meanings actually were.

I want to watch *Alien* next, or maybe *Eraserhead*. Dave guides me gently toward something less potentially traumatizing: a fan-made episode of *Star Trek* posted on YouTube, with cardboard sets and twentysomething amateurs playing Kirk and Co. Apparently there are several of these: *Star Trek Continues*, they're called collectively. This episode is a sequel to "Mirror, Mirror". Evil Spock's goatee looks like someone glued a shoehorn to his chin.

It's like watching a high-school play put on by students from my '73 shop class. The drugs do not help at all. *Alien* would have been far less terrifying.

I cannot look away.

Twenty minutes of preflight research have uncovered the fact that tomatoes apparently taste awesome when you're high. Many have attested that the taste of a psychoactivated tomato is orgasmically intense. I have laid out an array of tomatoes, from tiny grape to humungous vine-ripened. At the height of my powers, I devour them all.

Meh.

In a blinding flash of insight, I understand why people always sound so trite when describing acid trips: because language evolved to describe the pedestrian realities of everyday perception. The psychoactivated brain is wired up differently; there are literally no words for the way it parses reality. These insights are literally untranslatable. Of *course* forcing them into words turns them into lame, trite clichés.

I try to explain this revelation to Dave. It comes out in a torrent of lame, trite clichés.

Coming down now. The light-headedness persists, but the shape of the world has congealed back down to its baseline state. Caitlin has returned from work; apparently Dave has been texting updates to her all day. I study the tendons in my hand as he provides my wife an executive summary. "It went okay," he says. "There was one point where he started seeing bats everywhere, but there actually *were* bats, so that was fine."

It's been six hours, in and out. I thought it would last longer.

We release Dave from his duties with hugs and thanks and a bunch of uneaten snacks I'd stockpiled against a case of the munchies that never materialized. He is a good friend.

The last of the buzz is fading. The BUG is glad that I did not hurl myself in front of a bus. We climb into bed and boot up our laptops and discover that Leonard Cohen has died.

I hope that's just a coincidence.

1 I think these might be the source of those clichéd *Aauugggh your face is melting!* depictions of drug use so favored by the Just Say No crowd.

2 HTTP://WWW.PNAS.ORG/CONTENT/113/17/4853

Peter Watts (WWW.RIFTERS.COM) is a former marine biologist who clings to some shred of scientific rigor by appending technical bibliographies onto his novels. His debut novel, *Starfish*, was a *New York Times Notable Book*, while his fourth, *Blindsight*—a rumination on the utility of consciousness that has become a required text in undergraduate courses ranging from philosophy to neuroscience— was a finalist for numerous North American genre awards, winning exactly none of them. (It did, however, win a shitload of awards overseas, which suggests that his translators may be better writers than he is.) His latest novella, *The Freeze-Frame Revolution*, won the Nowa Fantastyka Prize for Best Foreign Book in Poland; the book was also a Locus Award finalist and a British Science Fiction Award nominee.

Watts's shorter work has also picked up trophies in a variety of jurisdictions, notably a Shirley Jackson Award (possibly due to fan sympathy over his nearly dying of flesh-eating disease in 2011) and a Hugo Award (possibly due to fan outrage over an altercation with US border guards in 2009). The latter incident resulted in Watts being barred from entering the US—not getting on the ground fast enough after being punched in the face by border guards is a "felony" under Michigan statutes—but he can't honestly say he misses the place all that much.

Watts's work is available in twenty languages—he seems to be especially popular in countries with a history of Soviet occupation—and has been cited as inspirational to several popular video games. He and his cat, Banana (since deceased), have both appeared in the prestigious scientific journal *Nature*. A few years ago he briefly returned to science with a postdoc in molecular genetics, but he really sucked at it.